SOMEONE WAS OUT THERE... WATCHING...WAITING

Kelly reached in the drawer for her automatic, and she was still digging through the clutter when a pebble shot toward her across the grease-stained concrete floor. She looked up, her fingers finally closing around the butt of the gun. The silhouette of a man filled the hangar's entrance. She stiffened, her gut filling with an odd mixture of fear and hate.

Nick Cavanaugh.

What was he doing here? Why had he come strolling into her life after all these years?

She watched as he calmly dropped his duffel bag and slowly raised his hands, his cocky grin never fading.

"It's good to see you, too, Kelly."

"What do you want?" Her voice was cold.

Nick nodded at the gun. "Didn't anyone ever tell you guns are dangerous?"

"Depends which end you're facing. It feels fine from this side."

He took a step forward. "I guess, but I've never been comfortable around a woman with a pistol in her hand, especially when she's pointing it at me."

SOMEONE SAFE
LORI L. HARRIS

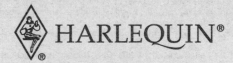

HARLEQUIN®

TORONTO • NEW YORK • LONDON
AMSTERDAM • PARIS • SYDNEY • HAMBURG
STOCKHOLM • ATHENS • TOKYO • MILAN • MADRID
PRAGUE • WARSAW • BUDAPEST • AUCKLAND

For Bobby Harris
With love.
You are my world.

And

For Bobbie Laishley
Who made me believe I could do anything.
Thanks, Mom!

ISBN 0-373-22830-9

SOMEONE SAFE

Copyright © 2005 Lori L. Harris

ABOUT THE AUTHOR

Lori Harris has always enjoyed competition. She grew up in southern Ohio, showing Arabian horses and Great Danes. Later she joined a shooting league where she competed head-to-head with police officers—and would be competing today if she hadn't discovered how much fun and challenging it was to write. Romantic suspense seemed a natural fit. What could be more exciting than writing about life-and-death struggles that include sexy, strong men?

When not in front of a computer, Lori enjoys remodeling her home, gardening and boating. Lori lives in Orlando, Florida, with her very own hero.

CAST OF CHARACTERS

Nick Cavanaugh—He was one of Immigration and Customs Enforcement's toughest investigators. And just as there's always one woman who lingers at the back of a man's mind, for every investigator there's one case that he can't forget. For Nick, the case is Princeton Air, and the woman is Kelly Logan.

Kelly Logan—She's the scrappy, blond beauty who owns Bird of Paradise airline. Seven years ago, she was in love with Nick, but then he destroyed her family….

Rod Griffis—Owner of the local dive shop and the kind of guy who is always helping out those around him. He's in love with Kelly, but her feelings for him are anyone's guess.

Myron Richards—He was the Agent in Charge and Nick's mentor. He and Nick have always had each other's back…until now.

Doug Willcox—Recently divorced; Special Agent Doug has his hands full with two kids and an ex-wife, and tended to disappear at all the wrong moments.

Benito Binelli—This big-time drug dealer was the No.1 bad guy on every federal agency's most wanted list and the headliner on Nick Cavanaugh's hit parade.

Chapter One

U.S. Immigration and Customs Enforcement special agent Nick Cavanaugh scanned the case file one last time before setting it aside.

The first day back after an investigation was completed meant hours compiling detailed reports. Nick preferred field work to paperwork and was a hell of a lot better at it. Unfortunately, the prosecution required both.

For the first time, he realized just how late it was and that the cramped office smelled of the Mexican food he'd thrown uneaten into the trash can. After three weeks of greasy fast food and doughnuts, he hadn't been able to face the enchilada and refried beans any more than he had been able to face going home to an empty condo.

With the office and his thoughts closing in on him, Nick stood and crossed to the window. He opened the blinds. Gray pavement and shale-colored buildings. Not a view that would make an Orlando travel brochure. Under the last vestige of dusk, the scene appeared as somber as his mood.

When he returned home last night, he'd found a note on the kitchen counter. Stephanie, his girlfriend of more than eleven months, had moved out while he tracked a load of cocaine up the Eastern Seaboard.

He really wasn't surprised. The job, his lifestyle, wasn't

conducive to long-term relationships. But in the beginning, he'd hoped this time might be different.

When they'd first dated, she had seemed independent enough to handle the occasions when a case kept him out of town and out of touch. In recent months, though, that had changed.

She talked about how, because he wasn't available, she'd turned down this invitation or that one. He told her often enough to go on without him. But even when he said those words, he knew they weren't the right ones.

The bottom line was he couldn't give her what she wanted. Marriage and kids. A husband who showed up at the dinner table every night.

It just wasn't in him. Wasn't part of his makeup. He wasn't a nine-to-fiver. He'd be bored with any job that kept him behind a desk or any relationship that became as predictable as his and Stephanie's had.

It really was better that she was the one to move on. Easier for her. She'd find someone ready to give her what she wanted. What she was entitled to. And he, no doubt, was getting exactly what he deserved.

Fatigue overtook him as he stood there, staring. He recognized the feeling that crept up on him more and more of late, from the dark alleys of his mind.

Regret.

Over cases gone sour, over failed relationships. Regret that he wasn't a better friend for Myron when his wife had passed away. That he hadn't mended fences with his own father before his death five years ago. That perhaps he was responsible for a man hanging himself. That, though he had no other choice, he'd killed a fourteen-year-old kid in a dark warehouse.

He couldn't seem to let go of any of them; instead, he kept them buried inside. They escaped some nights, and he welcomed them because they were all he had.

The phone rang.

He briefly considered ignoring it, then, relenting, turned and grabbed it. "Cavanaugh here."

"Can we meet?"

Recognizing his friend Ake Almgren's voice, Nick managed a tired smile. "That wife of yours must be giving you the night off for good behavior. Or she's tired of having you underfoot," he added as he sat again.

He envied Ake and Sue their solid marriage, their kids. Maybe tonight more than at other times. He rubbed the grit from his eyes. "Or does Sue think I need some cheering up?" Recently, Sue and Stephanie had been getting together for lunch or a movie, so Ake's wife probably knew about Stephanie.

There was a hesitation on the opposite end of the line.

"Hey, Ake. I'm okay."

"I was sorry to hear about Stephanie's decision, but that's not why I'm calling. I almost wish it was."

"What do you mean?"

Ake didn't answer him, and at the continued silence, the muscles between Nick's shoulder blades bunched. "Ake? Sue's okay, right? The boys, too?"

"They're fine. You alone?"

"Yeah. Why?"

"Does the name Kelly Logan mean anything to you?"

His hand clenching the phone, Nick straightened. He hadn't heard the name in more than six years. Except in his own head. The case, the woman, were some of his biggest regrets. Even now, if he closed his eyes, he knew he'd see her there.

"You investigated her back in ninety-six." Ake prompted, obviously thinking his silence was due to his inability to place the case. "Princeton Air."

"I recall the investigation. It was one of my first cases,"

Nick said. "We got a tip a small cargo airline was moving weapons for the Irish Republican Army. I went in under-cover."

Ake picked up where he stopped. "The father committed suicide before he could be taken into custody. Both the girl and Aidan Gallagher, a known IRA sympathizer, walked."

"Couldn't be helped," he said. "We had nothing to tie them directly to the guns. The only material witness, a courier, was dead before we could get to him, and the only prints found on the weapons were the father's."

"And just two of the crates were recovered," Ake said.

"That's right."

"The report I'm reading says Aidan and the Logans were friends, that he claimed his appearance in their home was innocent."

"And there was no evidence to suggest otherwise. The Logan girl even called him uncle." Nick reached over and switched on the desk lamp.

"Not a casual friend, then?"

"No. If I remember the story right, John Logan and Aidan grew up in the same Belfast neighborhood. Several months earlier, the old neighborhood had been ripped apart by a couple of bombs. John's sister was one of the ones killed." He recalled John telling him the story, the tears in the Irishman's eyes. Nick had never been an IRA sympathizer, but, in that moment, he had certainly been an empathizer.

"Why all the questions, Ake? Most of what you've asked so far must be in the report sitting in front of you."

"What do you know about Benito Binelli?" Ake continued.

With the question, the headache thrumming just below the surface, perhaps for hours, mushroomed, an atomic bomb going off at the base of Nick's skull.

He massaged the stress-tightened muscles. "Businessman. Scum. Has a team of lawyers to keep him out of jail."

"What would you say if I told you there's evidence Kelly Logan's in bed with him?"

Nick's fingers tightened on the handset again. "What would I say?" He came up with numerous possibilities. Most of which he was unwilling to voice. "I'd say he's a little old for her," he said, though they both knew Ake had meant *in bed* figuratively.

From all accounts, Benito Binelli appeared a happily married man with two teenage daughters. Currently, his only vices were the selling of illegal drugs and the occasional murder when someone was foolish enough to get in the way of business.

"Where are you going with this, Ake? Are you guys working Binelli now?"

"Yeah." After another brief pause, Ake picked his words carefully. "This isn't an official call. It's strictly one friend asking another for an opinion. It's important that it doesn't go any farther. At least for now."

"Sure." He stood to look out the window again. "Whatever you say."

"Kelly Logan's name came up in several of the reports. As background, I read over the file on Princeton Air." Ake hesitated again. "There're some unusual similarities between the two investigations."

"Unusual? In what way?" Nick asked.

"I rather you look at it for yourself. I may just be seeing spooks where none exist."

It was an odd choice of words. "Okay," he said, his tone cautious. "Do you want to meet? I could use some dinner."

Someone tapped at his closed door. He'd thought himself alone in the suite of offices. Myron poked his head in.

Realizing Nick was on the phone, the resident agent in charge offered a small salute, but remained mute. Nick noticed the strain around the other man's eyes.

"Myron just—"

Ake broke in. "Watch what you say."

Nick's gaze dropped away, and he reached for the empty coffee cup on the edge of his desk. "Okay. What do you propose?"

"We need to talk. Tonight. Alone." Ake suggested the top level of a nearby parking garage.

"I'll see you there in five." Nick replaced the receiver just as Myron dropped into the chair in front of the desk.

"Who was that on the phone?"

"Old college friend," Nick offered. "Wants to meet for a beer." He pulled his holstered weapon out of the top drawer and slipped it on. "Did you need something?" he asked when Myron made no move to stand.

"No. I was just finishing up and saw your light on. Thought we could catch a sandwich." He rubbed his knees. "Maybe another night."

"Sounds good." Nick said. "Everything okay with you?"

"Sure." With a forced smile and a soft grunt, Myron pushed stiffly to his feet. His shoulders sagged. "I guess I'm just restless. It's been a year today, and I still don't know what to do with myself. Pathetic, isn't it? I feel like a lost pup scratching at the back door of a dark house."

The previous July, Myron had buried his wife of thirty-four years. Nick hated seeing the pain in the other man's eyes. Myron was more of a father to him than his own had been, and still he didn't know what to say. So he said nothing. And regretted it.

"If you're on your way out, I'll walk down with you," he offered.

Myron opened the door. "I just need to stop by my office and make a quick call to my daughter."

When they reached Myron's office, Nick stayed outside in the hall. After several moments, though, he found himself glancing down at his watch. He'd told Ake five minutes. Something had rattled the experienced FBI investigator. Nick reached in his pocket for the pack of cigarettes he carried. Instead of taking one, he glanced with uncertainty at the bank of elevators twenty-five feet away and considered going on ahead, but then he remembered the look in Myron's eyes. A few more minutes couldn't hurt. As he waited, he did his damndest to keep his mind away from Kelly Logan. Without success.

He couldn't say he was surprised to hear of a connection between Kelly and Benito. Disappointed, though. He'd always hoped he was wrong about her.

He rested his head against the wall behind him and closed his eyes.

Why was it, when he could barely remember the color of Stephanie's eyes, he could still recall the way Kelly had looked the first time he'd watched her climb down from a plane and stride across tarmac?

Tight jeans and a baggy sweater. Long, loose stride. A smile that hit a man dead in the gut and kept going.

Myron closed the door to his office, and Nick straightened.

"How's Lily?" Nick asked as they headed for the elevator.

"Okay. Better than me." Myron shifted his briefcase to the opposite hand and reached into his pocket for his keys. "I finally agreed to put the house on the market, so we're at least talking again." He glanced at Nick, offering a weary smile. "She's like Bev. Determined."

"She's like Bev in other ways, too."

"Suppose she is," he admitted, seeming to give additional thought to the observation. "Can't cook like her mother, though."

Nick followed Myron into the elevator. "Different generation."

"You can say that again."

"You're a dinosaur."

"Lily has another term for it, a long word that manages to sound like a compliment, but isn't." Myron stepped out into the parking garage and Nick followed.

"How about we catch that sandwich tomorrow night? Maybe shoot a few games of pool?"

"Sounds good," Myron called and offered a small wave.

Four minutes later, Nick's car skidded into the parking garage.

After taking the ticket from the entrance machine, he entered the parking structure. At this time of night, the garage, which catered to bank customers and employees, was mostly empty.

What in the hell was going on? Was Kelly hauling for Benito? Nick felt his gut tighten at the possibility.

His sports car roared up to the top level. A clear, star-studded Florida night spread overhead. Tall buildings, several lit to reveal the bold architectural details of the New South, surrounded the structure.

As soon as he circled around the ramp's guard wall, he spotted Ake's car, one of the few vehicles parked on the unprotected rooftop. He pulled alongside the large sedan expecting to see Ake sitting behind the wheel, but the Buick was empty.

But, then, he was more than ten minutes late. Maybe Ake had decided to stretch his legs.

Nick climbed out, stood next to his own vehicle. In the distance, interstate traffic hummed. Closer, an ambulance wailed. He searched the lot for movement. What had made Ake think of a deserted garage as a meeting place? Only rookies considered deserted lots and buildings good places for private conversations. He preferred crowded restaurants with loud music and booths. As did Ake usually. So what was different about this time? What did Ake want to show him?

He walked out into the driving lane, looked toward the far wall, then behind him. Nothing.

Backtracking, he glanced inside the Buick, front seat, then back. John's child seat was strapped in place, a diaper bag sat on the seat, and Ake's briefcase lay on the floorboard.

He tried the door and found it unlocked. The damp stickiness on his fingers registered at the same time the interior light came on.

Dropping into a crouch in front of the open door, he released the strap holding the 9mm secure in the shoulder holster, flicked off the safety as soon as steel broke free of leather.

Blood glistened on the charcoal upholstery. At least one bullet had missed its mark and torn into the seat back, the blood-splattered guts of the upholstery leaking out like torn flesh. Not a lot of blood, though.

He could taste the vaporized gun powder against his tongue now. Only minutes old. Which meant whoever had done this might still be close by, might have Ake pinned down somewhere.

"Ake!"

Nothing.

Looking down for the first time, he spotted more blood leading toward the rear of the car. A lot more.

He shouldn't have waited on Myron. He should have sensed something was wrong. Reaching in, he removed the keys from the ignition. As he backed out of the path of the dome light, his shoe sent an object pinging across the pavement. A small caliber casing from the sound of it.

Stopping short of the rear of the car, he rested his back against the fender of his small car, distancing his body the same way he attempted to distance his mind.

He'd opened doors and trunks in his career, often knowing what he would find inside. He'd seen the bodies of men

tossed into large shipping cartons after their illegal contents
had been emptied, their remains left there undiscovered for
days, until the stench of death brought help too late.

Nick shoved the key into the trunk lock and turned it. As
the lid came up, the interior light blinked on.

He staggered back as if he'd taken a couple of shotgun
blasts to the chest and gut. The pain was real. Not physical,
maybe, but still burning and messy.

Ake's body was folded nearly in half, the gray carpet beneath him rapidly turning crimson.

The wave of nausea hit Nick with the solid vengeance of
a Louisville Slugger.

It was several seconds before Nick could move again. Refusing to look back, he calmly walked to his car, almost dar-
ing the shooter to take him out, too. Better the pain of a bullet
tearing into flesh than what he felt inside.

He called it in. As he waited for homicide, for the FBI and
the crime scene technicians, anger replaced shock; determination, the pain.

He could hear the keening of sirens. The muffled, mechanical scream as they climbed through the bowels of the parking garage. But they were nothing compared to the raw howls
roaring inside his head.

Ake and he went way back. Had gone to school together.
Played basketball on weekends. He'd been the best man at
Ake's wedding. Was godfather to both of his boys. Ake was
one of the few people he truly trusted.

And now he was gone.

Somehow, Nick would find whoever had done this. Someone would pay.

Chapter Two

Hell was probably ten degrees cooler than the Abaco Islands in late July, Kelly Logan decided.

Massaging the stiffness in her neck, she tried to ignore the way her clothing stuck to her skin. The corrugated metal sides of the airplane hangar, when coupled with the island heat and the ceiling fan revolving slowly in the dense, skeletal shadows overhead, turned the structure into a large convection oven. Everything seemed to cook faster. Except for the company books.

She lifted the top page of the bank statement. What she wouldn't give to just cram all six months' worth in the trash can. She could fly anything from a single-engine prop to a heavy cargo plane to a small jet, but even the simplest accounting managed to defeat her. She just wasn't a numbers person.

Fatigue overtaking her, she checked the time. Ten-thirty. No reason to take a dinner break at this point. In fact maybe she should just pack it in.

And maybe she could have if her mechanic, Ben, Bird of Paradise's only other employee, had managed to come back as promised after his dinner break.

Closing her eyes, she scrubbed her face. What was she going to do if the ads didn't bring in more business? Cutting fares again wasn't an option; the margins were already non-existent, and there was more meat in a poor man's stew than left in her operating budget. And fuel costs were expected to continue to rise to the record levels of early 1970s.

What was going to happen when she couldn't keep it together any longer? What then?

She studied the plane sitting thirty feet from her and wondered where in the hell she had gotten the dumb idea she could build an airline from the ground up?

Her father had taught her how to dream, how to reach for what seemed impossible when her feet were flat on the ground. He'd taught her to set goals, to work hard to achieve them. But, unfortunately, he hadn't taught her how to fail, which accounted for the sick feeling curled up inside her most nights when she closed her eyes.

A noise broke the silence in the hangar.

Kelly glanced toward the large opening at the front of the hangar, all thoughts of business vanishing. She couldn't quite identify the origin of the sound. An animal foraging in the underbrush along the edge of the tarmac? Or had the sound been of human making? Considering the time, she knew it wouldn't be her mechanic. If he was following his recent pattern, Ben was facedown on the pub's bar by now.

She continued to watch the doorway where the shadows of swaying palm fronds broke the halogen glare of the outside light. A gust of wind stole through the doorway, bringing the scent of the nearby Atlantic, and with it, the certainty that someone was out there.

Watching.

Waiting.

She reached in the drawer for the small automatic weapon that she usually kept locked on the plane, was still digging through the clutter when a pebble shot toward her across the grease-stained concrete.

Kelly looked up, her fingers closing around the butt of the gun. The silhouette of a man filled the opening, the lamp light from the desk barely reaching him.

She stiffened, her gut carrying an odd mixture of fear and hate.

Nick Cavanaugh.

What was he doing in Marsh Harbor? And why now? Why come strolling back into her life after all these years?

She watched as he calmly dropped his duffel bag and slowly raised his hands, his cocky grin never fading.

"It's good to see you, too, Kelly."

"What the hell do you want?" Her voice came out clipped and cold.

Nick nodded at the gun. "Didn't anyone ever tell you those things are dangerous?"

"Depends which end of it you're facing. It feels fine from this side."

He took a step forward. "A sound argument, I suppose. But I've never felt comfortable with a pistol in a woman's hand. Especially when it's pointed at me."

"Well, there's an easy solution for that one. You could pick up that satchel of yours and leave. Save me the trouble of putting a bullet in you."

Nick seemed amused. "Are you any good with it?"

"Good enough." She nudged the revolver's barrel upward. "How did you find me?"

"Your mechanic."

"Now there's a lie if I ever heard one," she said, her tone scathing. "Ben has no more use for you than I do. He'd tell you to take a hike off the nearest pier before he'd tell you a damned thing."

"Perhaps he didn't realize who he was talking to. He'd had a lot to drink." His eyes narrowed. "Come to think of it, I may have told him I was an old friend."

"Same Nick. Whatever it takes. Lies. Fabrications. It doesn't really matter, does it? As long as you get what you want."

He took another step, his hands dropping slightly. "I just came to talk."

Kelly thumbed the hammer back.

The definitive click as it locked into position brought him to a sudden halt. Nick pushed his hands several inches higher.

It was her turn to be amused, she decided. Not that he looked truly worried. It would take more than a gun leveled at his chest to shake Nick. Still, all in all, it wasn't a bad moment.

Feeling in control for the first time since he'd stepped through the door, she allowed herself to really study him.

The neatly clipped, chestnut hair of seven years ago had been allowed to grow longer, until it brushed the collar of his T-shirt. His shoulders had always been broad, his body well-muscled, hard, but now there was a power about him. Dangerous, her mind prompted.

It was still too dark to see the color of his eyes, but she remembered them. Too well. They'd be the same deep, steel-gray color of the Atlantic when churned by a hurricane. Unreadable. Unrelenting. Treacherous.

"You don't really want to shoot me."

The calm assurance of his words grated against her nerves like raw metal skidding across tarmac.

"Just how sure are you of that, Cavanaugh?" She stepped out from behind the desk. "Do you think I hate you any less today than I did seven years ago? Do you think I've forgotten about what happened? Forgiven you?" She moved closer still. "Forgiven myself for letting you use me to destroy my father?"

For the first time, she saw uncertainty in his eyes, an emotion she'd never seen there before. Nick had always been so blasted certain about everything.

"I know you don't want to believe it, but I regret what happened to your father. If I had known he was going to—"

She cut him off. "You're right. I don't believe you. My father's dead because of you and your investigation." Kelly's finger tightened on the trigger. "You were always so sure you were right. About everything and everyone. Did you ever, for even one moment, consider what the price of being wrong might be? And who would pick up the tab for your mistake?"

She found his silence patronizing. "Maybe you should have," she suggested as she tossed the small automatic on the desk behind her.

Slowly, Nick lowered his hands.

"No ammo," she offered as she leaned back against the desk with what she hoped passed for an amused and satisfied smile. "There's a full box of shells around here somewhere."

She gave a casual glance to where the checkbook and bank statements covered the desk, then at the nearby filing cabinets with their jumble of parts catalogs, invoices and airtime logs. "You didn't give me enough time to locate them. Of course, if I'd known it was you, I would have looked a hell of a lot harder."

He chuckled unexpectedly, the deep sound seeming to resonate in her middle.

Tightening her arms across her, she watched the play of muscles beneath his shirt as he moved into the hangar's shadows. Though she hated him now, she couldn't seem to quite forget how his chest had once felt beneath her hands.

Fragments of a thousand memories she'd kept locked away, came rushing to the surface. The way he had tasted. The strength of his body. The need he had created in her. She hadn't known who he was then, though, hadn't known what loving him would cost her.

He walked around the brightly painted King Air, with the

airline's trademark spray of bird-of-paradise blooms and thick jungle foliage, seeming to view it from all angles. "I see flying's still in your blood and your smart mouth is the same."

"You used to like my smart mouth."

"Maybe I still do."

The remark caught her off guard. She took a deep breath, let it out slowly. "Okay, Nick. You've had your fun. What do you want?"

Without answering, he prowled past her, his steps taking him to where a short hallway led to a supply closet, the bathroom and a small lounge. Nick stopped to examine the photos just to the right of the door, many of them the same ones that had lined her father's office.

"I always liked this one the best," he commented.

The black-and-white photo commemorated her first solo at age nine. She was perched atop her father's shoulders, her bare knees hanging from beneath her dress, both skinned. Her smile wide and happy, a duplicate of the man who held her aloft.

She wondered if Nick had actually expected her to play nice, to act as if they were old friends. She shook her head in amazement. "I didn't catch the evening news. Did hell freeze over?"

He gave her a tight smile. "I would have thought starting up an airline was a high risk proposition. Seems every time I open a newspaper, one has hit the dust."

Turning away, Kelly caught sight of the satchel on the floor. *Her satchel.* The full impact of the situation hit her. After all, Nick was with Customs.

Maybe she should have thought of it when he'd first shown up, but she hadn't. And there was no way he could know about the bag's contents, was there?

She just needed to remain cool, go on pretending she had nothing to hide. She would have liked to kick the bag under her desk, but knew the action would only serve to draw Nick's attention.

"Okay. Logan's business strategy one-oh-one. Some smaller commuter lines try to make a profit in a saturated market. Too much supply for the demand."

"And the Abacos aren't a tough market? Seems quite a few of the big hitters serve the area. Must make it rough at times."

"You're right. They're not as wide-open as they once were. Making a buck isn't quite as easy."

"There *are* other ways to make cash. Easier ways."

Given their history, she would have to be a complete fool not to realize where he headed with that comment. He thought she was smuggling. Which meant this was undoubtedly some kind of fishing expedition.

Kelly folded her arms across her again. "I think it's time you left. If you don't, I'll have you arrested for trespassing." Her gaze level with his, she picked up the phone as if to make good on the threat.

He waited to move, long enough to let her know he was more amused than worried. Nick pushed away from the wall and walked toward her, his dark gaze never leaving her face.

It was then she realized she wasn't immune to him. Maybe no woman ever could be.

He stopped just in front of her. "Okay. We'll play it your way."

She lifted her chin, tightened her arms and spine. Her heart battered the inside of her ribs, and it wasn't just fear this time. "I do have the home court advantage."

She sensed the tension in his lean body. Felt a more potent one uncurl deep in her own. Being this close to him, the hint of his aftershave reminded her just how grubby she was. Not that she gave a damn. She didn't care what Nick thought of her as long as he left her alone.

She forced herself to keep her gaze level with his. She

could see the small flecks of midnight scattered through steel. He wasn't here to leave her alone. He wanted something. From her.

He smiled slowly, until it was raw and sexy and knowing. "I'll be staying over at the Hopetown Hotel."

"Tell someone who cares."

"I'm just mentioning it because I want you to know I'm not going very far."

"Whatever it is you think you know, you're way off base, Nick."

"I doubt it, Flygirl."

At the door, he picked up his duffel. "Next time you pull a gun, make sure it's loaded. And be ready to use it."

"If I ever have you lined up in my sights again, I won't hesitate."

IT WAS PAST MIDNIGHT when Kelly placed the last crate of bronze castings on the scale. She listed the weight and contents on the manifest, then used a marker to number the top.

At several points during the past hour, she'd caught herself worrying about the reason for Nick's visit.

Obviously he suspected she was involved in some type of smuggling. Not the Ocularcet, she reasoned. The FDA would be more interested than Customs in the unapproved drug she carried in the side pocket of her bag. For Customs to get involved it would have to be something with a financial payoff. If she took their previous history into account, the answers would be guns.

Which meant she had nothing to fear. He wasn't going to find anything incriminating. There were no guns stashed beneath the lounge sink or in the luggage compartments of the King Air.

If Nick wanted to waste his time investigating her, that was his problem and not hers. She'd just keep to business as usual.

And as far as the Ocularcet, come morning, she'd deliver it as planned. If she got caught at Customs going in, so be it. The cause was a worthy one and, with any luck, she wouldn't get jail time. The way she saw it, with a child involved, she didn't have any choice. At least, none that she could live with.

"Hey, there."

Kelly jumped at Ben's greeting. Her earlier irritation rose again. "I thought you were coming back to load the plane."

"And here I am," Ben Tittle stated simply. He was fast pushing sixty. Most would call him scrawny, but that was just an illusion. In the past year, he'd gone native, taken to wearing shorts and T-shirts and often looked as if he'd slept on the beach. Despite his appearance, he was still the best aviation mechanic on the islands. And, after her aunt, the closest thing Kelly had to family.

The stink of stale Scotch and cigarette smoke reached her. She noticed the grin on his face remained uncontrolled, loose, and his eyelids drooped over his watery blue eyes.

Confronting him now about his drinking would be a waste of time. Morning would be more productive. Maybe, after some sleep, she might actually feel up to it.

Kelly secured the luggage compartment on the King Air. "I loaded the foundry's shipment." When Kelly crossed to the desk, Ben followed and stood just behind her as she checked over the flight plan.

"Why take the King?"

"It'll handle the weight well enough, and I have a passenger to pick up. World's most obnoxious passenger, Superjerk, is making another round trip. He's scheduled to go back on Sunday. Bringing a friend with him this time. I can't wait to see if it's male or female. Care to make a small wager?"

She almost wanted to chuckle at the sour expression the news brought to Ben's features. She didn't like Jeff Myers any more than Ben did. Occasionally, when she was out over the Atlantic and the attorney started in on just how rough the ride was, how the beer nuts were stale, how the fare was out of line, she fantasized about opening the door and booting him out.

She flipped through the manifest, thoughts of the lawyer fading. "Nick Cavanaugh dropped by tonight."

She looked up to catch Ben's expression. Though he seemed to be surprised, was he?

"Why would he do that?" Ben asked.

"I thought perhaps you might be able to tell me?"

His eyes narrowed in what appeared to be confusion. "What do you mean?"

"He said you told him where to find me."

"Then he lied."

She nodded. "Which doesn't come as a complete surprise, does it?"

Ben looked relieved at her easy acceptance. He glanced down at his flip-flops. "Did he say what he wanted?"

"No. He didn't come straight out and ask if I was smuggling, but he sure as heck was doing some serious trolling."

"Did you tell him he was wasting his time?"

"Yes. Not that it will stop him." She scanned the top of the desk, felt as if she were leaving something important undone. When nothing reached up and grabbed her, she dismissed the feeling. She was just too tired to think. Too exhausted to even care about Cavanaugh. "The plane needs to be washed and the cabin vacuumed before morning. It might be a good idea if you bunked down here tonight so you can take care of both those things."

Staying at the hangar would also keep him out of ditches, but Ben looked anything but pleased by her request.

He jerked a thumb toward the back room. "I can't get a decent night's sleep on that damn cot."

She sighed. "No matter where you spend the next five

hours, it's not going to qualify as a good night's sleep," she pointed out. "But at least you would be here to do your job." And she wouldn't have to worry about his hurting himself or someone else on the road.

She turned away, as annoyed with herself as she was with Ben. She wasn't being completely fair here. He'd stood by her through the very dark days following her father's death. Without him, she could never have even made a go at the airline. The first year, he'd taken only a small wage and, without the funds he'd recently put in, Bird of Paradise would already be out of business.

She faced him. "I'm sorry. I guess I'm just tired. And I'm worried."

"About Cavanaugh?"

"No. About you. About your drinking." As soon as she said it, the look in his eyes went from concern for her to wariness. There was no going back, though. "What's going on, Ben?"

"Nothing. I'm just having a good time."

"No, you're not," she said quietly and picked up her satchel. She stopped at the door and turned back. "This can't continue. It's not good for your health."

"I know," he said. "I'll handle it."

"I'm here for you," she said. "Just as you've always been there for me."

"I've never doubted it," he said and smiled before he, too, turned away.

AFTER LEAVING KELLY, Nick hiked toward the marina. He'd made arrangements earlier to be taken over to Elbow Cay by boat. Marsh Harbor was the most densely populated area of the Abacos, but at this time of night the streets were empty, especially of taxis.

With no traffic to watch for, he found himself thinking about the meeting with Kelly. She had changed, but her hatred hadn't. He hadn't expected it to. Just as he hadn't really expected Kelly to provide him with any answers tonight. He just wanted to make her nervous, give her something to worry about.

And, if he wanted to be truthful, he'd been curious enough to want an up-close-and-personal look at the girl-woman he'd investigated seven years ago. From what he'd seen, there was little of the *girl* left.

He recalled the way her shorts had exposed unbelievably long and tanned athletic legs. Where her blouse had been un-buttoned, smooth skin glistened. And above that were the pale green eyes filled with loathing.

Not that he gave a damn how she looked at him. The only thing Nick wanted from Kelly was information that would take him even one step closer to finding Ake's killer. That was it.

Not that he held out a lot of hope. She was his weakest lead at this point. Come morning, he'd start making inquiries on a more promising one. He had a line on a guy who had worked on Binelli's yacht up until several weeks ago. Disgruntled employees were usually willing to talk. And of course, Binelli wasn't the most understanding of ex-employers.

He needed to work fast, though. After all, he was functioning in some very gray areas.

Even showing up in Kelly's hangar tonight was likely to have repercussions. Officially, he was staying in the Abacos for a much-needed vacation. But, after tonight, he wouldn't be surprised if he didn't appear very prominently in several surveillance photos.

And once those photos landed on Myron's desk, Nick would be ordered back stateside.

He'd had to pull half a dozen favors to get what information he had on the FBI's current investigation. Which wasn't nearly enough.

What he did know was that they'd been documenting Binelli's business dealings, both legal and illegal, for over a year. The possibility of a connection between Binelli and Kelly had surfaced only recently, though, when Binelli's attorney, Jeff Myers, had used Bird of Paradise for repeated trips to the islands.

Early on, there had been no substantiating evidence. No cash had been uncovered during inspections, even when dogs were used, and all transactions within Kelly's bank accounts had remained consistent with those of a struggling company. At least, they had until the end of June, when a single large deposit of cash had been made. There had been no paper trail. Not conclusive, but when added to the previous history, it was highly suspicious.

Nick shifted the weight of the duffel higher on his shoulder. He still hadn't been able to figure out the "similarities" Ake had mentioned on the phone.

The rumble of a car motor broke the night's stillness. Nick glanced back at the approaching vehicle, only the second he'd seen since leaving the hangar. Edging over, he made room on the narrow road for the car. He looked over his shoulder again as the vehicle drew closer, but kept walking.

The car's engine roared suddenly. Tires squealed.

Nick dove sideways. But not fast enough.

The chrome bumper slammed into his thigh, the impact catapulting him across the hood.

He tried to roll with the impact, lessen its pounding effect, but pain exploded in his head as he crashed into the windshield.

Chapter Three

An hour later, Kelly took the winding road to the marina where she kept her boat. She had planned to stay at Aunt Sarah's tonight, as she had for the past two nights, because her aunt was out of town, but now wanted the comfort of her own bed.

Having parked at the far edge of the lot, she walked toward the rented slip behind the building. A breeze off the water cooled the night, brought the temperatures, which hovered close to a hundred in the daytime, down to the low nineties, almost bearable if you added a cold drink to the equation.

The squat, frame structure housing the water taxi lay dark. She glanced absently in the front window as she passed. Lights from the back filtered through, creating a shadowed army out of several dozen plastic waiting room chairs.

During the drive, she had managed to keep her thoughts away from Nick and focused on Ben.

She wondered if he was worried about Bird of Paradise going under. Sixty-year-old mechanics weren't exactly in demand. Especially considering the industry's recent problems. Within the past month, one of the big carriers had announced it was closing its doors for good. That meant huge layoffs and a glut of aviation workers scrambling for jobs. Not that Ben would be the only one faced with the prospect. It wasn't just ticket agents and flight attendants and mechanics losing jobs. There would be plenty of pilots walking the streets, too. Many of them would be far more experienced than she was.

Kelly turned the corner of the building. A bulb had burned out in the light fixture, leaving the sidewalk in deeper darkness. She shifted the weight of the satchel to her other shoulder. In all likelihood, to find work, she'd have to leave the islands and her aunt.

The sudden pain in her upper arm nearly drove her to her knees. She screamed. Someone—a man—a large man—grabbed her and hauled her back into the dark alcove of the side entrance.

He shoved her face-first against the building. Splinters from the rough wood siding scraped her palms as she tried to protect her face.

"Shut up." A knife blade flashed next to her cheek.

When she tried to look at him, he drove her farther into the corner.

"Do that again, you're dead."

Blood pounded in her ears. She gulped air, tried to stay reasonably calm by concentrating on fragments of information. He was dressed well. Not a T-shirt. A sports jacket. Hard-soled shoes. She could hear them against the concrete. His voice. Not rough, like his words. Maybe from the Midwest.

"There's some money in my bag. Take it. Whatever you—"

Not waiting for her to finish. He jerked the satchel off her arm, tossing it away, then forced a dirty burlap bag over her head.

She gagged violently. The scratchy cloth smelled as if it had been used to haul fish or conch. Or worse.

Blinded, she could still feel the blade resting against the side of her neck. He pulled her around, ripped open her blouse.

Air spilled from her lungs. "No!" She tried to pull away. He forced her flat to the wall again.

"Please. No," she begged in a harsh whisper, unable to find the breath to speak louder. "Please!"

The sound of his heavy breathing told her he was looking at her. As his fingers brushed the material covering her breasts, then explored more boldly, she attempted to emotionally disconnect. She needed to stay calm, to think. He didn't want her able to identify him. Maybe he intended to let her live.

Or was the blindfold meant to terrify her further?

He chuckled softly as a tremor went through her. "I said take it easy. *Kelly.*"

She went rigid at the sound of her name, was thankful for the wall at her back when her knees gave out. She wasn't a random victim. He knew her. How? From where?

The knife scraping the side of her neck cut short any further attempt to think.

He dragged the blade upward almost as if it were a razor, heat, the warm trickle of her blood, following the cool sting of steel.

She swallowed reflexively, felt the edge bite again. Instinct ordered her to jerk away. She fought the urge this time. "Please," she begged again through gritted teeth. "Please…"

Ignoring her pleas, or perhaps because he enjoyed hearing them, he used the tip of the knife, this time slicing the skin over her collarbone. She bit back the sharp gasp of pain. Living was all that mattered.

"I…I'll do whatever…y…you want," she repeated, the sour burn of bile mixing at the back of her throat with the metallic taste of fear.

"Sure you will. Now that I've got your attention. And because you're a smart lady and you want to live, don't you?"

She nodded.

Where was the knife? She couldn't feel it. Not at her throat. Not where he'd just cut her. Where was it?

"You've got something doesn't belong to you. All you have to do is return it."

"I don't underst—"

He forced a knee between her legs. "Mr. Binelli pays me to make sure no one screws with him. I'm damned good at it, too. So don't *screw* with me."

"I…I don't know what… I don't know any Bin…Binelli. A mistake—"

He used his grip on the burlap sack to slam her head back against the siding, used his forearm across her throat to keep her there. "No. You're making the mistake, Kelly."

He stroked a fingertip over the wound on her collar bone, the touch oddly gentle, at odds with his other actions, then traced a circle around each cloth-covered nipple. She clenched her eyes closed as if that would somehow block out the image in her mind. It didn't.

"Perhaps you remember him now?" he asked calmly. She could feel his erection now. Pressing against her abdomen.

She found herself nodding. *Give him what he wants. Appear to go along. Survive.*

"See. Isn't that easier? You have twenty-four hours to return what doesn't belong to you."

She numbly nodded again.

"There was a Customs man at your place. What did he want?"

He'd been watching her even then, knew Nick had been there. When she tried to speak, her voice shook. "He wanted to… He asked about flights."

His fingers continued their play. "You wouldn't be stupid enough to lie to me, would you?"

She swallowed. "No. I wouldn't—"

"I didn't think so. And it better stay that way. Return what doesn't belong to you and you'll live." He leaned down until his mouth was next to her ear. "Play games, talk to Customs or the police, the only thing you'll be good for is shark bait."

He abruptly shoved her down into the corner. She cowered on the cold concrete.

Pulling her blouse together, she felt for buttons with stiff fingers; finding none, she tied it together. She could feel him standing over her. Clasping her arms, she fought to control the sharp shudders that came endlessly, one after the other.

When enough minutes had stretched, soundless and expectant—when she had finally convinced herself she was wrong about her attacker still being there—she felt the first glimmer of relief and reached for the burlap still covering her head.

His low chuckle stopped her in midmotion.

He'd been watching her cringe like some beaten animal at his feet. Anger twisted in her.

She left the blindfold in place, but pushed her way up the wall until she stood unsteadily. "You won't kill me. We both know it. Not until Binelli gets what he wants."

He laughed. "Don't go thinking you're too smart, Kelly. Or I'll be forced to finish what I've started here."

"You'd like that, wouldn't you, you sick bastard?"

He stepped closer. "No. I'd love it."

At his words, Kelly took a sharp breath. She listened to the crunch of his footsteps as he walked away.

With the first heave, Kelly ripped off the hood. Doubled over, she emptied her stomach in the corner. She scraped at the dampness on her cheeks, wobbled back a step, then, straightening, dragged her fingers through her sweaty hair. She tested her bruised cheekbone.

Binelli? Who in the hell was Binelli? Why did her attacker think she knew him when she'd never even heard the name before?

She grappled to make any sense out of what had happened, but no matter how she turned it, she was in deep trouble. The kind where people ended up dead.

She'd been right all along. Nick's showing up tonight hadn't been by chance. He'd been after something. She couldn't even begin to figure out what was going on, but she was sure Nick already knew what the attack had been all about.

She stood there in indecision. She needed to move. But where? Going to the police would be a waste of time. They couldn't help her. They'd fill out a report. Send someone out to gather evidence, including the vomit. In the meantime, she'd be like a blind woman. She didn't known what her attacker looked like. He could walk up to her in broad daylight on the street, in a crowd, or anywhere, and kill her.

Who was Binelli?

Taking a sharp breath, she bent forward, pushing hard against her abdomen, the panic so sharp it felt as if a knife were being driven between her ribs. When she finally managed to straighten again, sweat poured from her.

If she wanted to live, she needed answers.

And the only one likely to have them was Nick.

THERE WERE NO LIGHTS ON inside the hotel, most tourists having fled the intense heat of July and the threat of hurricane season. The air was heavy and hot and suffocating; the moon, nearly full and high in the sky, was bright enough to throw sharp shadows beneath the trees.

A hunter's moon.

Kelly circled the long, low-slung structure until she spotted a single room off by itself where the drapes were drawn.

She approached carefully. If there had been anywhere else for her to go for the answers, anyone else for her to turn to, she wouldn't have come here.

After looking nervously over her shoulder, the memory of her attacker's warning to stay clear of Nick still prominent in her mind, she tapped lightly.

"Nick, open up. It's Kelly."

Nothing. Not even the sound of someone moving around inside. She rapped again, this time with more force.

Then, when there was no answer, with desperation.

The panic she'd barely kept under control broke loose inside her and she pounded harder. Had he lied about where he was staying?

And, if he wasn't here, what was she going to do? Where would she go? Who could she turn to?

"It's a little late for social calls."

Though the slow drawl of Nick's words had barely broken the night's silence, she jumped.

As she spun to face him, her hand climbed to her throat, remained there.

He leaned against a pillar not more than five feet away, his stance seemingly as lazy as his voice. And yet, even with the distance between them, she could feel the tension in his body, the sharp interest in his gaze.

He wore the jeans he'd had on earlier and a dark shirt, which hung from his shoulders unbuttoned and untucked. As her glance swept down to his bare feet, she hesitated on the automatic he held in front of him, the barrel currently pointed at the concrete.

He thumbed on the safety before palming the piece.

"I would have figured this was the last place you'd show

up tonight, Kel." He arched a brow. "Or any night, for that matter."

She shut her eyes briefly, forcing her thoughts into some semblance of order, and was thankful for the deeper shadows of the covered walkway. She didn't want him to see just how terrified, how desperate she was feeling.

Hugging the green hooded jacket she'd pulled on over her ruined blouse, she looked down, the shakes still wracking her body. "I want some answers."

As he closed the distance between them, Nick watched for signs of a weapon, but saw none. A satchel weighted her left shoulder, a good spot to conceal a gun, but she seemed barely to notice it hanging there. Her hair was windblown around her face.

Stopping in front of her, he couldn't seem to stop his fingers from lifting a strand of it, testing its texture, getting closer to her than she wanted him to be. Invading her space.

He realized he'd forgotten just how short she was. Maybe five-four at most and a hundred and ten pounds of hard muscle and flowing curves. Soft skin. An appealing package if you could ignore her taste in business partners.

"What kind of answers are you looking for?"

As he tucked the hair behind her ear, he saw the scrape on the side of her neck. Or was it a burn of some sort? "What's this?"

When he tried to touch her, she jerked away, covered the area with her hand.

"Nothing," she said and met his gaze.

It worried him that the usual directness was oddly absent, her pupils appearing overdilated. As if she were on something.

Nick felt his nerves take a little joyride on him. He needed to be damned careful. It had been after leaving her hangar tonight that someone had tried to resurface the local roads with his hide. Either she'd made a phone call after he'd left or she was being watched and whoever was doing the watching had followed him.

"Kelly?"

She looked up at him. "I want… I need to know the real reason you came to see me. No more games," she added.

Without answering, he reached around her and turned the doorknob. He sensed her withdrawal as he once more got too close. "Let's take this conversation inside. Where we can talk without any interruptions."

She remained where she was, her arms locked around her body, across the jacket. Out on the water, it might have been needed, but why continue to wear the coat? Especially zipped up tight as it was now?

Unless she was hiding something beneath.

"Inside is safer." Without waiting for her agreement, he shoved the door wide and, simply by advancing, forced her backward.

All of the rooms had been furnished pretty much the same. Inexpensive hotel furniture from the eighties, worn terrazzo floors, cotton spreads. A refrigerator in one corner.

"You wouldn't have brought any surprises with you?" he asked as he kicked the door shut and slid the Glock into the holster concealed beneath his shirt. "Maybe in that bag of yours?"

He stripped the satchel off her shoulder and tossed it toward the bed, heard it land on the mattress. "I need to check you for a weapon."

"There's no need—"

"We can make this fast and easy, or difficult. It's your choice. But I don't plan to have a gun stuck in my face twice in one night."

Making a sound somewhere between disbelief and disgust, she held her arms away from her sides.

He patted her down, his hands moving over her quickly, efficiently, finding those areas where concealment of an automatic weapon might be possible. He could feel her rebelling when he checked the area between and below her breasts, then lower.

Touching her in the nearly dark room, even in the rapid, fluid motion of a professional body search, even with the possibility someone might bust through the door behind him, brought back memories of the last night they'd spent together. His hands had done a hell of a lot more in Key West. And, yet, he recalled how, at the time, it hadn't been nearly enough. Another of his regrets, he realized, and tossed it into the basket with the rest of them. One of these days, he was going to run out of room.

Nick stepped back abruptly. After dragging a small dresser in front of the door, he picked up the satchel and grabbed Kelly loosely by the upper arm. "Should I expect company?"

"Like who?"

The edge of irritation and impatience in her voice sounded more like the woman who had confronted him with a gun earlier that night. Moments ago outside, he'd thought he'd sensed something far different, something he hadn't been able to identify. And, because he couldn't, it had worried him. "Maybe you brought a few friends along."

"I think I would remember if I had."

"But would you tell me?"

He wasn't surprised when she ignored the question.

"Next door," he ordered, ushering her toward the connecting opening.

After twisting the lock and shoving a straightback chair under the knob, he crossed to the window. He didn't like it. Kelly showing up like this. First the hit-and-run attempt and now Kelly's nocturnal visit.

What did it mean? Who wanted him dead? No one from

the States had known where he was going or what his intentions were. As far as Myron knew, he was taking a few weeks off to get his head straightened out.

"Stay there," Nick ordered when she tried to follow. As she sank onto the bed, he briefly scanned the stretch of lawn ending at the incline to the beach below, then dropped the satchel at his feet and stooped next to it. He used one hand to do a rough search. Finding no weapon, he tossed it on the closest bed. "You packed light tonight."

She retrieved the bag. "Did you really expect to find a gun in there?"

"Call me cautious."

Something Ake hadn't been on that final night. Which was only one aspect of his murder that worried Nick. How had the killer managed to get close enough on a wide-open rooftop to put two well-placed bullets in Ake's skull? Nick didn't like any of the possibilities that came to mind.

He again looked out the window. If trouble came, it would be from out there. "You wanted to talk, so have at it."

"Why are you over here? Out of your jurisdiction?"

"Vacation." He glanced at her and added, "To do some scuba diving."

In obvious impatience at his answer, she shoved a hand through her hair. She glanced away briefly, maybe in indecision, then met his gaze again, her lips thinned.

"You expect me to believe that? That you just happened to run into Ben tonight over at Gilroy's—a meeting Ben says never took place? That you decided to stop by the hangar for the sake of old times?" She took a sharp breath. "The *old times* weren't that good, Nick. In fact, I could have gone my whole life without ever laying eyes on you again."

She tightened her arms across her. "So can we just cut to the chase here? What is it you're after? What is it you think I'm involved in?"

"Come off it, Kelly. Wasn't it you who said no more games?"

"Who is Binelli?"

His expression hardened. "The innocent act won't play this time. I may have bought it seven years ago, but I know better this time. Tell me, what are the chances of an *innocent* citizen's name coming up twice in connection to the same type of crime?"

She remained in the shadows. "You think I'm smuggling again."

"If you came here hoping to convince me you're not laundering Binelli's drug money, you're wasting your breath." He glanced out the window again.

"Laundering drug money? You're wrong, Nick, about me, about my being involved with anyone named Binelli. As wrong as you were about everything seven years ago."

He turned and faced her. "Do I need to remind you that your father's prints were on the two remaining crates we found in the storeroom that morning, on the guns inside them?"

"Do I need to remind *you* that, except for the prints, except for the word of a weapons dealer who had previously perjured himself on the stand, the evidence was circumstantial? Photos of me and Dad with Aidan. He'd been a guest in our house for years. Not often, maybe, but he still stopped around to talk about old times, about flying. God, Nick, they grew up together."

"On the streets of Belfast. Where they both lost family."

"Dad hated war, violence of any kind."

"Yet he welcomed a man with known terrorist connections into his home. Invited a man who supplied weapons that killed and maimed to sit at his table."

"You sat there, too. He trusted you just as he did Aidan. Look how wrong he was about *you*. You betrayed the friendship in every conceivable way."

"Are you suggesting he didn't know about Aidan?"

She let out a sharp breath. "I don't know. Maybe he did. Perhaps he turned a blind eye to Aidan's connections. He never discussed Aidan with me. But my father can't defend himself, can he? He never got the chance."

"No, he didn't. But does an innocent man hang himself? Leave a note admitting to a crime he didn't commit? In that same note, exonerate his daughter? I'm sorry for what he did, but he *was* guilty."

"And me? Because I didn't hang myself. Does that mean I wasn't guilty? Is that why you guys didn't charge me?"

Nick rubbed his face. Had she been guilty then? Had she known what her father was doing? It was a question he'd wrestled with for the past seven years. And as far as the reason Kelly hadn't been indicted, it had been a judgment call made by prosecutors. There had been no direct evidence linking Kelly to the guns. And they'd thought that selling nineteen-year-old Kelly as a desperate gun runner with connections to a terrorist organization to a jury would be a real uphill battle. One they might not win.

"Nick?"

"You'd do better to worry about the present, Kelly. If you want to talk, really talk, I'll listen. I'll do whatever I can to help you."

"Just as you did in New Jersey?" She picked up the satchel from where she'd laid it on the bed, and then hesitated. In the dimness, he couldn't read her eyes. "Maybe you've forgotten how it was, Nick. How you left me in that holding cell. How you walked away without ever once looking back.

"I had just watched my father be cut down from that rafter." She took a deep breath, met his gaze again. "I thought I was in love with you back then. It was your arms I turned to, your arms I wanted locked around me. Until that moment, I trusted you. Even when I learned who you really were.

What you were. I don't think I'll make the same mistake twice," she offered and, without waiting, crossed to the door.

"Kelly?"

She stopped, her hand already on the knob.

"Be careful. Binelli plays by his own rules." Nick didn't know why he felt it necessary to offer the warning. Maybe because he knew the people she'd chosen to associate with, was worried she might not know the full extent of what they were capable of.

"I already got a taste of it tonight." Turning, she unzipped her jacket, pulled it wide.

Confronted with the torn and bloodied blouse, Nick hauled her forward into the moonlight coming through the window. What he'd thought was a burn or scrape on the side of her neck, what she'd been careful to conceal from him by the hooded collar of her jacket, he now recognized as the work of a knife. Though it wasn't, the cut in the area of her collarbone had bled enough to look serious. He didn't miss the pattern some scum had drawn on her bra. All wounds easily concealed beneath clothing. Her attacker obviously had some practice at terrorizing women.

"Who did this?"

"We didn't exactly get around to formal introductions."

"Why did it happen?"

"Why? Because Binelli thinks I have something that belongs to him?"

Kelly stepped free of his grasp, rezipped the jacket as he moved back half a step. "I don't suppose it matters that I have never set eyes on Binelli."

"And that's why some of Binelli's muscle messed you up? Because you don't know the man?"

"If I knew what was going on, I wouldn't have wasted my time coming here, would I?"

"Oh, I don't know," he said, his tone hard-edged. "With

your back plastered to the wall, I might look like your best hope."

Something, maybe indecision about his next move, made him look out the window at that moment.

A man sprinted across the lawn. A second followed.

Busy watching the two, he hadn't seen Kelly reaching for the door again until it was almost too late. He grabbed her before she could get it open. "Don't go out there. You're safer with me. For now."

She tried to shake free of his hold, but he only tightened his grip on her upper arm. "Damn it! Listen to me. There are two men outside watching the room next door."

"I don't think I was followed. I was careful."

"Which means it's me they're after."

"Why would they be after you?"

"Doesn't really matter, does it? The outcome will be the same. For both of us."

"I was warned not to contact you or the police."

He stared outside again. "So why did you come to me, Kelly, and not the police?"

"The police wouldn't be able to protect me, not against someone like Binelli. And they'd only have questions. You, on the other hand, have answers."

"None you'll like." He pushed her back into the shadows next to the wall, out of harm's way, then flicked off the automatic's safety.

"Hell of a first night of vacation, don't you think?" he added as he took up a position next to the window.

Nick watched the shadows of two men sweep past. He didn't question the decision to take Kelly along, told himself it was because she just might be able to provide him with some of the answers he needed. But he knew better.

"How did you get here?" he asked.

"Boat."

Nick eased forward and, as he watched, one of the men rolled around in a smooth, practiced motion and kicked in the door to the adjoining room. Furniture thudded and banged. Nick's attention shot to the connecting door between the two rooms as a solid blow landed against it.

He checked back outside to where the second man stood guard. He needed him to follow his partner inside. Otherwise, they were as good as trapped.

Another kick landed against the connecting door. He could hear the jamb splinter.

"Be ready for anything," Nick said between gritted teeth, but didn't look in Kelly's direction.

The chair under the knob exploded across the room.

The second man followed the first in.

Nick ripped the front door open, grabbed Kelly and shoved her outside ahead of him.

Chapter Four

"No matter what, keep moving!"

Nick dragged her along with him. Moonlight splashed down on the wide expanse of yard, forcing them to hug the shadows of the cement block building.

At the sound of footsteps behind, he glanced back. "We've been made." His fingers tightened around her upper arm. With the automatic held easily in his right hand, he looked more like a warrior than anything civilized. She took comfort in that. Nick was a tenacious fighter, a survivor. If anyone could keep them alive, he could.

He crowded her closer still to the building, until her shoulder scraped the block's roughness. She gritted her teeth against the pain.

When she looked up at him, she noticed his attention focused on the walkway ahead. In another dozen yards, they'd run out of cover; they'd have to sprint across open lawn. "Is there another way to the dock?"

"Not without going back."

"Where are the keys to the boat?" he asked sharply.

"In the ignition."

Glancing back, he swore and roughly shoved her ahead of him, his body blocking hers as he lifted the gun. He squeezed off three quick rounds.

The vibration of sound slammed through her, sharp staccato punches to her chest. At any moment, she expected to feel the impact of bullets. She lost her hold on her bag and grabbed for it as Nick pulled her forward.

"Leave it!"

"No." She jerked free.

With a grim expression, he retrieved it, passed it to her.

Thirty feet out, motion-sensitive outdoor flood lamps captured them in a searchlight glare. A shot, muffled by a silencer, popped. A second and third followed. The ground at their feet exploded.

Nick turned, fired quick rounds at the wall where their pursuers sought cover, then two more at the spotlights. Glass exploded and rained down as they continued to run.

Kelly shifted the weight of the satchel to the opposite shoulder. She pushed herself, yet still slowed Nick. If she hadn't been such a damned coward, she'd tell him to leave her, but when it came to men with guns…

Another shot snapped. Her knees buckled. Nick grabbed her hand, and she half stumbled in his wake toward the stairs and the cover of trees ahead.

More shots. A barrage that chewed the air, the ground. Yet she could barely hear them over the roar of blood in her ears. They weren't going to make it. It was all going to end here. She was never going to know *why*. Never going to know *who*.

Nick faltered beside her, then, with a sharp intake of breath, went down.

In horror, she watched as his face twisted with pain. He'd been shot. In the leg.

Cursing, he rolled and unloaded the remaining bullets from his position on the ground as the two men vaulted the wall. One fell, remained doubled over. Not dead, but wounded.

Nick ejected the spent clip. He slammed in another and

immediately tapped out additional rounds, forcing the remaining man to seek shelter again.

Climbing to his feet, Nick pushed her ahead of him. "When we get to the top of the steps, I'll drop back and slow him. If I'm not there by the time you have the motor started, get the hell out of here." His fingers tightened. "Don't wait on me."

Her lips thinned. "You didn't leave me back there."

"I don't have time to argue."

"Just make sure you're there."

Kelly focused intently on the trees ahead, the shade beneath them. The possibility of some cover. But it would also make the steep stairs difficult to handle.

Her foot was already on the top step when she saw the man on her boat and dove to the ground. She barely heard the rustle of land crabs around her or felt their hard bodies brushing against her. The man now ripped open the compartments where bait and freshly caught fish were usually kept. Fiberglass covers slammed against the boat deck.

With the next burst of gunfire, he glanced up, appeared to gaze directly at her, though she knew he couldn't really see her.

In the next instant, he vaulted over the side of the boat and onto the dock.

"More company," she said when Nick dropped next to her.

For a brief second, breathing hard, he watched the man sprinting the length of the dock, then glanced over his shoulder, possibly gauging how much longer they had before they were squeezed. "I've always liked a challenge."

"Well, I don't." She wiped the sweat from her forehead. "What now?" Her lungs still burning, she looked toward the hotel, but couldn't locate the man closing in from behind. "I can't run much farther. With your leg, neither can you. I know a place," she said and fought to breathe. "Not too far.

A house. We should be able…" She saw his hesitation. "If you have a better solution…"

The man was at the bottom of the steps now. In seconds, he could be right on top of them.

"Nick?"

He pulled her up. "Which way?"

As soon as they stood, they were spotted. The man below held fire, perhaps briefly afraid the shadows belonged to his friends, but the man behind didn't hesitate. Bullets ripped savagely at leaves and twigs and hunks of bark.

After half a dozen steps. Nick pushed her to the ground. Dropping to one knee beside her, he unloaded yet another clip. Explosion after explosion went off until she lost track of which protected her—the ones from Nick's gun—and which came from the weapons of their pursuers.

A bullet slammed within inches of her hand, then closer still until she felt the heat of its impact as it chewed a hole in the soil. Her chest ached as if she'd been pummeled. She couldn't seem to breath. Or think. Or move. Instead of seconds and minutes, time was measured in never-ending explosions.

Then deafening silence.

Nick remained kneeling over her, his left hand keeping her down, his face barely discernable in the shadows as he waited. Instead of its usual saltiness, the night air tasted of spent powder. And of fear.

He wrapped his fingers around her upper arm and bent down until his mouth was close to her ear. "When I give the signal, run. I'll be right behind you."

She looked around her for the first time. They were closer to the hotel's maintenance alley than she had realized.

"Now!"

Kelly scrabbled to her feet, headed for the cover of a Dumpster as more rounds attempted to force them back to the ground. Nick followed.

They worked their way around the back of the hotel by way of the service courtyard and alley. The beach was an easy sprint just beyond and offered the cover of trees and dunes.

Ten minutes later, they ducked into a narrow lane created by tall, vine-covered fences. Nick rested behind a group of trash cans, while Kelly slumped against the side of the building, her lungs on fire. Her leg muscles, after running close to a mile in the soft sand, cramped. In fact, at that moment, there wasn't much of her body that didn't hurt, ache or burn.

"I don't like it," Nick said. "That was too easy."

"Easy?" she managed between heaving breaths. "I'd like to see your idea of hard." She closed her eyes. "I take that back." She exhaled harshly. "I'd rather not."

Nick's expression remained grim. "Even if the one I hit wasn't just wounded, one of the other two should have continued to chase us."

"Maybe they were afraid of the police."

"Men like that aren't worried about the law."

"You were well prepared," she commented. "As if you were expecting them."

"I was warned." He placed the gun next to him on the pavement while he removed his shirt.

"You said those men might have been looking for you?"

"Yeah." He didn't elaborate.

Earlier, she'd noticed changes in him. But since she'd knocked on his door those differences had become even more apparent. There had been no hesitation, no change in his voice when he talked of killing a man.

Seven years ago, there had been a softness in Nick. It had been so deeply imbedded at his core it had been nearly impossible to reach, but in those last few weeks before her father's suicide, before everything had changed, she'd seen glimpses. She suspected it no longer existed. He was now as ruthless and determined as the men following them. The bare, well-muscled chest and shoulders and the leather holster weighted with a very serious piece of steel did nothing to lessen her impression of him. Nor did the closed expression on his rugged face.

With her forearm, Kelly swiped away some of the sweat continuing to bead her forehead. What had happened in the intervening years to harden him. The job, no doubt.

"How many bullets do you have left?"

He stood to wrap the shirt around his thigh. "Enough to keep us alive a bit longer."

The wound didn't look so bad from where she was sitting, though she suspected, listening to his harsh intake of breath as he pulled the material tight, it was causing him quite a bit of pain.

Kelly followed suit and got to her feet. The last thing she wanted to be was left behind. "Are you going to be all right?"

"Yeah." He started to take her arm, then seemed to decide against it. "It'll need to be cleaned out when we get wherever we're going. Perhaps now would be a good time for you to let me in on our destination."

Kelly picked her way along the alley. "My aunt's house. She's out of town until tomorrow."

Nick caught up and pulled her to a stop. "I don't recall any aunt." He tightened his fingers around her arm.

She sensed his distrust. "I'll tell you what, Cavanaugh. You can believe whatever you want. You can put your ass right back on the ground and stay here with your leg the way it is, but, right now, I want more cover than this alley is providing and maybe some kind of bed."

With that, she jerked free of his hold and turned and walked away. Nick caught up, fell in step beside her.

They were a strange pair, he decided. Neither trusting the other, yet linked together again by a second twist of fate. He glanced over at her, studied her profile. The hair, red-gold when caught in sunlight or in lamplight, turned a paler, more muted shade in the moonlight. The tail end of a breeze played with it now.

He recalled the feel of it earlier. Silky and cool. Just like her skin… Nick kicked that door shut. Kelly was no less desirable now than she had been back in Jersey, but he was a hell of a lot smarter now.

They passed no one as they traveled the narrow streets.

Brightly colored cottages and shacks jumbled along the waterfront like cereal boxes on a shelf. The muggy night air offered odors. Age and uncollected trash. Hibiscus and frangipani blooms. The stench of oyster beds at low tide.

Though Elbow Cay was a decent-sized island, the settlement was compact, small enough they'd be easy to spot.

"I'd liked to get off these streets. How much farther?

"We're close."

He followed without comment when she ducked down a narrow alley between a pair of two-story clapboard structures. Though she didn't knock before entering the unlocked door of one of them, caution made him pause to check the area.

A cat, curled in sleep, was braced against the front door of the other building as if waiting for it to open. A flag barely fluttered overhead. Otherwise, there was no sign of life, no lights on inside either home.

The door through which Kelly disappeared groaned softly with the breeze. Tension tightened in him as he considered the possibility he'd walked into a trap. Not of Binelli's making, but of Kelly's. There was no aunt. He'd done the background check on her seven years ago and knew as much.

Nick removed the magazine clip from his weapon, switched it with the full one in his pocket. Safety off, he edged inside, halting next to her.

Except for the subtle scent of a recently cooked meal, the dark room smelled much as the outdoors had. The French doors along the opposite wall were open, moonlight angling into an enclosed courtyard beyond.

Something moved in the shadows and he aimed the Glock.

"No!" Kelly ordered in a desperate whisper and nearly tripped over a suitcase. "It's a cat."

Nick dropped the muzzle of his weapon. "A cat?" Most of the furniture suddenly seemed alive as tabbies and Persians and calicos spilled like an advancing army onto the floor. Some mewed in quiet greeting, others in a complaining meow.

"Looks like the local feline rescue."

He nudged a suitcase with a foot. "Your aunt's? The one who is out of town?"

He didn't like it. He was still weighing his options when she suddenly tried to shove past him and out the door.

"We can't stay here."

Instead of letting her go, Nick pushed her farther inside, closed the door behind them.

If she was worried about who was upstairs there was a fifty-fifty chance it was an aunt. They were better odds than he'd get with Binelli's people.

"We stay here tonight and get out before first light."

"No we don't. I won't put her at risk."

"You should have thought about that before now." He wrapped a hand around her upper arm. "But since you didn't, you can make some introductions."

She tried to twist free. "Like hell, I will! Just look at us. Your leg. My clothes. The only thing that would accomplish is scaring her."

"Where does she sleep?"

"Upstairs. But, Nick, please don't—"

"Save it, sweetheart." He escorted her roughly to the steps, Kelly continuing to fight him.

"Damn it, Nick!"

He only tightened his hold. "Maybe you've forgotten just how well I knew you at one time. And maybe you've forgotten that touching performance you gave the press about how your father was the only family you had? How you had been left alone in the world?"

Nick felt her anger even before it manifested itself into the small, but hard fist she threw at him. The blow was glancing, but still carried enough power that when it landed on his already bruised ribs, he fell back half a step.

She didn't fight like a girl. He realized he should have remembered as much. When she would have tried a second, he caught her wrist. "Take it easy. I just wanted to get the story straight."

Eyeing him, Kelly pushed a section of hair behind her ear. There was no way he was ever going to believe her or trust her. And no reason to continue fighting the inevitable.

Besides, at the moment she wanted a shower and a bed. "Okay. Whatever."

He waited while she zipped the jacket, did her best to straighten her hair.

They climbed into the darkness. The air was warm and musty, the daytime heat trapped in the narrow stairwell. The wooden treads, weak with age, gave slightly under his heavier weight. Ahead of him, Kelly moved with the sureness of familiarity.

Near the top, he pulled her to a stop. He could feel the rigid anger in her body. Or perhaps it was fear.

Was she afraid she'd be caught in the cross fire? He had proof of her complicity. Binelli wouldn't be after her if she hadn't double-crossed him. If she would double-cross someone like Binelli, why not a Customs agent?

This time, when Kelly tried to move ahead, Nick tugged her back against him. "Not so fast." His hand crept beneath her hair as he eased her more tightly against him with the hand still holding the automatic.

He was suddenly very aware of the soft feel of her body touching his. "I'd hate to see anything happen to you, so don't do anything foolish." He dropped the hand holding the gun, allowing their bodies to hide the weapon.

"Aunt Sarah?"

Nick heard the shift of sheets. As light leaked from beneath the closed door, he eased back, taking Kelly with him. The door opened slowly.

The woman was somewhere in her eighties. Her white hair hung in braids on either side of her face.

"Has something happened, dear?"

"Just a boat problem. Nothing serious. I hope you don't mind if Nick uses the guest room?"

"Of course not. Let me pull on a robe and I'll help you freshen the linens."

"The sheets are fine." Kelly offered a reassuring smile. "Go back to bed. I'll take care of Nick. I just wanted you to know we were here in case you heard us moving around."

"If you are certain?"

Kelly nodded. "I didn't expect you back until tomorrow."

"I missed my kitties."

"Of course you did," Kelly murmured. "Good night, then,"

As soon as the door closed, Kelly faced Nick. "Unless you're afraid of eighty-two-year-old women and what they might do to you in your bed, you should be satisfied now, Investigator."

When she shoved past him, he let her go.

Kelly waited for him at the bottom of the steps. "The bedroom's this way." She led him through the kitchen, then down a cramped hall at the back of the house.

"The bed isn't the most comfortable," she said as she opened a door.

The glow of the small lamp she turned on seemed to mellow the scratched and dented surface of the brass headboard. A large crucifix hung in the shadows just above and reminded him of the one over his grandparents' bed.

On the opposite wall, a dresser stood, topped by a mirror.

Except for the large, boldly done oil painting of a calico cat sitting in the sculptural shade beneath a tree, the room was dated and, Nick suspected, rarely used.

Kelly switched on the ceiling fan before facing him, her expression grim. It was the first time he'd seen her in reasonably good lighting since leaving her at the hangar. A bruise darkened on her forehead near the scalp, a cut marred the left corner of her swollen lower lip.

His gaze traveled lower still, to the closed jacket. He knew what it covered. "Maybe I should take a look?" Without asking, he pulled the zipper down.

She stopped him. He could feel the tremor of her hands where they loosely wrapped his wrist. "No. I'll do it later. It's not as bad as it looks."

"So he just roughed you up?"

After several long moments in which he sensed she fought to stay in control, she answered him, her voice so low he barely heard her. "If you're asking if he raped me, no. He was too busy showing me what could be done with a steel blade and a burlap sack."

She lifted her eyes to his and, making no move to cover herself, seemed to almost invite his gaze.

Her words, the added details, made what she'd gone through that much more real for him. Though he tried not to, he envisioned the attack, the sack covering her head, a knife pressed to her throat. The anger came, as he'd known it would. Maybe even as she'd known it would.

The blood on her blouse had long ago dried, as had the dark circles the psychotic bastard had drawn on the material covering her breasts, but the cut at her collarbone still seeped.

The most intense wound, though, shone in her eyes. She'd been terrorized, and even now he suspected the assault played over and over and over in her head like a gritty film clip.

Nick forced himself to look away. He'd keep her safe. For tonight. For longer if she'd let him, but he was afraid she wouldn't. Maybe he could convince her to turn herself in, turn state's evidence against Binelli.

"I'm sorry," he murmured and, lowering his hands, stepped back. Now wasn't the time to think about the future. Right now he needed to focus on their immediate survival.

"I dropped my phone back at the hotel. Do you carry a cell or does your aunt have one I can use?"

"Battery is dead on mine. There's a pay phone two blocks over. Occasionally it even works."

"No good. Too risky."

"The dive shop has one. Rod's a good friend. He usually opens early."

Nick nodded.

"In the meantime," she said, "we should take care of your leg."

"Maybe we should talk first. About what you know. And exactly what it is Binelli wants back."

"I'll say it one more time. I don't know Binelli."

Nick rubbed his face. "You expect me to believe a criminal intelligent enough to run an operation the size of his, breaking every law on the books without leaving enough evidence for any government agency to get him off the street, doesn't know who works for him?"

Kelly's chin edged up. "Do I expect you to believe it? No. I don't even believe it." She arched a brow. "But it's true."

Nick shifted to ease the ache in his leg. "That's bull!"

"Okay, Nick, what evidence do you have linking me to Binelli? More photos?"

"For starters."

"That's not possible."

"Isn't it?" he asked. "Since February, Binelli's attorney has been using your airline on a weekly basis, always flying into Marsh Harbor on Fridays, back out on Sundays."

"Jeff Myers is Binelli's attorney?"

With one brow raised, he offered a hard smile. "You want me to believe you didn't know that?"

"The only thing Jeff Myers is to me is a fare. As far as his frequent trips, he claimed he had a boat over here. Liked to dive. I didn't believe him, of course."

"Why?"

"It's hard to spend any time on a boat without getting a suntan, or at least a burn."

"Then what did you think he was doing on all those trips?"

"Actually, I didn't much care. But if I thought anything, I suppose I figured he had a boyfriend over here and that whatever he was doing was none of my damned business." She crossed her arms. "What else, Nick?"

"Past history, of course."

"That would play a prominent role. Do I need to remind you once more that I was never tried in a court of law, never found guilty of anything?"

"Doesn't make you innocent. Where did the extra fifty thousand in your account last month come from?"

Her eyes narrowed. He'd hoped to surprise her, and per-haps he had. But there was no way for him to be certain.

"Ben," she said after a several-second hesitation.

"And where did Ben come by that kind of money?"

"A relative passed away. A distant uncle or something. He left Ben his estate."

"Estates aren't settled in cash, Kelly."

"The deposit was in cash?"

Nick arched a brow. "You didn't know that, either, huh?"

"Ben insisted on taking care of the banking." She kept her gaze level and steady with his.

"Didn't you find the inheritance story a bit coincidental? Ben producing cash just when you were turned down for a loan?"

"No." She paced away. "Maybe. I don't know," she said, her frustration coming through in her voice this time.

"Is it possible Ben works for Binelli? Could he be loading and unloading the money without your knowledge?" At her hesitation, he added, "It wouldn't be difficult for him to convince Binelli you're in on the scheme."

She shook her head. "I do the preflight checks. I handle most of the cargo. To smuggle something without my stumbling onto it at some point is nearly inconceivable."

"Which, since you're a two-man operation, leaves you."

"You would see it that way." She flattened her lips and frowned. "This is getting us nowhere."

"It's getting us to a consideration you haven't even entertained." Kelly might not fear him, but there was one thing she was truly frightened of. "The scum who assaulted you tonight wasn't playing at being tough. Binelli only hires the best. And he'll use whatever methods are necessary to make sure you either *can't* or *won't* talk to the government. My guess is, if he can't get to you, he'll start with those closest to you."

He saw the horror in her eyes. There was a part of him that regretted being the one to lay it on the line for her, but she needed to know what she was up against.

"Don't you think I've thought of that?" She turned away. "I'll get a towel and some supplies for your leg," she said, her voice dull and flat. "The bath is through the door."

WHEN SHE RETURNED ten minutes later, he had a towel wrapped around his waist. A small amount of blood trailed down his damp leg. She placed the gauze and alcohol, along with scissors, tweezers and tape, on the mattress, then indicated the space next to the supplies.

He sank onto the edge of the bed. "Just take it easy with the alcohol. I'm not big into pain."

Kneeling in front of him, Kelly shifted the towel slightly to get better access to his upper thigh. The bullet had punched a hole through the thick cord of muscle, taking only a slightly larger piece of flesh as it exited.

"Maybe I should be thankful he was using a copper jacket."

Kelly lifted her gaze to Nick's. She could feel her vision narrowing and the nausea climbing her throat.

"You're not going to pass out on me, are you, Kelly?"

Pass out on him? *Not likely. If anything, she'd keel over on the floor.*

She took a deep, steadying breath. "I'm fine. It's just I've never done this before."

"Wish I could say the same."

Though she'd been careful not to for the past few minutes, she lifted her eyes briefly to the faded scar just above his left nipple. It hadn't been there seven years ago.

Nick's instructions interrupted her thoughts. "Any bits of cloth, even threads you can reach, need to be removed. The rest can wait until tomorrow when I get to some kind of medical facility."

Kelly carefully cleaned the area with a white washcloth soaked in alcohol, first loosening the crust of dried blood, then swabbing the tissue beneath. When the cloth turned red, she refolded it and poured more alcohol onto it. Then came the tweezers.

As she probed the center of the wound, his breath stalled

abruptly, then rushed out in a drawn out hiss. "It didn't hurt that much when it went in."

"Sorry."

"Don't be," he said between gritted teeth. "You're doing fine."

With only a glance and without a word, she went back to removing the last few bits of denim. As she covered the area with gauze, he nudged her unsteady fingers aside. "I can finish here. Grab a shower."

Ignoring the stiffness in her calves and hamstrings as best she could when she stood up, she picked up two bottles of medication from the nightstand. "I found some antibiotics. The second bottle is a painkiller."

He finished smoothing the tape in place. "A regular pharmacy, aren't you?"

"Use them or not. I had a small accident a few months ago."

She headed for the bathroom. At the door, she hesitated, but didn't look back. "Thanks for not leaving me behind tonight. I know you didn't have to do what you did."

Nick didn't say anything.

Twenty minutes later, when she emerged from the bathroom, the bedroom was dark. Having just experienced a close encounter with the mirror and having been given a few minutes alone to contemplate her next move, she felt depressed and weary. She was in way over her head. If there were a way out of the mess, she couldn't see it.

She crossed to the French doors.

Evidently, she wasn't the only one who had been doing some thinking. Nick paced the narrow, enclosed courtyard. He'd pulled on his jeans, the dried blood stain a darker badge on one leg, but his chest remained bare.

To Nick, she knew, there were no degrees of guilt. Either she was innocent or she was guilty.

Which meant she'd just have to find some way to convince

him of her innocence, didn't it? Or, at the very least, open his mind to the possibility.

She thought about the Ocularcet now buried at the bottom of her purse and felt…and felt…worried. It was hard to feel too guilty about smuggling a small quantity of a pharmaceutical grade substance when she was so damned afraid of other, more immediate and life-threatening problems.

The smart thing, she realized, would be to flush it down the toilet. She had tried, though, only moments earlier and hadn't been able to. Cutting out now on her promise to the Kicklighters wouldn't particularly help her current situation. And would destroy the possibility of Amanda getting what she needed.

EVEN BEFORE Kelly stepped outside, Nick sensed her behind him. "Better?"

"Yes," she murmured. "Much."

"Want me to have a look at that cut now?"

"There's no need." She wrapped her arms across her. "I could get us a gin and tonic or some Kahlúa? Or are you hungry?"

"I'm not hungry, and I took one of the pain pills, so I better not drink. But maybe you should. It might take the edge off. Help you sleep."

"I don't like drinking alone." Kelly scanned the courtyard, but her gaze returned almost immediately to Nick. "What happens now?"

"That's up to you."

Seeing the fear in her eyes, Nick reached out and stopped her when she would have turned away. "Come here."

As he pulled her close, he realized, dressed as she was, her hair hanging wet around her pale and bruised face, she was beautiful.

But it wasn't her beauty bothering him right now. It was her vulnerability. He'd never seen her this way. Even in the darkest days before charges were dropped against her, when there was every possibility she'd do time behind bars, she had been tough and beautiful, spirited. Determined. But never vulnerable.

He hadn't come to the Abacos to save Kelly Logan. But, innocent or guilty, she was damned well going to be one of the reasons he stayed.

He tilted her chin up with his fingertip so he could study her face in the shifting shade beneath the tree. Her eyes had always been as startling for their direct gaze as for their unusual shade of green. But right now they collected tears, the first ones he'd seen from her since she'd watched her father carried out in a body bag.

In what he suspected was an effort to hide them, she slipped free of his finger. "I'm going to end up like my father. History is repeating itself, isn't it?"

Nick tightened his arms around her, tucking her body to his as he contemplated her words.

She was frightened. He understood that. What he didn't quite want to face was why he should give a damn.

He inhaled the warm, clean dampness. When she trembled, his fingers strayed, caressing her smooth cheek, tracing the outline of her lower lip with his thumbs. Without giving any thought to the action, he lowered his head until his mouth found hers.

He hadn't meant to kiss her, but he did, and she kissed him back in a way that had him spiraling into sensations he'd long ago forgotten.

He tugged cautiously at her lower lip, opening her mouth.

Her fingers twisted into his hair, dragging him harder, deeper into the kiss. She made a tiny sound deep in her throat.

Nick groaned, his hands sliding down her back, then upward to the curve of her hip. Even through the thin silk of her nightshirt, he felt the warmth of her skin, and his body tightened.

He'd wanted to comfort her. Instead, as she twisted against him, he found what he'd wanted all along.

Chapter Five

At the touch of Nick's lips against hers, every muscle in Kelly went limp. For the first time in hours, a sense of safety coursed through her exhausted body. She knew it would be so easy to give in, to take what Nick was offering. But she also knew it would be a mistake.

Kelly broke off the kiss. "I can't." She attempted to duck out of his arms. When he didn't release her, she lifted her chin again. "This isn't wise—"

"Wise?" His gray eyes appeared warmer, concerned. Neither of them advanced or retreated, almost as if they were caught on some middle ground, held there, unmoving, by some indefinable power.

Even as she swayed toward him, she shook her head slowly. "No, Nick. I can't…"

Instead of letting her go, Nick twisted his fingers into her wet hair again and dragged her back up to him. "The hell with wise." His lips took hers in a demanding, openmouthed kiss.

If there had been any thought of resistance left inside her, the avalanche of raw emotion buried it.

Nick tore at the cloth-covered buttons of her nightshirt. Her breath caught as he tugged aside the garment.

She met his gaze and would have spoken if she'd been able to form words or coherent thoughts.

"I've imagined you like this," he whispered, his voice rough-edged as his hands released the material.

She stood there unmoving, the air in her lungs trapped by the look in his eyes. She could see her own desperate need mirrored in his dark gaze.

He reached out and caressed her slowly, his fingertips gently avoiding the cuts and bruises as they skimmed downward to her breasts. She was mesmerized by the sight of his long, blunt-tipped fingers against her skin. He collected her in his palms. Without releasing her gaze, he massaged the callused heel of his hands upward across her nipples.

The ragged groan may have started in Nick's throat, but it ended somewhere deep, deep inside her. Where reason and caution meant nothing. Where heat and want ruled.

Then he was kissing her again. His arms felt so strong, as if they could protect her, as if they *would* protect her. And for this one night, the illusion was nearly impossible to resist. But it was just that. An illusion. A very dangerous one for her.

She turned her head aside, managed to put enough distance between their bodies that, when she raised her gaze this time, she could look into his eyes.

Only seconds earlier she'd seen desire. Similar to what still racked her insides. Now there was…a stillness. As if he'd disconnected. And, if not for the ragged thump of his heart beneath her curled fist, she might have believed she'd imagined what had gone on seconds earlier.

"Nick, I…" She took a deep, steadying breath. "I can't do this. Not like this. Not now. I…"

The shadows made it impossible to track the progression of his thoughts in his eyes, but she could feel them in his touch, in the way his fingers first loosened, then drifted down her arms. As a shiver followed their retreat, they dropped away.

"You're right, Kelly. That should never have happened." He rubbed his face. "I'm sorry."

She felt too emotionally raw to offer a comment. What could she say? That it felt good to be held? That it had been too long since she had been? That it wouldn't have mattered whose arms she had found herself in? Nick wasn't that big of a fool.

And neither was she.

"Mark it down to the adrenaline," he said and eased farther away from her. "Maybe we should get some sleep."

By the time he joined her in the bedroom, she had already grabbed a pillow and was in the process of pulling the extra blanket from the foot of the bed. "You can have the bed. You'll need the room for your leg. I'll manage well enough in the chair." Alone.

"No. I want to be able to keep tabs on you."

Only moonlight and the narrow bed separated them.

"You think I might go somewhere?"

"Yes."

She couldn't believe it. He was actually serious. "Where? At this time of night?"

He eyed her. "You're a very resourceful lady. I suspect you could think of one or two places to disappear." Nick pulled the quilt back, releasing the clean muslin scent of the sheets beneath. "Which side did you want?"

"I'd be a fool to wander the streets with Binelli's people out there."

"Yes, you would. But I'm not certain that would keep you from doing it." Freeing his belt buckle as he moved, he limped around the bed, grabbed up the pillow and blanket from the chair and plopped them back on the bed. "I usually sleep on the right side."

She folded her arms across her. "Well, of course you do. As an agent of the U.S. government, it's the only side you'd feel comfortable on."

Nick's mouth only tightened. "Cut the arguments, Logan,

and get in. Before I come around there and put you where I want you."

"Are you suggesting you don't already have me there?"

"What I'm *suggesting* is we both get some rest."

Admitting she had little choice and even less energy for sparring, she sank onto the bed cautiously, then stretched out full length, balanced on the very edge with her back to him.

After several seconds Nick joined her, his weight forcing her to tense as the mattress dipped beneath them.

He wrapped his belt around her waist.

Kelly flipped to face him. "What do you think you're doing?"

"The phone wasn't the only thing I left back at the hotel."

"You mean you left your handcuffs? That you would be cuffing me now if you hadn't?"

"Something like that." He ran one end of the belt through a loop on his jeans.

"You've got to be kidding."

Still ignoring her, he tightened the belt until her lower body was forced intimately against his, then fastened the buckle. As he shifted, her breasts briefly compressed against his chest. "Believe me. This will be more comfortable than trying to sleep with one hand fastened to the headboard."

In an awkward maneuver, she turned away from him, her hip brushing his crotch before she settled spoon fashion. As she attempted to stretch her nightshirt down her thighs, her elbow bumped Nick's bruised ribs. His sharp exhale brought a smile to her lips.

Nick settled at her back. When he draped his arm across her, she stiffened again.

"Sorry," he offered. "There's not much room here."

Kelly ignored the apology.

But, no matter how much she pretended otherwise, she continued to be aware of Nick's arm resting over her, his inner arm shifting across her breast as he breathed deeply and in an easy rhythm.

Though she was both physically and mentally exhausted, even after Nick succumbed to the effects of the painkiller, her mind remained trapped on a never-ending treadmill of its own. There had to be some way out of this mess. Some way for her to convince Nick she wasn't involved with Binelli.

As she started lining up the facts, she once more realized what an insurmountable task it would be. And it wasn't just Nick she needed to worry about.

A madman not only believed she hauled his dirty money, he also thought she'd stolen something. Given what she now knew about Binelli's money laundering, the obvious answer would be cash from a shipment.

Returning the money was no longer an option. When she'd gone to Nick's room tonight, she'd sealed her fate. She was a dead woman. With few alternatives and fewer guarantees. It went without saying Nick wasn't just her best shot to stay alive. He was her only one.

And yet he appeared to have an agenda of his own. One he wasn't talking about.

Why hadn't he tried to arrest her, offered her some kind of deal, even put more pressure on her to talk? Something didn't feel right.

Shivering, more a result of the adrenaline once more pumping through her than the room's temperature, she worried about what would happen come morning. What were Nick's plans for her? More important still, what were her plans?

She couldn't afford to sit back and wait for whatever came down the tarmac. She needed to go on the offensive. She needed to find answers. How was she going to clear her name? How, if everything blew up in her face, was she going to keep Sarah safe?

Before Kelly would let anything happen to Sarah, she'd do anything, including, if it came down to it, to giving herself up to Binelli.

Sarah and Ben were family. Her *family*. And she wasn't going to let anything happen to either one of them.

Kelly finally allowed her mind to break through the mental guardrail of denial she'd carefully erected around it hours earlier.

Was Ben involved in the smuggling?

No matter how much she wanted to believe her mechanic, her friend, wouldn't do anything to harm her, Ben had easy access to the planes. He knew the schedules and destinations for charters even before she did.

Then there was the money he'd come up with. Fifty thousand. It wasn't a small amount, unless you measured it against what a drug king would take in from a single shipment.

Was it possible Ben had been protecting his own gravy train from extinction when he'd suddenly produced money to invest in the airline? It had been only days later when he'd gone on his first drinking binge.

Confronting Ben would be the quickest route to some answers. But would it be safe?

She shivered, the trembling starting at her toes and creeping upward to her shoulders, then her mind. Tonight had been loaded with firsts. First assault. First gun battle. First time coping with a gunshot wound.

First time she'd ever questioned Ben's loyalty.

Kelly stared straight ahead into the darkness. What if she'd been wrong about him all along? Maybe she didn't know Ben, didn't know what he was capable of.

Nick shifted in his sleep, the rough denim of his jeans catching on the silk of her nightshirt and hiking it up around her hips. Kelly maneuvered the shirt back down and scooted closer in an attempt to lessen the discomfort of the leather biting her waist.

She was running out of time here. If she were going to go on the offensive, it needed to be now.

Very carefully, she twisted until she faced Nick.

"Nick?"

He didn't so much as shift in his sleep. The painkiller she'd given him contained a strong narcotic. After a run-in with fire coral, she'd taken only one of the tablets and had slept through two alarm clocks.

"Nick?"

She waited to be certain he remained locked in a drugged sleep before reaching for the belt buckle. The metal felt warm to the touch, as did his skin when the backs of her hands briefly brushed against him.

The hair that trickled from his chest to disappear at the waist of his jeans tickled her knuckles as she manipulated the leather. Thoughts of what lay behind the material inches from her hand filtered in and she briefly hesitated before resuming work on the buckle.

Even when free, Kelly continued to lie there in the dark, listening to his measured breathing. She counted out the seconds and then the minutes in her head. When she was completely certain her movements hadn't awakened him, she backed out of bed onto the cold floor and collected what she needed.

In the small laundry room, she located a clean uniform of khaki shorts and a tropical print blouse. As she dressed, several of her aunt's cats poked around in the dark, searching for the usual night prey of mice and lizards.

Kelly let herself into her aunt's bedroom.

Lilacs, the scent of the lotion her great aunt favored, lingered in the stuffy air. The thick rug, a faded Aubusson, deadened the sound of her steps, but the floorboards beneath let out subtle creaks. She knelt next to the bed.

"Aunt Sarah."

The sheets shifted as the older woman sat up. There was a disoriented quaver in her voice. "What is it, dear? Is something wrong?"

When she would have turned on the bedside lamp, Kelly placed a hand on her arm, stopping her. "No. Everything is fine. I just need to leave. I have a flight scheduled later this morning." Kelly had already decided it would be better if, for the time being, her aunt thought everything was fine, strictly business as usual. "Nick's asleep in the guest bedroom. I forgot to tell him I needed to leave so early."

"Don't you worry about your young man."

Young man. Her father had called Nick that once when he'd warned her to be careful. She should have listened.

"I won't worry. I know he's in good hands. Just as you are."

Kelly prayed she was doing the right thing. For all of them.

With a sharp edge of guilt, she reached for her aunt's hand. "Everything will be fine. I'm leaving a note for Nick on the kitchen table. Please see that he gets it."

KELLY WALKED AROUND the plane cautiously. The beam of her flashlight slid along the airline's painted trademark of a bird-of-paradise bloom, then leapt out into the dark hangar to check the shadows. Two additional planes hunkered back in the corners like predators coming late to a kill, their windshields flashing as her beam stabbed each in turn. Feral eyes.

Maybe coming here had been a mistake.

She poked the light into the interior of the King Air. Ben had been hard at work. The floor was vacuumed, the outside of the plane freshly washed. She climbed up inside and sat in one of the rear seats.

She'd had some time to do a bit more thinking. Jeff Myers

would want to accompany the shipments. Which meant one may have been scheduled for tomorrow morning. It rankled to think the creep Myers thought she'd been in on it from the first. She recalled some of his obscure remarks about how she should be serving lobster instead of the small packages of beer nuts, seeing the kind of money she was raking in. At the time, she'd thought he referred to her already discounted fare. Maybe he'd just been trying to be friendly—in a jerk-like fashion.

She should have booted him out while she had a chance. Without a parachute.

Kelly opened the cargo compartment and scanned the flashlight over the packing crates. No reason to search them. Whatever she was looking for wouldn't currently be on board, but would be loaded stateside, either disguised in cargo or in a hiding spot so ingenious she'd never come across it in any of her preflight checks.

But had Customs found it? Were they just lying back? Perhaps attempting to track the dirty cash to determine its final destination? Did they just want to round up as many as possible?

She wondered how many people would be going to prison. A few might get the opportunity to turn state witness—the lucky ones. The rest would see just how bleak the inside of a cell could be on a rainy day—an experience she didn't care to repeat.

Kelly climbed out of the plane. If anyone was looking for her, the hangar would be one of the first places he'd show up. With her attacker's promise echoing in her mind, she didn't intend to stay any longer than necessary.

Kelly nudged open the door to the employee lounge, a small room with a concrete floor and cheap paneled walls. Reaching in, she flicked up the light switch. The fluorescent ceiling fixture flickered benignly to life and hummed softly.

It took several numb moments for the scene to register. When it did, Kelly reached for the door casing.

Ben, dressed in only his shorts, lay spread-eagled on the floor in a pool of blood that leaked from the garish gash across his throat. Pushing a fist against her mouth as the wave of nausea hit, she turned away. Doubled over, she forced air into her lungs.

Everything assaulted her at once. The smell of the room, the heat. The utter silence of death. The recriminations.

He wouldn't even have been here if she hadn't insisted. This was all her fault, then.

The sound of one of the big, outside doors being rolled back jerked her upright, as if she'd been backhanded across the right cheek.

Then the echo of voices. Inside the hangar. Drawing closer.

Her knees gave out.

NICK'S MOUTH tasted like dried seaweed. The kind that had been baked on the beach, seasoned with fish carcasses.

As the painkiller haze lifted, he noticed the dull ache stretching from his right shoulder to his rib cage. He tested it by flexing the underlying muscles. Not too bad. Then he shifted his left leg. His lungs emptied as if they'd been squeezed like a tube of toothpaste. The only good thing he could say about the pain was, if he'd had any doubts he was still alive, they'd been answered.

It took him several more seconds before he remembered he shouldn't be alone in the bed.

He pushed his unwilling body to a sitting position, then stood shakily, his head swimming with the sudden change in altitude. He used the bedside table to hold himself upright and waited for the dizziness to fade.

Asinine idiot!

He should have known he couldn't trust her, but, hell, last night, he'd almost started to buy the possibility she might be innocent. That it might be the mechanic working on his own. But like all guilty suspects, at the first opportunity she'd made a run for it, hadn't she?

Nick tugged on the shoulder holster, then reached for his automatic. When his fingers didn't immediately locate it between the mattress and box spring, he pushed his hand in farther. Still no gun. He shoved the mattress aside and came up empty again.

He left on the empty holster. He'd catch up to Kelly and his gun. He only hoped Binelli didn't catch up with her first.

Chapter Six

Kelly shoved the light switch down and prayed the light hadn't been seen.

Voices echoed. Two. Three. All men. Cops? She hesitated a moment in indecision. Not likely.

Footsteps advanced just beyond the closed door. With her only escape route cut off, she skirted Ben's body and, dropping to the floor, awkwardly shoved herself beneath the narrow cot.

Almost as if it sensed Kelly's unwillingness to move and saw it as an opportunity to escape, a large spider suddenly scrambled across her cheek. Her eyes, which had been closed, popped open, staring into the darkness around her, seeing only shapes and shadows.

The door slammed open. The overhead light came on. A man stood in the doorway. From her position, she could see only his running shoes and the dirty cuffs of his jeans.

She watched as he crossed to the small sink. He hummed softly now, a Christmas jingle, and Kelly imagined him checking his appearance in the mirror. With the second verse, the tune suddenly ended.

It took several seconds of listening for her to identify his actions. He had opened the medicine cabinet and now rooted through the contents. In her mind, she saw his fingers checking the eye rinse, the sunscreens, the antacids, the adhesive bandages.

She desperately willed the man to find whatever he was after and leave. But not before he turned off the light. Even now she was careful not to let her gaze meet Ben's lifeless stare.

Several containers crashed into the sink. Kelly jerked, her arms and hands tightening across her chest, her heart slamming against her ribs. A plastic jar of multivitamins dropped to the floor and rolled across the concrete toward her.

With each revolution of the bottle, Kelly felt the fist around her lungs squeeze tighter. Too late to move. Too late to do anything but wait like some trapped animal.

She watched the man's poorly manicured fingers chase the container's slow progress. Instead of capturing the bottle on the first try, he nudged it faster, the bottle locking on her like a heat-seeking missile.

"What are you doing in here?"

A second man—this one wearing cordovans with tassels and cuffed slacks—stood in the doorway.

There was something familiar about the voice.

"Just after something for this headache," the first man answered. Instead of picking up the bottle, he kicked the vitamins beneath the cot. Just missing her, it bounced off the baseboard. "Can you believe it? Everything but friggin' aspirin."

The second man walked to the cabinet. She listened to the sound of pills sliding about in a nearly empty container. "Try one of these."

"Screw that!" the first man again. "That's for female cramps."

"Just take the stuff and shut up."

"I know you're calling the shots just now, but don't go thinking that's a permanent situation." Kelly could hear the edge of suppressed frustration. And the wariness.

"Whatever." Sounding unconcerned, the second man side-stepped the pool of congealed blood. "Have another look in here. Check the insulation above these ceiling panels."

"I already did both."

"And I'm telling you to do it again. The girl didn't have it. Which means whatever the mechanic planned to show Binelli has to be here somewhere."

"Maybe the bitch was holding out."

"Believe me. With a knife pressed to her throat, a woman will give you whatever you want. And as much of it as you want."

"So a blade does away with the boring details of fore-play?"

"Foreplay. The postcoital crap. The need to be discreet."

"Love them and leave them? Dead?"

"Not every time." A soft chuckle followed.

At the lifeless sound, a cold, hard knot twisted inside her. The second man, the one in the expensive cordovans, had been the animal who had brutalized her. Had killed Ben.

Kelly tried to breath, tried to keep it together, but she could feel the leak of tears already. She wanted to close her eyes, to cover her ears, to draw her body up into a fetal po-sition, but she could do none of those things. So she prayed. And watched as he nudged Ben's shoulder with the toe of his shoe.

"He knew he was a dead man. That we couldn't let him live even if he gave us what we wanted." He circled the body. "If we can't find it, we'll have to do the girl. And without her sitting in the pilot's seat, we will have to go back to the beginning, rebuild Benito's confidence with another pilot."

"I'm not waiting weeks or even months. I didn't put my kuchangas on the cutting block just to walk away without a payoff."

"Neither did I. So get busy. Find it. Before it's too late."

Kelly stared at the web of rusted bedsprings overhead, the stained mattress, the army-green blanket which had once been neatly tucked in but now dripped off the edge and into the ever-widening red pool.

Too late.

Too late for Ben.

Too late for all of them.

IF THE CAT sitting at the Formica table hadn't yowled as he passed, Nick might have missed the envelope propped against a ceramic canister. A faded Atlanta Braves baseball cap and a pair of dark aviator sunglasses rested next to it. He ripped it open, unfolded the note inside.

Nick,
I know I have no right to ask, except for human decency, but please be sure Sarah gets somewhere safe. Sorry for skipping out on you like this, but I had something I needed to do alone. I'll explain later. Meet me at the dive shop.
—K
You can count on Rod to help with Sarah.

Nick shoved the note into his back pocket, then glanced at the large gray tabby. A small plate of cat food—at least Nick hoped it was cat food, since Puss was eyeballs deep in it—had been placed on the table.

The back door opened as Nick contemplated his next move. Kelly's aunt stepped inside. Jumpy in spite of the narcotic hangover, Nick had reached for his empty holster.

"Good morning," she offered as she hung the broom behind the door and took down a faded apron. She tied it around her as she entered the kitchen in a slow, shuffling gait, the right heel of her sensible black shoe dragging occasionally.

A throng of cats trotted along with her, but made a mad dash for a large bowl of dried food when she stopped in front of the sink.

She smiled, and he realized the daylight intensified the sense of fragility about her. Until you looked in her eyes and saw something far different. Energy. The same driving life force Kelly possessed. Until that moment he'd doubted a blood tie between the women.

"I have cross buns in the oven," she said, "and I'll put on some tea. I know most Americans prefer coffee, but I'm afraid I don't keep it in the house. I just popped down to the market, but, as you probably know, most islanders don't adhere to time schedules. But then, that's why I like it here. None of that hustle and bustle. A person can think. Can breathe. Can create." She used her hands as she spoke.

Nick had no idea what he was going to do with her. Leaving her here was out of the question. He hadn't lied when he said Benito would use whatever means available to control Kelly. But, if he wanted to catch up to her, there wasn't time to put Sarah on a plane to somewhere safe or to drag her along.

Nick slipped on the glasses. "Did your niece say where she was going?"

Sarah took the kettle off the stove and filled it. "She had an early flight this morning."

He just bet she did. For Bogota or Caracas.

Had she gone to the hangar? Binelli's people would be staking it out. But even if she was naive enough to think she could get anywhere near one of her planes, how would she get to Marsh Harbor? She'd need a boat. Her own boat was out of the question. Which left the dive shop.

Nick took the kettle out of Sarah's hand before she reached the stove with it. "We're leaving." He reached past her and flicked off the oven.

"But…I can't…I—" she broke off as if she suddenly realized something was terribly wrong. "What's happened to my niece? Is she okay?"

Nick regretted there was no time for consoling lies.

"There's a man who wants Kelly dead. And because of your connection to Kelly, you're also in danger."

She shook her head, her pale green eyes showing real concern now. "Why didn't she… She didn't say anything. Just that she had a flight. That she didn't want to awaken you."

Sarah nodded at the piece of paper still hanging out of the front pocket of his jeans. "What about the note?"

"She wants to meet at the dive shop and she wants me to see to your safety."

Her hand shook as she raised it to the loose skin of her pale throat. "Oh, my lord," she murmured.

"Do you have someplace you can go for a few days?" Nick prompted.

"I don't know." She leaned over and picked up the cat that rubbed against her legs, and held him in front of her. "On such short notice…"

"A friend?"

"I suppose I could stay a night or two with Alice." She glanced at the cat she held. "But what about my kitties? I can't just leave them."

"Put out plenty of dry food. It should only be for a few days." He took the cat from her. "Just go pack a bag. We'll figure out the particulars as we go. If you have a passport, bring it."

He was hustling her out the back door less than four minutes later when she suddenly stopped and looked up at him. "You don't think she's coming back, do you? You think something has already happened."

Nick hesitated before finally giving her the truth. "She

was in a lot of trouble. I think she's decided to run. I'm afraid the man who's after her will get to her before I can."

May have already gotten to her because Nick had let his guard down.

"Oh, my lord," she whispered, and this time it sounded like a prayer.

NICK STOOD in front of Rod's Reels and Dive. The business was housed in the only new building he'd seen in town. A deep veranda surrounded the shop. From the look of it, Rod's was one of the few shops in the area that was prospering.

He had left Sarah at the friend's house, but still felt uneasy. Perhaps having Rod take her to Marsh Harbor and put her on a plane to the States would be the best solution. The sooner she was moved from the vicinity, beyond Binelli's ready reach, the better.

Nick climbed the front steps. The walk over had helped loosen the muscles of his injured leg, but it had started to ache again. After last night's fiasco, painkillers were no longer an option.

"Hello?"

When no one answered, Nick prowled the front of the shop. Glancing behind the counter, he noticed a speargun sitting on the shelf beneath. Flyers offering dive trips were piled neatly next to the register. The wall just behind held antique fishing gear, some early pieces of dive equipment and a door.

Nick took the short hall toward the back of the building. "Hello?" he called, pushing open a partially closed door to find a cluttered business office. A single, large window with drapes drawn across it and a solid back door filled one wall. A calendar hung opposite, the page still turned to July. Either time held no meaning for Rod or he was hesitant to give up the brunette sprawled in the sand.

Nick had just reached across the desk for the phone when he heard someone on the front stairs.

He returned to the public area of the shop just as a shirt-less man in his twenties came in hauling an air tank over one shoulder and a weight belt in the opposite hand. He wore cut-offs loose at the hips and had bare feet. Your average beach bum. With the suntan and bleached-out hair, he could have been the poster boy for a trendy sunscreen lotion.

In spite of his all-American looks, Nick didn't trust him. The kid was obviously Kelly's friend. Since she trusted him to help with her aunt, he must be a good one. Which meant, for the moment, Nick needed to assume they were on oppo-site sides of the fence.

"Can I help you?" Rod dumped the air tank onto the floor. As he straightened, his gaze dropped to Nick's bad leg. "You would be Nick. Kelly said to be on the lookout for you."

"Did she? Any idea where she is now?"

"No. She borrowed a boat."

"How big a boat?" Large enough to get to Florida?

"Seventeen-foot. All the twenty-ones were out."

"Too small for open water," Nick commented.

"Wouldn't take out even a twenty-one at this point. Storm system building down south." Rod crossed to an old-fashioned cooler and slid back the top. Nick saw both the speculation and the hesitation in the other man. Rod used the attached bottle opener, then stepped to the opposite side of the counter.

"Mind telling me what's going on here? Kelly seemed pretty upset, but wouldn't say much more than she was wor-ried about Sarah."

"I left her over at Alice's. I had planned to place a few phone calls to make other arrangements, but perhaps, since you're here, you could put her on a plane to Naples. She has friends there." And Nick could have her picked up once she was stateside.

Rod took a swig and used the back of his hand to swipe his mouth. "Kelly's obviously in some kind of trouble. As you can tell, we're tight."

"So tight she didn't tell you a damned thing?"

"She was in a hurry."

"As I am. If you want to help Kelly, take care of her aunt."

"And you'll take care of Kelly?"

Nick could tell the kid didn't much like the division of labor. Not that he cared what the kid did or didn't like.

"Something like that. Kelly said you might have a phone I could use."

"In the back room."

Nick waited for Rod to make a move. Was relieved when he finally backed toward the door. "I'll lock up behind me. Kelly has a key."

Nick waited until Rod went out the front door before heading to the office.

This time, as he reached for the phone, he noticed the photo on the desk. His hand skipped the phone to pick up the framed shot. Kelly sat on the wing of one of her planes, a relaxed smile on her face, a breeze in her hair. Sitting just to her right, his arm looped across her shoulder, was Rod. The smile on his face was just as wide, just as relaxed. Recognizing Kelly's messy handwriting, Nick studied the scrawled words at the bottom.

Enveloped in Heaven's clouds or caressed by Poseidon's warm waters. July 4th, an afternoon of firsts.
Love, K.

The overtly poetic words reminded him that, like Kelly, John Logan had also exhibited a sentimental bent.

Nick jerked up the phone handset. If he'd been wondering what Kelly had been doing with her life since he'd last seen her, he now had a fairly clear picture of one aspect. She obviously liked them young and blond.

He punched in Myron's phone number and waited. No answer. Hanging up, Nick contemplated his next option. He didn't really expect Kelly to show. She either would try to get to one of her planes or she would find somewhere to hide out. One thing she wouldn't do was sit still. Which meant he couldn't afford to, either.

Decision made, he picked up the receiver again and dialed the home of another Immigration and Customs Enforcement investigator. He and Doug Willcox had been working several cases together, including the one that had wrapped the day before Ake's murder. Separated from his wife, Doug just might be home on a Saturday morning.

When the phone on the other end was answered by a little girl, Nick thought he must have dialed the wrong number. Doug's wife had custody of their two boys. "Hello."

"Daddy?" the little voice asked.

A dog barked and children screamed in the background, nearly drowning her out.

Daddy? Did the little girl think he was her father? "Is Doug there?"

"Dunno."

"Can I —" The sound of the handset being laid on the table was unmistakable, as was Nick's irritation.

He was about to hang up when he heard his friend's voice. "Who answered the phone?"

More squealing and laughter and barking.

"Doug's Madhouse," Willcox said into the receiver, his voice sounding distracted.

Before he could even speak, Nick was cut off.

"No! You can't ride the dog! John, get your friend off Buster Brown before she gets bitten and I get sued. If that happens, I won't be able to afford your allowance."

Nick waited.

"Doug's Madhouse. Padded rooms extra."

Nick chuckled. "How much allowance are we talking here?"

"Nick."

Nick's voice turned more sober. "Sorry to call you at home, but I need a favor."

There was a brief, unexpected pause.

"Am I catching you at—"

"No. No, Nick. It's John's birthday party. Marci was supposed to have it over at her place, but something came up."

Nick tried to envision his well-dressed, uptight friend knee-deep in birthday cake and Pin the Tail on the Donkey. He couldn't.

"Hold on," Doug said. "Let me get to another phone where I can hear."

Screeching and whooping continued even after another extension was picked up. "Okay, John, hang up." The empty ring of silence filled the connection. "Where you calling from?"

"Dive shop in Hopetown."

"Then you probably don't have any idea just how hot your ass is at the moment."

"What are you talking about?"

"Myron Richardson has been asking some damned hard questions."

"Like what?"

"Oh, you know. Like what kind of backup weapon you were using these days, had I noticed any changes in your spending habits? Have I ever seen you help yourself to confiscated drugs or money? And if that wasn't enough, Myron and a couple of supervisors from over at the Bureau met behind doors. No one's talking about what went on. Maybe you have some idea."

Nick shifted to take the weight off his bad leg and considered what he'd just heard. The FBI stopping in for a chat. Myron asking questions he already knew the answers to.

"Well?" Doug prompted after several seconds.

"Yeah. My guess is that some of Ake's friends over at the FBI are checking everything out for themselves."

"Just like you are."

If Nick hadn't needed Doug's help, he would have gone on lying about his reasons for being in the Abacos. "Yeah. Just like I am."

"Have you come up with anything?"

"Just the woman," Nick said, his mind still playing with what Doug had just told him.

"And?" Doug prompted again.

"She's not talking."

"She'd have to be stupid to talk to you. Binelli sees her anywhere near you, she's a dead woman."

"Which just about sums up the reason for my call."

"Which is?"

"Binelli has marked her."

"Damn. You've really stumbled into it this time. Myron told you to stay clear. The friendship won't smooth this one over," he added.

"I can't worry about that right now."

"I know you can't. And I know this call wasn't strictly social. So what can I do for you?"

He'd known he could count on Doug. They weren't close like he and Myron were, or like he and Ake had been, but they had solid history between them and mutual respect. Nick knew Doug to be a conscientious investigator, a real team player when it counted.

"What I need right now, or will need in a few days, is some kind of transportation out of here. Binelli will have commercial airlines watched and will probably monitor the flight plans of both charter and private planes. See what you can come up with. Even a decent-sized boat—twenty-seven feet or bigger—will do."

"I'll see what I can come up with."

"And it might be a good idea if you didn't mention any of this to Myron. For now."

"No argument from me on that score."

"Anything else?"

"This gets a little trickier. Kelly Logan's aunt should be on an incoming flight at Southwest Regional. You'll have to monitor the flights. Name's Sarah Hopkin. Can you pick her up and put her somewhere safe?"

"Okay. I'll see what I can do."

"She won't be expecting you," Nick warned.

"That should be fun. Any suggestions how I get her to go quietly?"

"She's a nice lady. She won't give you any problems."

Doug chuckled. "It's the nice ones you need to watch out for." His tone changed. "I'm not sure why I'm asking this, but is there anything else I can do? Anything that's guaranteed to cost me my job?"

"One more favor."

Doug chuckled again. "Why start limiting yourself at this point, sport?"

"Run a check on an airplane mechanic. Ben Tittle. He was John Logan's mechanic and now works for Logan's daughter. And while you're at it, check out Rod Griffis. He owns a dive shop over here."

"What am I looking for?"

"I'm not sure. Check all the databases."

"Okay. Give me your number there and I'll call with whatever I find."

"Won't work. I'll be on the move as soon as I hang up. I'll have to contact you later this afternoon. Once I get the girl."

"She's not with you?"

"Long story."

Nick thought he heard something at the store's entrance and glanced at the open door of the office.

"Nick?"

"Yeah," he answered, but his thoughts were on the speargun under the front counter.

"Maybe you shouldn't have gotten involved."

In the background of the phone line Nick could now hear "Happy Birthday" being sung. Someone had obviously opened the door of Jack's study.

"There's no reason," Doug continued, "that you can't cut your losses now and get out."

"Its too late for that. They've tried twice to kill me."

"Who?"

"Probably Binelli, but I didn't get the chance to ask. I may have killed one of them last night."

"That should guarantee you a spot in the unemployment line." Again his tone changed. "What's really going on, Nick? Does this girl mean more to you than you're admitting?"

"No. Why?" Nick asked.

"There was talk around here after you left. About how this Kelly Logan was more than a suspect seven years ago."

Nick didn't bother to deny the words. She had been more, seven years ago. This time was different, though. And he'd make damn sure it remained that way. The only thing he wanted from Kelly was answers.

"I just want to find Ake's killer."

"As we all do. But is this the best way?"

"Ake wanted to talk to me about something that night, about Logan and Binelli. I plan to find out what in the hell was worth his life."

"Just watch out it doesn't cost you yours," his friend warned in a flat tone just before hanging up.

Nick replaced the receiver as he glanced at the back door. Whoever had been out front moments earlier now worked at the back lock.

It wasn't Rod. He would use the front door. Nor was it likely to be Kelly. Which, by process of elimination, left some of Binelli's people.

Feeling naked without his weapon, Nick scrambled to the speargun beneath the front counter and loaded it as he sprinted for the back office again. Stopping in the doorway, he lifted it to waist height.

Chapter Seven

Dressed in shorts and a golf shirt, Myron Richardson sat at the desk in his paneled den.

Bev had been gone for more than a year now, and he'd become a prisoner in his own home. The small bedroom, filled with her trinkets and clothes and scent, was the cell he returned to each night, while this room, the one place where Bev didn't confront him at each turn, had become his exercise yard, a refuge from the memories.

Myron glanced down at the ballistics report he held in his hand. No one had made the connection yet, but they would. If not in hours, then in days.

He opened the passport to stare at the photo and the name beneath. Money could buy anything, up to and including a new identity and a second chance.

And a smart man, no matter what he believed, hedged his bets.

Laying the passport aside, Myron picked up the one-way ticket to South America. Four hours away and without U.S. extradition.

The doorbell rang.

Myron considered ignoring the summons. Probably some idiot wanting to sell him aluminum siding or religion. At the beer's stale taste, he realized he was in the mood to torture the salesperson who had been foolish enough to intrude on a peaceful Saturday afternoon.

He was surprised when he pulled open the door to find Doug Willcox standing on the front stoop.

Myron gazed at the younger man. Though running five miles a day had kept him in good shape, Doug had been pushing his way through his forties for several years now. His deep-set eyes missed very little. The man was a damned good investigator. He possessed a sharp intellect and an almost uncanny ability to read people.

He was also a pain in the ass.

Doug stepped past Myron without waiting to be invited in. "We need to talk."

"Sure. You look worried." He closed the door. "Something happen?"

"Yeah."

"Come on back to the den." Myron led the way.

As he sat, he noticed Doug's glance skimming over the contents of the packing boxes Myron had stacked in the middle of the floor earlier that day, and the three large suitcases he'd pulled out of the attic with the intention of filling.

"Going someplace?"

"Not really." His own gaze found the passport and airline ticket where he'd left them in plain sight. "Just getting a head start. My daughter's convinced me to put the place on the market. I think she's worried I'll die and leave her with this mess."

As if he hadn't heard, Doug paced to the closed drapes and pushed them aside.

"I just heard from Nick." Letting the curtain drop, Doug faced Myron.

Myron saw Doug's hesitation. "And?"

"I'm concerned."

"What's going on, Doug? Nick called you and…?"

"He's in the Bahamas, but he's not on vacation."

The news didn't surprise Myron a hell of a lot. He knew Nick well enough to guess what was going on. What he didn't understand was why Nick hadn't called him.

"So he's gone looking for the girl." Myron rubbed his unshaven face, looked up at the other man. "I told him to stay clear of the investigation."

"And now he's ass-deep and sinking. He fired his weapon. He thinks it was some of Binelli's people. He also thinks he might have killed one of them."

"Damn. Did you check it out?"

"I called the local authorities. There was a shooting reported, but by the time they showed up, the party was over. They found some blood in several places, but no bodies."

"So you think Nick wounded the guy and his buddies helped him home?"

"Could be." Doug sat on the couch.

Myron sensed from the other man's tight face there was more to come.

"What else?"

"He wants me to arrange safe transport out of there. For him and the girl."

"What in the…what is he thinking?"

"He isn't. Hasn't been since Ake's murder. You know that and I know that. Unfortunately, the boys over at the Bureau aren't going to see it that way. From their perspective, he's screwing with the investigation."

Myron nodded. "I'll call Jeb over at the Bureau. Maybe I can smooth things for a few days."

Doug leaned farther forward over his knees. "With her testimony, we might finally get a direct shot at Binelli."

"And if Nick gets her to talk, the boys over at the FBI will back off some. Is that what you're thinking?"

"Yeah." Doug stared down at his hands. "I guess I am. I

hate to see an investigator of Nick's experience screwed up because he went off half-cocked. We've all been there."

Myron eyed the other investigator. This was the first time the kid had surprised him. He'd never thought of Doug as a real team player. Perhaps what was going on in his life, the imminent divorce, the loss of the family home, had made Doug realize no man is an island.

Amazing what having the fabric of your life rent in half did to a man. The big *D*s, as he'd started thinking of them. Divorce wasn't so far removed from death. Or defeat. Test a man and you might just be surprised by the road he'd take.

"Each of us makes our own decisions," Myron pointed out, "then we live with them the best we can." He stood, anxious to get Doug on his way. "Leave everything in my hands. If Nick contacts you, tell him he'll need to talk to me directly, that whatever arrangements are being made, I'm handling them."

Looking relieved, Doug followed Myron's lead and got to his feet.

NICK REMOVED HIS FINGER from the speargun's trigger, but didn't lower the weapon as his glance shot past Kelly to the open doorway.

She appeared to be alone.

Hauling her forward, he kicked the door shut, then threw the dead bolt even as he rounded on her. She'd just shocked the hell out of him, and he wasn't easily surprised by much.

Why hadn't she run?

She'd had ample time, undoubtedly the resources and contacts. And just cause to think it her best move.

Then Nick took a really close look at her. Her eyes were wide and dark and unfocused. Her lips stiff and colorless. As if she were in shock.

She held his gun in her left arm, which hung at her side as if the weight of the weapon was too much.

Then he noticed the dirt and blood smeared on her clothes. His gut tightened at the sight. Was it her blood?

He propped the speargun within easy reach next to the door and cautiously removed the loaded automatic from her grasp. "Easy does it there."

His gaze steady on her, he waited for some movement, some sign of just how bad her emotional state really was. He shoved the handgun into his holster.

"Where have you been?"

With a harsh sob, she tried to throw herself at him, but Nick caught her shoulders and held her away.

She didn't have delicate shoulders. They appeared to be delicate, just as there was an appearance of fragility in her face. But when you looked into her eyes you felt the strength that bunched just beneath the smooth, soft skin.

"What's happened, Kelly? I want answers. Now."

"He's dead," she said and shook her head as if in denial. Nick's fingers flexed, biting into her shoulders. "Who?"

"Ben." She suddenly broke through his attempts to withhold comfort, to stay disconnected, and buried her face against his shoulder, her fingers twisting into his shirtfront, holding on to him as if the ground had suddenly dropped out from beneath her.

"Blood. Everywhere."

An understatement, he suspected, given how much caked her clothing. He should have known it would take something drastic to drive her into his arms a second time in twenty-four hours.

"I've got you," he whispered, his arms momentarily locking her rigid body to his own. Not in an effort to comfort her, but to calm her enough he could get some reliable information from her. "You're safe."

Her fingers tightened on his shirt. If she were any closer, she would be inside him. And maybe she already was. In spite of the fact he didn't want her there. Couldn't allow any-one to get too close. Least of all her.

When he finally managed to force Kelly's gaze to his, it was still unfocused.

"Talk to me. Before it's too late."

Her eyes narrowed but still didn't connect with his. Instead, they remained in a flat, fixed stare. With no other choice, he shook her again, this time with harsh firmness, his thumbs digging into her shoulders until he could feel her wince.

"Kelly. Before it's too late," he repeated, suspecting she hadn't really heard him the first time.

"It's already too late." She whispered the words.

He could feel the hard shudder rip through her body.

"No, it's not. It's not over until I say it is. You're going to have to believe me on that. I'm not giving up, and I don't want you to, either. You got that?"

After several seconds, she nodded.

"Good girl. Now tell me what happened. Where was Ben?"

"The hangar. The lounge. He…he was dead when I found him. His throat…" Her body stiffened and she looked away. "It's my fault. I made him stay."

"It's not your fault. Did you see anyone?"

"Two men. I was under the cot. All I could see was their feet moving around. Their voices. I was so scared."

"What did they say?"

She took a deep breath. "I have to get to Sarah before…"

"Rod's putting her on a plane."

Tears collected in her eyes, but Nick knew she wouldn't allow them to fall. Not in front of him. Maybe not in front of anyone but Rod.

The thought rankled. It shouldn't, but it did. As did the fact that at a time like this, he couldn't quite ignore the words scrawled at the bottom of a photo, couldn't help but wonder about the gory details of their relationship.

Couldn't help but wish he hadn't walked away in Key West. But back then, he'd always played by the book. No more, though. From here on out, he was going to have to make and play by his own rules.

Nick released Kelly. He raked both hands through his hair, then turned away, needing even that brief distance to recenter his thinking.

"We better move it and fast," he said as he faced her again. He looked down at her, at the blood beneath her nails, the streaks on her forearms and bare legs and on her clothes. Like it or not, he was going to have to trust her. Now more than ever. Between the two of them, they might actually live to see the sun go down.

"You know these islands, Kelly. We need a place people won't be looking."

"I don't know."

"Think!"

"I can't! Not right now!"

"A house that isn't being used?"

Kelly glanced up. "The Camerons' place."

"How far?"

"By boat, an hour."

"Okay. Wash up while I see to a few things."

For the first time, she seemed to notice the blood. "Oh, my God," she whispered. He knew she was remembering how the blood had gotten there.

"Recriminations will have to wait." Nick grabbed her satchel. Though she must have made the trip from the hangar to Hopetown dressed as she was, she couldn't continue to walk around smeared in blood. Not without drawing attention. Which was about the last thing they needed right now.

He found shorts and a clean T-shirt and tried to give them to her. "Put these on."

When she didn't immediately take them, he dropped the

clothes at their feet and reached for the buttons of her shirt. By the time he got to the fourth one, she pulled away. "I'll do it." Scooping them up along with the canvas bag, she headed for the bathroom.

As soon as the door closed, Nick phoned Doug again, intending to alert him to the change of plans. But when the other investigator didn't answer, Nick decided not to leave a message.

He checked the cabinets for additional weapons, found only a filet knife and a few marine flares before Kelly came back.

"Gather what you can in the way of supplies. We won't be stopping at any stores."

Again she nodded but her expression remaining otherwise blank. He knew she was working hard not to fall apart, using every method known to mankind to cope under intense pressure: staying focused on survival, refusing to think about the emotionally incomprehensible, putting one foot in front of the other.

From the small refrigerator, they took a couple of containers of yogurt, a small block of cheddar cheese, cheese crackers and several small bottles of water from the front room. Kelly even emptied packages of fish from the freezer into a nylon mesh catch bag. On the way out the door, she reached for the speargun at the same moment he did. He passed it to her.

They used the boat she'd arrived in. Fifteen minutes later, as they sped toward a destination, a cottage on a small island north of Hopetown and Great Abaco, Nick glanced at Kelly. She stood less than a foot away, one hand wrapped around the aluminum upright of the Bimini top, the other around the console's grab bar. She kept her knees bent to absorb the repeated shock of the hull slamming against the surface.

To the west, mean clouds continued to build. The first signs of bad weather to come.

"How much farther to this cabin?" Though she stood nearly shoulder to shoulder with him, he raised his voice to be heard over the roar of the motor.

"Another twenty or thirty minutes." She turned her head enough to allow the wind to tug her hair away from her face. A single strand caught on her lower lip. Without thinking, Nick fingered it away.

She flinched.

He wasn't surprised by her reaction. Just because she'd thrown herself into his arms back at the dive shop didn't mean she trusted him. Or wanted him touching her. He'd just been a convenient harbor during a very rough storm.

Soon after, Kelly suddenly pushed past Nick and grabbed the throttle, pulling it back into neutral just as the boat plunged across coral.

He jerked the wheel hard to the left. Still beside him, Kelly hung on to the grab bar as the motor slammed into the coral.

Supplies that hadn't been stowed in bait wells and dry lockers flew forward; some went overboard to float like chum.

Wave after wave battered, driving them across the lone coral head. The deck heaved beneath them as the boat rolled.

"Get the motor up," Kelly said, but reached to do it herself. The hull bucked like a theme park ride.

Then they were free, yet remained at the mercy of currents pushing them with relentless force toward the center of the reef.

"Get us out of here!" Kelly called as she desperately hung on to the bar.

Nick lowered the motor and engaged the throttle. The boat lurched against the current, the vibration and sound of the engine like an eggbeater chewing rocks.

When they were clear, Kelly sank to the bench seat, her knee brushing against his.

She massaged her shoulder joints. "Sorry. I wasn't paying attention and I should have been."

"Neither was I." Nick spared a glance for the damaged motor. "Just tell me we're close to this cabin of yours."

"Swing around the end of the island here." She pointed to a spot where there was a void in the distant vegetation. "There's a small inlet and a dock on the other side."

Nick eased the noisy skiff through the narrow inlet overhung with branches from both banks. Looking back, he realized that from open water neither the inlet nor the dock would be visible. Though he would have preferred someplace completely unconnected to Kelly—a rock that no one would think to turn over, it wasn't bad as far as hideouts went.

"Are you certain the owners won't show up?"

"Not likely. The Camerons only come over during the winter months. Off-season, I check on it every few weeks."

"How many people know the routine?"

"A few."

"Rod?"

"Yes."

Of course he would.

"How long have you and Rod been acquainted?"

"Before I settled here, he checked on Aunt Sarah every day, shopping for her and doing the odd maintenance job around her house."

"That would make him a regular Boy Scout, wouldn't it?"

"No. That makes him a decent guy. If you're worried Rod will talk, you needn't be."

"How *well* do you think you know this *decent* guy? As well as you did Ben?"

Her lips thinned. "Point taken. Maybe I've been too trusting. And maybe I continue to be too trusting," she said pointedly.

"Trusting?" He gave a dry, lifeless chuckle. "Yeah. Right."

And perhaps because he realized his interest in the relationship wasn't strictly professional, he was going to let the topic drop.

He took his eyes off the water long enough to glance at her. There were moments when he looked at her and he'd see remnants of the way she'd been. The sadness was still there, the pride, the stubbornness and the loyalty that had left him both frustrated and envious of those whom she protected with it. John Logan had been a lucky man. Too bad he hadn't had the guts his daughter possessed, Nick decided as he let the boat glide the last few feet to the dock, where he killed the already maimed engine.

"Can you cook any better than you used to?" he asked, needing a safe subject.

"Not much." She moved with efficiency to grab lines. "How about you? Taken any cooking courses in your spare time?"

"I can handle the odd grilled cheese sandwich or omelet."

She smiled, a tepid warmth briefly filling her green eyes. "What you're saying is starvation may do us in before Binelli has another chance at us."

He didn't respond right away and she hesitated in what she was doing. "What?" she asked.

"It suits you," he commented.

She held the line looped loosely in her hand. "What, starving? If you're suggesting I need to drop a few pounds—"

"No. The smile. It's the first time I've seen it since I've been in the Islands."

"I guess I haven't had much to smile about."

"And now you do?"

Kelly ignored the question as she hopped onto the dock to tie off the stern line to the cleat with the ease of someone who spent a lot of time around boats.

He tossed a few of the supplies onto the dock behind her. "Looks like we have a little climb ahead of us."

The house was perched atop a bluff like an osprey's nest, the water a good sixty feet below the randomly configured deck. Wooden steps were covered in coarse sand that sifted unceasingly down the slope to melt into the man-made inlet.

"The island's called Ransom Cay. Pirates used it for holding their hostages." She looked at him pointedly.

"You're not my hostage."

"What am I, then?"

"That's up to you," he said. "In the meantime, let's get these supplies taken care of."

She picked up the mesh bag of frozen fish and her satchel and started up. "The view's great from up there. So's the breeze."

They couldn't have done much better, he realized. The position of the house would make it easy to see if anyone was coming, and from his current vantage point, the steps appeared to be the only easy way in from this side of the island. He'd check out the rest once they'd unloaded the boat.

While he made trip after trip with supplies, Kelly dealt with the cistern and the generator that ran the pumps and the lights. Dropping the last of the bags on the living room floor, he wondered how many women would know how to do either. As John Logan's daughter, dragged from one pub to the next, raised in a cockpit with mechanics and other flight hounds as her only example, she'd grown up tough and capable. He only had to recall the punch she'd thrown at him last night and the way she'd handled finding Ben dead to realize just how tough she was—both physically and emotionally. Nick doubted she'd truly leaned on even one person since her father's death.

Until now.

Chapter Eight

More than two hours later, Kelly opened the sliding glass doors of the smaller front bedroom on the lower level.

The ocean breeze whistled through, clearing away the mustiness of disuse. The vertical blinds fluttered, their gentle clacking mimicking that of the palmettos covering the dark slope outside.

As she stepped closer to look out at the lonely night, she shivered. Not in reaction to the breeze, but in reaction to the uncertainty of what lay ahead.

Somewhere out there, men searched for her. Men who had killed Ben and wouldn't hesitate to kill her. Or even Sarah.

If Kelly had never come to the islands, her aunt would be safe now. That fact alone was enough to make her sick inside.

Last night, she'd thought her situation couldn't get any bleaker, and yet it had. Less then twenty-four hours ago, she'd watched Ben leave for a dinner break. As he'd ambled away, he'd lifted his left hand in that small backward wave of his. He'd probably called a "See you," but she couldn't remember hearing the words.

There had been no ugliness, no pain, no fear of what the next hour would bring. Just the struggle and worry of building a business.

Then she had looked up to see Nick standing there, and it all changed. More basic human needs had suddenly taken precedence. Staying alive. Seeing her aunt safe. Getting the packets of Ocularcet through to Amanda. Amazingly, at the moment, staying out of jail was the least of her worries.

Kelly rubbed her bare arms. What evidence did Customs have? Nick hadn't really said last night. More than just photos? More than Jeff Myers's frequent use of her airline and Ben's cash deposit?

Of course, there would be nothing to tie her directly to the money or Binelli. Not that it would matter.

With no way to refute any of it, and with the only man capable of corroborating her innocence dead, she knew how it would play out. Just as her father must have known how it was going to end for him.

As she had a million times since that horrible day, she tried to imagine how it was possible that a man as strong and as determined as her father could take his own life. Why had he run out on her when she needed him the most?

Had he even been thinking of her?

Kelly grabbed a set of sheets from a dresser drawer and tossed them on the bed, her thoughts shifting to the moments she'd spent cowering beneath a cot last night.

In hopes of finding some way to prove her innocence, she tried to recall what the men had talked about.

They'd been looking for something. Something they hadn't wanted Binelli to see. Her eyes narrowed. No. That couldn't be right. They worked for Binelli. Her attacker had been certain *she* had something belonging to Binelli. They had killed Ben for it with the very same knife that had been used on her.

A slight scent of mildew filtered up as she unfolded the linens and picked up the closest pillow with trembling fingers, but it was the scent of warm blood that lingered in her mind now. She doubted it would ever fade completely. Death could be peaceful and quiet, like a whisper dissolving into a night breeze, or it could be as ugly and mean as Ben's had been.

She should just be thankful to be alive, she realized. Even though, from the start, Nick had thought her guilty, he'd kept her safe. And not only because he thought she had what the government needed to put Binelli away. But because, when you got to the very bottom line, he was a good guy. Because, unlike most of the men she'd met, Nick Cavanaugh would always do the right thing.

Whether it was easy or not.

She knew that much about him. But what about the rest of what he'd told her back in New Jersey? Fact or fiction? Bad childhood? A father he hadn't gotten along with? Lies fabricated to gain her trust? To gain her father's?

Nick was obviously good with lies. Knew how to twist them just right.

Kelly tossed the pillow on the bed and picked up the remaining pillowcase. As she unfolded it, something made her glance toward the open sliders. A man stood there.

Adrenaline scrabbled through her unchecked. Her muscles knotted for flight.

In the next second, she realized her mistake.

Though she hadn't heard Nick descend the stairs, the reflective glass of the doors revealed him leaning in the doorway behind her, one arm braced against the frame, his broad shoulders filling the narrow opening.

As she took a deep breath, his gaze collided with hers in the glass. "Sorry. I didn't mean to startle you." Pushing away from the casing, he took a step toward her. "I made us something to eat. Are you hungry?"

"Not very." Needing to keep her hands occupied, she reached for the second pillow.

Nick walked past her to look out the sliding glass door. He'd showered. He wore the same blood-stained clothes, but droplets of water bled into his collar from where his dark hair curled damply against his neck.

Nick chose that moment to look over his shoulder and caught her staring.

He was the first to speak, to glance away. "As steep and overgrown as it is, the slope might be hard to climb, but not impossible."

"Before someone got that far, they'd have to make it across the reef, which, as you saw this afternoon, can be a bit tricky."

"How about if you anchored out and used scuba gear?"

"With the way the surf has kicked up, it would be dangerous. And they'd require light to navigate."

"Night vision equipment would easily take care of that."

He scanned the room briefly, then, without saying another word, ambled past her and out into the hallway. Seconds later, he was back.

"You don't need to finish here," he informed her. "You'll sleep in the back bedroom."

Her chin popped up. "No way! That room's like a prison cell. It doesn't even have a window. It must be over a hundred degrees in there."

"So I won't have to worry about anyone getting in it without my knowledge or you slipping out of it, will I?"

"I won't be running."

Nick tugged the pillow from her grasp. "So you said last night."

"That was different. I had to—"

"Had to go to the hangar? For what? A plane?"

"I needed to confront Ben."

"And you did, sweetheart. And nearly got yourself killed in the process."

"As if you give a damn. We both know the only reason you're holding on to me is because you think I have something you want."

He cut her off. "It's either the back bedroom or share my bed again. Your choice."

She swallowed the rest of what she was going to say. "When you put it like that, I'll take the oven."

He gave her a tight smile. "I thought you might." He tossed the pillow onto the bed.

When she tried to turn away, he stopped her with a hand on her upper arm. "When you came to my room, I told you it would be done my way. I meant it."

"I know you did. It's the only way you know how to do anything, isn't it?"

"Yes. So you might as well get used to it."

She shrugged away his touch. "I'll be up in a few minutes," she added as she left the room.

Kelly turned on the shower, stripped off her clothes. Ignoring the fact they were using a cistern, she took her time showering, scrubbing over and over with the rough cloth. No matter how many times she went over her skin, in her mind Ben's blood still clung to her. As did the image of his sightless eyes.

The tears came suddenly and, slumped on the tub bottom, she cried for Ben. In spite of what he had done, she couldn't find any hate inside for him. She cried for Sarah. And, even though it felt weak, she cried for herself.

When the worst of it passed, she stood and let the water rinse away the signs, then flipped off the faucet.

One of the Cameron boys had left behind some faded T-shirts and she helped herself. From her bag, she dug out a hair clip and makeup. She used just enough foundation to cover the signs of her crying jag and the bruise above her temple.

As she dropped the bottle back in her satchel, her fingers touched the strip of condom-like packages. They had some-how managed to find their way up from the bottom of her bag. Like a deep thought working it's way to the front of the mind where it could no longer be ignored.

Each foil packet contained a dose of Ocularcet, the only hope for a little girl.

Kelly stood there uncertainly. She had no choice, she told herself. She couldn't risk Nick finding them. If he found them, there would be no convincing him she was innocent of the other charges.

She lifted the seat of the toilet, carefully opened the first packet and watched the clear fluid flow into the bowl. With the second, she ripped and squeezed, but refused to watch.

Her fingers shook by the time she got to the third. In her head, she saw Amanda's face, the clear blue eyes, the turned-up nose and freckles. Heard five-year-old's laughter and high-pitched squeals.

Kelly sank back, her spine resting against the wall, her eyes closed in horror at what she'd almost done. And in de-spair at her situation.

Nick knocked on the door. "You okay in there?"

Startled, Kelly stumbled to her feet. "I'm fine. I'll be up in a moment."

She waited until she heard him walk away, then shoved the packets to the bottom of her bag. Her thoughts, she knew, wouldn't be so easily forced from view.

Nick was already sitting at the table waiting for her. He'd tossed the frozen fish—dried-out grouper—onto the grill. He'd also thrown together a meager salad and opened a can of green beans he must have found in the pantry.

"You obviously were playing down your talents," she of-fered as she tugged out the folded paper towel from beneath the fork.

"You'd better hold judgment a bit longer," Nick suggested as he did the same.

He poured red wine into a water glass.

She picked up the glass, tried it in the hopes it might settle her nerves. "I don't recall bringing wine."

"I found it in the upper cabinet. Well-aged, if the layer of dust is any indication. The vintage's a little questionable, but uninvited guests can hardly be choosy, can they?"

"No." She flaked off a corner of the overcooked grouper and lifted it to her mouth. She chewed for nearly a minute before forcing the still dry, tasteless meat down her unreceptive throat.

"How is it?"

She took her time separating another mouthful. "Not bad for bait."

Nick hesitated, his own fork hanging midair. "Bait?"

"That's all Rod keeps at the shop. Anything he doesn't eat fresh, he freezes for bait or chum."

"Why didn't you say something?"

"Because it wasn't important. Protein is protein. And as you said earlier, we aren't in a position to be overly choosy. About what we eat or where we sleep."

The next morsel she washed down with more of the room-temperature wine. She noticed Nick did the same.

Though she had little appetite, she forced herself to eat. She needed energy. She also needed sleep, which would have to wait a bit longer.

When she looked up again, Nick watched her. The unexpected sharp thrum of male-female awareness had her looking away. But in that second before she did, she admitted something she'd been denying for the past twenty-two hours. No matter how much she didn't want it to be so, she was still vulnerable to Nick on a physical level. Last night, she'd told herself she'd allowed Nick to kiss her, to touch her, because she hadn't wanted to feel so damned alone, but she'd been wrong. There was more to it than simple neediness.

The sudden wedge of self-contempt made swallowing difficult. She shouldn't feel anything but hatred for him. He'd used her to get close to her father, to further his investigation, then walked away without once looking back.

He refilled her wineglass, set the bottle aside.

"A penny for them."

She met his gaze, but remained mute. There were questions she needed answers to, but she had been holding off asking them, certain that as soon as she voiced any of them, Nick would start in with his own interrogation.

But he'd be asking those same questions before long anyway, wouldn't he? She was actually surprised he hadn't already done so. But perhaps the sneaky bastard was waiting until the wine kicked in.

Kelly picked up the wine bottle by the slim neck and refilled his empty glass to the rim. "You said Rod was putting Sarah on a plane?"

"That's right. To Naples. She'll be picked up once she's stateside."

"By whom?"

"By Doug Willcox."

"And he's with Customs?"

"That's right."

Kelly took a sip, more to soothe away the tightness in her throat than to quench her thirst. "How safe will she be? Will Binelli be able to get to her?"

"No."

His assertion didn't fully ease her worry. The question she'd most feared, though, needed to be asked. "What did you tell her?"

"Tell her?"

"About what was going on. About what you think I've done."

"You're worried that I told your aunt about the smuggling? About your involvement with Binelli?"

She nodded.

"I just told her you were in some danger. And that the best thing she could do for you was make it so you wouldn't have to worry about her right now."

"She was okay with that?"

"Sometimes you ask a lot of people, Kelly. She was scared. For you, though. Not for herself."

Kelly closed her eyes and looked away. She should have stayed away. If anything happened to what was left of her family, she could never forgive herself.

"What now, Nick?"

"We wait."

"For...?"

"Until transportation is arranged." He took a bite of his salad. "You didn't think we could just catch the next plane out of here, did you?"

"I suppose I did."

Nick leaned forward. "You're hot stuff at the moment, Flygirl. Everyone wants a piece of you. Binelli. The FBI. Customs." He shoved his chair back so he could stretch his legs.

The use of the Flygirl nickname irritated her. "What about you, Nick? Shouldn't your name be on that list?"

His mouth tightened, even as his pupils darkened. "No. I just want to help you."

"Into a jail cell."

"Cutting a deal with us, telling me what you know, is your best shot."

She took another long gulp of the bitter wine. "I'd do anything to save my aunt. Anything. But I can't do what I can't do." She grabbed her plate and carried it into the kitchen.

Leaving the light off, she turned on the water and squirted

soap into it, then waited for the sink to fill. She could feel Nick standing just inside the door, watching her.

After several moments, he set his plate on the counter near her elbow.

"We could start slow. Like some details about what you saw or heard at the hangar last night."

"They talked about killing. About how easy it was." She squeezed her hand into a fist around the dishrag. "They killed Ben because they wanted something he either didn't have or wouldn't turn over to them."

"But they didn't say what it was?"

"No."

"Do you think it was the same thing your attacker was after?"

"Yeah. And if I had had it, Ben would still be alive."

Nick cut her off. "Don't play that game, Kelly. Don't start holding yourself responsible for things beyond your control."

She made a small sound at the back of her throat. "I have very little control now, Nick. Over anything."

She shoved her hands into the warm water and found the rag again, wrung it out with her fingers more viciously than necessary. She needed to keep her anger honed and ready. It was the only weapon she still possessed, one of the few things still in her control.

"You can trust me, Kelly," he said from just behind her.

The muscles across her upper back and shoulders tensed. Even though he didn't touch her, it was as if she could feel him.

It would be so easy to sway, to let her spine rest against his solid body. He'd catch her, probably even hold her there in the dark silence.

Nick cupped her shoulders, moved half a step closer until she could feel his chest pressed to her back. His fingers flexed into her bare skin with warmth and what felt like need. "I want to help you." He said it so softly she wondered if he had said it at all.

She took a deep breath and let it out slowly. She glanced over her shoulder and up at his face. Not for the first time she had the sensation that there was something more personal at stake for Nick in this case.

"I can handle this," she said after several seconds. "You don't need to watch over me."

Withdrawing his hands, he backed away.

Turning her attention to the dishes, she rubbed at the first plate, going over it half a dozen times before setting it in the other sink to rinse later. She could feel the emotional and physical fatigue overtaking her as she reached for the second plate. She slipped it silently beneath the water, almost wishing she could do the same.

Nick's voice jarred her. "So, how about a new subject?"

"Okay," she answered cautiously.

"What have you been doing since I last saw you?"

She hesitated. "You mean since that holding cell where you left me?"

When he didn't respond, Kelly glanced at him, both of her hands still covered in suds. He stood unmoving in the shadows, waiting silently, his handsome face implacable. He could have easily returned her attack, but he hadn't.

She felt some of the anger drain away, enough that she could see reason. She was obviously going to be stuck with him for the next few days. Until Nick got her back to U.S. soil. It might be smart to look for some way for some safe ground, some way for them to deal together. And who knew, given enough time, she might be able to convince Nick he was wrong about her.

She found a fork on the sink bottom. "I flew for several small charter companies. Mainly in the Midwest and mostly cargo."

She flicked on the light over the sink. As with the slider downstairs, the window in front of her became a mirror. "The pay wasn't great," she continued, "but at least I spent my day in a cockpit." Her quick, dry chuckle sounded hollow. "Not that I had any other marketable skills."

With Nick's silence, she continued. "The small company I worked for fell into financial problems. I was forced to look for work outside the industry."

"What kind of work?"

She picked up the next piece of silverware. "Barmaid, for starters. I figured I'd spent enough time in pubs as I was growing up to know the general mechanics of serving."

"What happened?"

"I lasted three nights. Then I tried working in a dental office. Pay wasn't as good, but the hours were regular. And the doctor was an okay guy."

"And?"

"Someone offered me a job flying." She rinsed a plate and handed it to him, along with a towel. "Might as well make yourself useful."

Nick took both without hesitation.

"How about you, Nick? What have you been up to?"

"I moved to the Orlando office about four years ago."

"Why?"

When he didn't answer immediately, she glanced in the window. He was still drying the plate, polishing it, really, his expression filled with something resembling regret. When he realized she studied him, he turned to put the plate in the cabinet. "No reason. The timing was right for a change."

There was more to it than that, but it was unlikely he was going to share any more information about the move with her. She guessed that he hadn't relocated for a promotion. Had his move involved a woman? "How about a personal life?"

"What do you mean?"

"You know, friends, girlfriend?" It was a question she should have asked last night but hadn't. She found herself waiting for the answer. "Nick?"

"You had it right before. I'm not much good at relationships."

The knot in her middle eased with his answer, but immediately tightened again when he leaned in and helped himself to several pieces of the rinsed silverware in the bottom of the sink. For a brief moment they were only inches apart. If she had turned her head, their lips would have been all but touching. Kelly swallowed the urge, but couldn't quite ignore the way her pulse continued to pound even after he retreated.

Nick filed each piece of dried silverware into the drawer. "Are you and Rod serious about each other?"

Kelly pulled the drain plug for something to do. The question had taken her by surprise. "No. Just friends."

"That's not the impression he gave me."

"I think he wanted more at one time. But, as the saying goes, we can't choose who we love."

"But if you could?" Nick closed the drawer.

"I don't know. Maybe. He's a good man. Honest and kind. Generous with his friends. Attractive." She closed her eyes against the image that came to mind when she used the last of those words. Nick standing inside Princeton Air's hangar. The grin cocky. Eyes filled with a reckless light that had seemed to somehow match the craving deep inside her.

She felt the rhythm of her heart climb behind her ribs until it filled her throat. She'd been nineteen at the time. Inexperienced, but damned eager to learn, and Nick had seemed the perfect instructor. Just the man she'd been looking for.

"Has there been—"

Kelly rolled around and leaned back against the counter, her arms locked across her chest. "I'm not going to discuss my sex life with you."

"Sorry. I didn't mean to step on any toes." Nick tossed the towel over his shoulder with practiced ease. The action made Kelly wonder again about the women in his life, about the one woman who had taught him to dry dishes and silverware, to mop up the counter when the last dish was slid away. To drape the towel over the edge of the counter to dry when there was no towel bar in sight.

Even if her own sex life was off-limits, she realized she couldn't help but wonder about his.

"What about your aunt? How did you find her? Or did she find you?"

"It took me almost three years to get up the courage to go through Dad's personal papers. It was Christmas Eve. I was stuck in a cheap apartment and the couple next door was having another one of their shouting matches. I opened a large bottle of red wine and a box of tissues. By the time I found her letter at the bottom of the box, I'd already emptied both and the couple next door had made up."

"How did you know they—"

"Like I said. It was a cheap apartment."

His eyes hinted at sympathy. "Where were you at the time?"

"Iowa, I think." She squinted, trying to recall where it had been. All she could seem to remember, though, was the cold gray emptiness of the apartment. And of her life. "Or maybe it was Illinois. In any case, it was one of those flat states starting with an *I*."

She glanced around, searching for something to occupy her hand. Picking up the rag again, she wiped down the clean range top. "I don't know why Dad kept the letter all those years. There was no love between my mother's family and my father. He was afraid they'd take me away if they realized I hadn't died at birth."

"Maybe he planned to give the letter to you when you were older."

"I suppose." But she didn't really think so. She suspected he had simply overlooked it. Not that his motivation mattered. After all, did anyone ever really know why someone else did something?

She moved to the counter and continued wiping, forcing herself back to the present. "I also found at the bottom of the box a bank book for a small savings account. It wasn't much, but it helped to buy the first plane."

"John would have liked that."

She nodded, but made no further comment. A day didn't go by that she didn't remember her father in some way. Especially when she climbed through dense cloud cover to the waiting blue of clear skies. It was there she felt him the most. It was as if he were with her, a part of the skies he had loved.

There were other times, too, when she sensed him nearby. She would be startled from a sound sleep by his voice. She'd never told anyone, afraid there was some logical explanation. She didn't want logic. She wanted something much more dear. And impossible.

Kelly flicked off the light over the sink. Nick was still there when she turned. She attempted to push past him, but he refused to let her by.

"I'm glad you found your aunt," he said, sincerity a heavy thread in his voice.

She took a deep breath. "I wish more than anything I could talk to her, or at least talk to someone who saw her today. Saw her safely away from the islands." She lifted her eyes to his. "We could try the radio."

"No," he said without hesitation.

"I wouldn't say anything to give away our position. So even if someone were listening—"

"But they'd know we were still in the islands. And we have a better chance if they think we may have already slipped by them."

She nodded her understanding. "Thank you for seeing to Sarah's safety, Nick. I know I should have said it before, but—"

"You're saying it now," he finished for her. He looped a strand of her hair behind her ear. She lifted her gaze to Nick's again. A solid punch of raw, sexual awareness replaced the disappointment of seconds earlier.

Nick felt something, too. His fingers twitched as if they'd touched something they shouldn't, then slowly dropped away, the brief physical bridge broken.

He motioned toward the door. "Come on. We both need sleep."

Flipping off the remaining lamp next to the sofa, he led the way downstairs.

Stopping her before she could enter the back bedroom, he said, "Wait here."

The room's only light source was the lamp on the nightstand, but Nick left it off. She waited in the hall while he inspected the closet. Nick's glance hesitated on the bed. She wondered if he, too, recalled their night in Key West and just how close they had come to consummating a physical relationship. She had been totally naked and vulnerable when he'd suddenly left her sprawled on the rumpled sheets.

Still a virgin.

As he stepped by her this time, she noticed he favored the leg more than he had earlier.

"How's the leg?"

"Stiff and sore."

"Any infection?"

"Some redness. Antibiotics should take care of it."

"You need a doctor."

"And I'll survive until we can get to one. There's a lock on the door," he said in an abrupt change of subjects. "Use it. If you need to get up for any reason during the night, bang on the wall, but don't open the door unless I tell you to."

"Isn't that a little extreme?"

"Perhaps, but—"

"You're calling the shots," she finished for him. She decided opposing him on the issue would be pointless.

MORE THAN TWO HOURS LATER, Nick pulled on the jeans he'd kicked off earlier. With another day's wear, they'd be able to stand as straight and stiff as a guard on the Citadel's parade ground.

The comfortable breeze of dusk had faded shortly before midnight, the heat in the house climbing by the minute, reminding him of the heavy heat of Charleston, South Carolina, where he'd grown up. He'd been back only once in recent years. To clear up his father's estate, to see the family home sold, a house that had been in the family for more than two hundred years.

Some would say he'd turned his back on his heritage, and perhaps he had. He hoped he had.

Nick hesitated outside Kelly's door just to listen, to assure himself she was safely tucked away. At least, that's what he told himself, and yet his hand wrapped around the doorknob, and he pressed his forehead to the cool wood. He hadn't for the past few hours just been ruminating about the investigation; he'd also been thinking about Kelly. Dangerous thoughts about how easy it would be to cross the line a second time, to forget who he was, to forget just who she was, what she had done.

There had been a moment in the kitchen when he had nearly done so. If she had reached for him there in the darkness, he wouldn't have been able to stop himself.

He'd also found himself contemplating the small possibility she might be telling the truth, that she might be innocent.

But that line of thought had more to do with wishful think-ing than with sound reasoning. The angle just didn't play very well. The chances of a law-abiding citizen getting mis-takenly named in a smuggling investigation twice seemed highly improbable.

But not impossible.

He should have pressed Kelly back at the dive shop when he'd had the chance. She had been close to both emotional and physical exhaustion, the ideal time to force a suspect into making a mistake or even into confessing. But he hadn't. A tactical error, perhaps, but, surprisingly, he had no regrets.

Nick moved soundlessly down the hall now, intending to do a routine check of the house.

It was unlikely Binelli could have a line on their location this fast. By now, he might even have turned his attention away from the islands and toward U.S. soil. But when Kelly didn't show up stateside in twenty-four to thirty-six hours, he would again look to the islands and redouble his efforts to find her. Which left a very small window of opportunity to get her out without it getting messy.

Come morning, he'd find a phone to contact Doug for the arrangements.

Nick found the upper level to be cooler. It was also brighter than the lower floor, the moonlight having plenty of access through the bank of sliding glass doors.

Opening the middle one, he stepped out onto the deck. Below him, the Atlantic shimmered, the moonlight a flow of silver on its surface. Off shore, he could see where the surf crashed across the reef, the sound an endless, harsh metro-nome. He searched the slope and, when nothing moved, he turned away, locking the door behind him.

And wished he could lock away thoughts of Kelly just as easily.

IT WAS PAST MIDNIGHT when Myron Richardson carried the last of the boxes and the heavy suitcases out the condominium's back door. Behind him, the French doors stood open, the inside light pouring out to welcome insects into cool, conditioned air. He loaded the luggage into the trunk with the others, then quietly shut it.

By this time tomorrow, a search warrant would be issued allowing Nick's condominium to be turned inside out. The carpets would be ripped back to reveal the concrete floor beneath, the attic would be examined and the small patio area would be dug up, the flowers and bushes left bare-rooted on hot pavement.

Myron pulled off the latex gloves he'd worn. For the past seven hours, he'd gone through Nick's place with meticulous care, packing what needed to be removed, leaving behind what wasn't important. Adding that which was missing from the picture.

He'd spent a career, a lifetime, untangling and sorting evidence, following the tangible trail to its end. Tonight, he'd worked in reverse, creating enough evidence to confuse even the most seasoned government agent.

Chapter Nine

Kelly stared up at the dark ceiling. She hadn't slept in more than thirty-six hours. Sleep was crucial if she planned to continue functioning, but before she could give into her fatigue, she had to know her aunt was safe.

Which wouldn't be easy. She'd noticed during dinner Nick had removed the handset to the shortwave. Had he also discovered the spare stashed in a cubbyhole near the radio itself? If he hadn't, and if she could get to it…

There were risks, but there always were. Consequences, too.

Kelly piled the pillows at the head of the bed and sat up. If she could reach Rod, if he was listening in on his shortwave…

Tonight would be her best opportunity, perhaps her only chance. She couldn't be certain where she'd be tomorrow.

She closed her eyes, intending only to rest them for several moments as she waited for Nick to fall asleep.

The nightmare jettisoned her to consciousness. With her heart still slamming against her ribs, she glanced around her, momentarily confused about where she was. Then memory overtook her. She sat there for several minutes more, panic slowly receding until she managed to draw a steady breath.

There was no clock in her room and no window, either.

No way for her to be certain if she'd slept mere seconds or hours. Was it still the middle of the night or nearly dawn?

Kelly slipped off the bed and crossed to the door. She opened it and waited for movement from Nick's room. When she was satisfied that he slept, she groped her way down the dark hallway, the bottom of the steps her first goal.

Before she reached the stairs, she'd have to walk past the small alcove containing the entrance door. Anyone could be waiting for her there, waiting to reach out and grab her just as her attacker had last night. She stopped to lean against the wall.

Get a grip, Logan.

She forced herself to slide along the wall until it ended. A small eddy of air swirled around the corner. She heard the sounds of the wind and of the surf, and of her own rapid breathing.

And the sound of a gun being cocked.

"Going someplace, Kelly?" Nick asked as he lowered the weapon.

"The kitchen. For some water."

"Anything wrong with the bathroom?"

"I wanted a glass to put on the nightstand."

He stepped back and reholstered his weapon. "There's a glass on the sink. Use it. I'll wait."

MORNING DAWNED cloudless. Unfortunately, Nick's head didn't feel quite so clear as he stood at the top of the stairs leading down to the dock.

Below him, the boat strained at the ropes. The tide had gone out farther than he had anticipated. He shouldn't have retied the lines. Should have trusted Kelly to know the correct amount of slack.

Something made him glance back at the cottage where she still slept. He wasn't worried she'd slip off. The closest island was more than six miles to the south. But he hadn't bought her lie about wanting a glass of water last night. She'd been headed upstairs for more than a drink.

This morning, he'd checked out the cottage further. In the desk near the radio, he located a second handset. He smiled, imagining her irritation when she realized it was gone, and that he knew just how her mind worked.

He even wished there were some way to contact her aunt. Just to ease Kelly's worry. But the shortwave was just too public for his comfort.

Nick descended the steps, the household toolbox clanking as the contents shifted with his stiff, uneven gait.

He'd spent the morning with his leg elevated while he'd compiled notes on the investigation. There were a hell of a lot of leads he would have liked to check further. Not that he had any idea who he would call at this point. To request anything more of Douglas would be asking the man to risk his job.

And, until Nick knew more about his supervisor's meeting with the Bureau, contacting Myron was out of the question.

An angle Nick hadn't considered before had been riding him hard for the past hour. From the moment he'd discovered Ake's body, Nick had assumed the killer had followed Ake to the rooftop. That the timing of the hit had little to do with their meeting.

But what if his assumption had been wrong? What if the killer had been tipped off Ake was on to something, that he was about to talk?

What if the phone call Myron made that night wasn't to his daughter?

The possibility left Nick uneasy. Twenty-four hours ago, he'd have bet his life on Myron. They went way back. Back to the beginning of his career. It had been Myron who'd been responsible for hiring him. But the relationship hadn't stopped there. Nick shoved the possibility away once more, but knew it would continue to lurk in his head.

As he boarded, the boat moved restlessly beneath him. He set the tool kit on the deck before removing the automatic from his waistband and placing it inside the box along with the two handsets.

Trimming up the outboard motor, he examined the first signs of damage. A broken skag and a bent propeller. The mangled prop accounted for the engine vibration and the boat's inability to come up on plane. Unfortunately, without a new one, there was little he could do to fix either.

Nick pulled off his jeans, then slipped over the side, the warm water stinging his thigh and shoulder. Fitting the diving mask over his face, he dropped beneath the surface and into the shade cast by the boat. The scrapes along the hull were consistent with the type of damage caused when fiberglass tangled with coral. He paused to study an exceptionally deep gash, then moved on again when he was confident the outer skin hadn't been breached.

Below him, the sunlight piercing the inlet's twelve feet of water shimmered across the sand bottom. A horse conch moved slowly and silently through the surreal world.

Coming up near the stern, Nick removed the mask and tossed it onto the dock, before hoisting himself in after it. He pulled on his jeans.

Another theory he didn't much like had also played at the back of his mind.

The Abacos weren't the end of the line for Binelli's money, just a transfer point. Grand Cayman was the ultimate destination. Which meant, since Bird of Paradise didn't cover the area, someone other than Kelly had to complete the final leg. Who better than Rod?

There had been a pamphlet on the dive shop's front

counter advertising diving junkets to the Caymans. Had Binelli's cash been hauled as far as Marsh Harbor on a Bird of Paradise's plane, where Rod had taken over, using the junkets as a cover?

Mulling the possibility from different angles, Nick grabbed a screwdriver from the toolbox.

He was still bent over the motor twenty minutes later when he sensed Kelly's presence behind him.

"Good morning," Kelly offered as she dropped to sit on the edge of the dock. She propped her feet on the side of the boat, the coffee mug cradled between her hands.

She wore wrinkled shorts and another borrowed T-shirt, this one a bright orange with faded lettering. "You should have gotten me up."

"You needed the rest."

She sipped the coffee. "What about you?"

He tossed the wrench he'd been using into the toolbox. "I slept, if that's what you mean."

"Did you? I heard you walking around several times during the night."

"I'm restless sometimes."

Especially since the night he'd found Ake. First, John Logan had haunted him, then the kid Nick had shot four years ago when an investigation he'd been working had taken an unexpected turn and now it was Ake's murder that kept Nick awake at night.

"Yeah, restless," she responded.

Something in Kelly's voice, in her tone, pulled Nick away from thoughts of his own demons. He turned, spark plug in hand, to study her more fully. She'd showered and had taken the time to apply makeup. Her attempts had come close to concealing the shadowed circles and even her injuries, but it would have taken the sunglasses she'd worn yesterday to hide her fatigue. Whatever Kelly had spent the last eleven hours doing, it hadn't been sleeping. Maybe she had her own demons to cope with.

Empathy came unexpectedly and took him by surprise, like the first dip on a roller coaster. "It gets easier," he said as he again turned away.

She didn't pretend not to know what he was talking about. "Maybe for some."

"Perhaps easier is the wrong word. I suppose in time we just learn to cope with the truth of death."

"What truth would that be?" she asked and stood, the boat rocking with her movements.

He paused in tightening the spark plug to consider his next words. "That life goes on, and we need to go on with it or curl up and die beside those we've lost."

She sat again. This time on the bench seat three feet from where he worked, her legs stretched out casually, all that cool, smooth flesh not going unnoticed by him. He felt his pulse kick just beneath the surface.

"It sounds as if you lost someone recently."

Nick hesitated. Except in an official capacity, he hadn't spoken to anyone about Ake's death.

"Was it someone you knew well?" she pressed.

"A very good friend," he answered after another short pause.

"What happened?"

He turned and looked her full in the face. "Someone put a gun to the back of his head and pulled the trigger."

Swallowing the sip of coffee she'd just taken, Kelly stared at the half-empty cup she clasped. "I'm sorry, Nick."

He had seen the brief flare of shock in her eyes, then the pity. The shock he could deal with. The other he couldn't.

"Maybe you should be. He was investigating you. And Binelli, of course. But it was *you* he wanted to talk about the night it happened."

In the next instant, he regretted the cruelty of his words. She glanced off in the distance, seeming to study the water at the inlet's opening. She had a strong profile, a sharp-angled jaw she'd inherited from her father, lips that wore both laughter and sternness with the same ease. But it was her eyes, which were now turned away, that had always been the most revealing. He found himself wondering what they said.

"I suspected there was more to it for you than just a job," she said finally, her voice tinged with something sounding like remorse. "No wonder you hate me, believing what you do."

"I don't hate you, Kelly."

"Maybe not. But you don't much like me, either."

She looked at him then, and something in her gaze, a vulnerability, reminded Nick it hadn't been just John Logan, Ake and the kid who'd kept him company last night. For some reason, she seemed to have the same hold on him alive as the others did dead.

He just couldn't seem to forget what had been between them at one time. Nor, no matter how implausible it was, could he completely ignore her adamant assertion she was innocent. Stranger things had happened, hadn't they?

And smarter men than him had been taken in by a pair of long legs and a good mouth.

He'd traveled between those same two opposing thoughts so many times they'd carved a rut across his brain. Still, he had no answer.

Nick turned his attention back to the motor. "I need the large Phillips head." Without looking at her, he held his hand behind his back.

She found the screwdriver among the others in the box and snapped it into his palm with the precision born of many hours of handling tools.

"How bad is it?" she asked.

"We won't be going anywhere today. The bottom's pretty torn up, but it appears to be watertight at the moment. As far as the engine, the lower unit has some damage, but I can't tell how much without pulling it."

"The propeller?" she asked.

He straightened. "I was saving the best for last. It's severely bent. If it comes to any kind of chase, without a new one we're dead in the water."

"Nice analogy," she said.

"Would you rather I lie?"

"No. I've always preferred the truth. Even when it's unpleasant." Kelly stood. "There's a lot of gear and tools in the generator room. There might be a spare prop."

"When I'm done here, I'll check it out." He turned to apologize for his earlier words, but she was already halfway up the steps.

Kelly returned ten minutes later with a replacement prop.

"I didn't realize you knew so much about boat motors," she offered as she placed it within arm's reach.

"There's quite a bit about me you don't know."

Crossing her arms, she fixed a tight smile on her lips. "I suppose that's true. I was the one who did all the talking seven years ago. Maybe that should have been the tipoff."

"About what?"

"Usually people who talk very little about themselves are hiding something."

There was a cool note of condemnation in her tone. He liked it, liked the fact, even now under the present circumstances, she hadn't turned meek or mute. There was a resiliency to Kelly he still found appealing. And a sharp intellect to go with it.

"And now it's you who's refusing to talk," he observed.

For a brief second, when their gazes met and before she camouflaged it with her thick lashes, he saw that she was hiding something, but decided not to pursue the tack head-on. They weren't going anywhere for at least another twenty-four hours. He could afford to be patient for a bit longer. Let her relax. Let her start considering her options. She was a smart woman. Eventually she'd start acting like one.

"Okay, Kelly. For now, you can ask the questions and I'll supply the answers."

As he torqued the last spark plug loose, Nick could almost feel Kelly mentally walking possible alleys of conversation, carefully looking for trouble.

"So you have a boat?" she asked finally.

He grinned at the innocuous choice of subjects. The wrench clattered on top of the others in the box. "A small one that I use for fishing up at my cabin in North Carolina. I don't get up there often, so the motor always needs work." He used a small rasp on the point to clean it, then wiped off the plug.

"How long have you had a place?"

"A few years. It's old and on the small side, just a couple of rooms, but it was constructed from logs cut on the property back in the thirties. It has character."

"When a man uses that word, it can mean one of two things—either it's dark as a cave or there's no running water."

"I take it you're not much for bathing in a cold lake in November?"

"No. But I don't suppose I'll have to worry about that any time soon."

For some reason, the image of her doing just that came to him. He realized he could picture her there at his cabin, a fishing line dangling in the water, her feet bare. Curled up by a roaring fire on an autumn night. After several seconds, he cleared his mind, then his throat. "I've been fixing it up a little more each time I go. Last fall, I put in a new kitchen."

"What about neighbors?"

"A few, but it's on the remote side."

"Sounds peaceful." She moved to the starboard side of the skiff to dump what was left of her coffee, then settled on the hull's edge. "At least for the first few days. Then the lack of company must get lonely. Unless…I guess I assumed you went alone, but—"

"You're now wondering about my sex life."

"Not quite, Cavanaugh. I was just wondering if you're still the loner you seemed to be back in Jersey."

"It comes with the territory."

"Maybe. Or maybe you're a loner because it's easier that way. Less work. Less of yourself on the line."

"If you're looking to psychoanalyze anyone, it seems you might want to start with yourself."

"Why? I'm an open book to myself. I know what makes me tick."

"Mind sharing a run down with me?"

"I would, but I have this little problem."

"What's that?"

"I'm a loner, too. I have a hard time opening up to people, and a harder time trusting those around me. Especially if history says they can't be trusted."

"Don't kid yourself. Even if New Jersey hadn't taken place, you still wouldn't be talking to me."

"You're probably right. You government guys aren't very good at listening. Seems to me you draw a conclusion, then work backward to find the substantiating evidence."

"Sometimes it's the only way."

"Have you ever noticed, though, depending on the way you shuffle facts, the different result you can get?"

He stopped what he was doing. "So you're saying a line of evidence might be misread?"

"Not just misread, but selectively gathered to support a set of conclusions." She uncrossed her legs, ran the heel of one up the length of the other until it rested across her knee. "It explains innocent men behind bars."

"You're right. The system is imperfect."

Perhaps the conversation wasn't going anywhere, but at least it was a diversion from his own thoughts.

"Mind telling me something, Nick?"

"Depends."

"Was any part of what you told Dad and me the truth?"

"Most of it." He usually stuck to the truth as much as possible when he was undercover. The closer he kept to the facts, the less likely he was to slip up.

As he gave the wrench a final tug, the only sound in the clearing was that of the water slapping against the fiberglass. Having nearly convinced himself he was alone again, he turned to look for Kelly. She sat in the same spot, but not the same position. Eyes closed, she had leaned way back, out over the water and into the sunlight which broke through the branches, only her grip on the Bimini top keeping her from taking a swim.

His reaction to the sight of her was both instantaneous and primal.

As he watched, she opened her eyes and looked directly at him, as if she'd known she was being stared at. But then, she was the type of woman who drew male attention yet never seemed to notice it. Never seemed to realize just what she did to a man.

Kelly pulled herself back into the shade of the top. "When do you think we'll need the boat?"

"Tomorrow. I know you're worried about your aunt and would like it to be sooner, but we have to be careful." He waited several beats before adding the question, "Any idea what Rod's plans might have been after he put Sarah on the plane?"

"He wouldn't let her travel alone. So he probably went with her. From there maybe on to the Caymans."

"Why the Caymans?"

"He's got a friend he goes diving with. He said something about making a trip soon, anyway, so I wouldn't be surprised if he decided to head on down."

"Do you ever go with him?"

"Once or twice."

"Did you meet this friend?"

Kelly's eyes narrowed. "Why, Nick? Why would you be interested in who Rod visits?"

"No reason."

She stood. "Then why do I get the feeling that I've been manipulated one more time?" She stood. "I think I'll head back up to the house."

Nick watched her go. Something made him glance down at the toolbox where he'd left his weapon and the two handsets.

All present and accounted for. Which meant she couldn't get into too much trouble.

KELLY TWISTED the shortwave's channel dial slowly, the disjointed garble of other radio users sounding almost like an orchestra during warm-up. She stopped on one of the frequencies Calvin Kicklighter or Rod might be tempted to monitor.

She'd been lucky enough to find a third handset when she'd been checking for the spare propeller.

"This is Blind Faith looking for Kicklighter. Come in." She released her finger and listened intently to nothing but open-air static.

Rod had to know just how anxious she'd be for news. So why wasn't he listening in? She used the back of her hand to rub her forehead. Unless he wasn't able to. Unless he and her aunt hadn't escaped.

"Blind Faith looking for Kicklighter. Need to firm up those fishing plans."

Twenty-five minutes later, she was still at it, but now worked to keep the desperation out of her voice. Nick might finish up with the boat at any minute.

"Blind Faith to Kicklighter. Over."

Open-air static. "Kicklighter, please come in. Blind Faith looking for an update on plans."

Slumping, the radio handset still clasped in her fingers, Kelly switched to the frequency Rod monitored at the dive shop, a frequency that wouldn't be nearly as safe as the others.

For several minutes she just listened to other radio users. What Nick said about Binelli monitoring the different channels made sense, as did his argument that, if Binelli thought she was no longer in the islands, it would be easier to slip by him.

Kelly glanced toward the stairs. But this also might be her last opportunity to use the radio, to get news of her aunt, to give hope to the Kicklighters.

She clicked the button in.

NICK ENTERED the cottage. He'd replaced the prop and finished checking over the motor. There were no guarantees the engine would hold under stress, but he'd done everything he could. Tomorrow they'd find a phone. With any luck, within hours of making a call, they'd be back in the States and Kelly would be stashed somewhere safe.

He wondered what Douglas had turned up on Ben and Rod. The way Kelly had walked away earlier suggested Nick might be on the right track where the dive shop owner was concerned.

As Nick turned toward the bedrooms, he heard the staccato scratch of the shortwave come to life in the dining room upstairs. He suspected Kelly had turned it on hoping Rod might try to get some kind of message to her about her aunt.

Shortwave radios were the main communication device in the Abacos, which meant most conversations involved either the locals ordering bread from a woman who ran a bakery out of her kitchen or the latest bootleg video.

The floor plan was open enough so that he could now hear one local resident instructing another to change channels for a private conversation. As he listened, the volume was eased down. It took him a moment to realize it was Kelly's voice.

When she spoke again, her voice was stronger, her words distinct.

"This is Blind Faith looking for Kicklighter. Go to sic, eight." Open-air static. "Kicklighter—" Nick could hear the hard edge of desperation in her voice. "Go to three, four for an update on delivery."

He took the stairs three at a time. Kelly looked up startled as he ripped the handset out of her palm.

"Where in the hell did you get this?"

"In the storage room downstairs."

"I told you last night using the radio could—"

She jerked away when he tried to capture her wrist. "Give me a little credit. I was careful." She stalked into the kitchen.

He followed.

"Careful doesn't cut it. These are trained people hunting us. You can bet they're listening in. They're out there beating the bushes right now, talking to everyone you know, every pilot, every water taxi. It only takes one person opening their mouth to blow us out of the water."

Possibly only because further retreat had been cut off, she turned to face him when she reached the counter. Nick crowded her against the cabinets, his arms blocking any escape and his body only inches from hers. It was a blatantly male stance meant to intimidate. But it didn't.

"So is this what you were doing up last night? Trying to get to the radio?"

"Yes. I was trying to reach Rod."

"So if you're trying to raise surfer boy, who the hell is Kicklighter?"

"It's a code name. A handle," she lied. She attempted to look away, but he pulled her chin around, forcing her gaze to meet his. She'd tied her hair back with a yellow scarf, leaving her long neck exposed. Her pulse beat rapidly in the hollow of her throat.

"Code name, huh?"

Her scent filled his nostrils, blending with the shared heat of their bodies. She moistened her lips with the tip of her tongue. His body tightened as it had earlier.

His gaze dropped to her lips. He remembered how they'd felt beneath his two nights ago, how even now he could taste her in his mouth.

Cursing himself, he lowered his mouth, settling his lips against hers. She stiffened at the contact, but made no move to escape him. Nor did she join in the kiss. Her very detachment fueled his own need to push her beyond it, to make her feel some of what he was feeling.

His fingers found the scarf holding back her hair. He tugged, his gaze now level with hers, his mouth hovering over hers, their breaths mingling. He watched her pupils darken as the scarf dropped from his fingers to skim her neck before falling to the floor. Nick twisted his hands into the cool, rich texture, lifting it away from her face. The finest silk. Soft, yet deceptively strong. Like the woman. Tough on the inside. Resilient. And, on the outside…

He kissed her temple, inhaling her scent, reimprinting the memory in his brain. He was tempted to linger, but instead worked his way downward to her jaw. A shallow moan slipped past her parted lips.

He sensed the moment she caught fire. Her chin edged up, giving him the access he craved.

He recalled how it had been with her before…the heat, the need…and realized time had only intensified both. He forced her mouth up to his.

This time, though her hands lay in loose fists against his shoulders, she opened for him. As his tongue slipped across hers, her fingers curled into the material of his shirt. His own hands held her steady as he took what he wanted from her.

Then she moved against his erection suggestively, and he felt his limited control escaping more rapidly. God, he wanted her. Here. On the kitchen floor. Anywhere, he realized as he pushed up her T-shirt.

She was naked beneath.

By the time he broke it off, he was short of breath and even shorter on reason.

Instead of letting her go, which, given the thoughts going through his mind at that moment, would have been the wisest thing to do, he rested his forehead against hers.

"You're going to have to trust someone, Kelly. Eventually. So why don't you tell me what it is that you are delivering to Kicklighter? Save us both some trouble." He pulled back to study her face. Her breath was as unsteady his own. His unshaven chin had chafed the side of her neck.

Her lips trembled as he traced a finger across where her pulse leapt. She was so damned beautiful. He could almost have drowned in the green of her eyes. So deep, so murky with unspoken intent and emotion.

"Kelly?"

She swallowed, looked away, evidently as shaken as he was by what had just happened. "It was just a code name I hoped Rod would recognize."

"People who are lousy liars should keep to the truth. Why would you be trying to raise Rod if he was on his way to the Caymans?"

She suddenly wedged her arms up between their bodies, her elbows and forearms digging into his chest. "Let go of me."

When he again refused to back away, she met his gaze. "I'm tired of this. Tired of being pushed around. Tired of fighting you and the whole damned world. You're right. I will have to trust someone…but it won't be you. Never you. Never again."

When she pushed this time, he stepped away. At the door, she turned back. She raked her hair from around her face, but the weight forced it to flow forward again onto her cheeks.

"I'm not sure Rod is on his way to the Caymans. He said he might head down there, but…I was hoping if he hadn't gone, he might be listening in, waiting to hear from me. I wanted to at least assure myself Sarah made it safely to Florida.

"You can hardly blame me, Nick. She's *all* the family I have, all the family you left me."

Sunset was still an hour away.

Nick sat on the railing with his back braced against the side of the house, the binoculars he'd been using momentarily forgotten where they rested on his thigh. A stiff breeze blew in off the water, making it hard to imagine in a few hours the night would turn still and hot and muggy.

Lifting the binoculars, he had no problem finding the lone snorkeler at the outside edge of the reef. She wore a purple one-piece swimsuit she'd pulled out of her travel bag.

He'd started to wonder, after Kelly's attempt to raise someone on the radio this afternoon, what he might have missed in his hurried search of the satchel two nights ago and his hasty retrieval of clothes from it the previous afternoon.

Assuming Kelly would have ditched anything too incriminating, Nick hadn't been particularly surprised or disappointed when all he'd initially found was another swimsuit, a pair of shorts and a sweatshirt, a prescription bottle for some medication he'd never heard of but which seemed legitimate. Then there had been the usual makeup and tampons, flight maps.

Only one item in a side pocket of the satchel had given him pause, and it had nothing to do with Binelli or the case.

Two strips of a dozen silver packets with a familiar logo. Condoms.

He didn't question why the last item bothered him. No matter how much he tried to tell himself he didn't give a damn whom she slept with, the truth was he did. And considering the number of packets she seemed to carry on a regular basis, she might have a number of bed partners. A hangar for the night at every destination.

Nick reached for the wine bottle he'd left on the rail and poured more into the tumbler. Like it or not, Kelly was trouble for him. Real trouble. He had definitely lost control earlier. And now he was using a bad bottle of wine to ease his sexual frustration.

Nick watched her fan her legs apart, the black flippers she wore moving gracefully at the end of her long legs. She jackknifed beneath the water. Moments stretched as he waited for her to resurface. When his own lungs ached, he realized he'd been holding his breath and he exhaled.

Seconds later, she broke the surface and shoved a lobster into the catch bag. That made four. Instead of swimming back in as he had hoped, she headed to the right.

He was getting tired of waiting for her to come in.

Which made it time for him to rein in his prisoner and set some new ground rules. For both of them.

Nick dumped the contents of the glass over the rail.

KELLY'S ARMS AND LEGS burned from the hour and a half she'd spent fighting the tidal currents.

With dusk, the reef had turned more somber, more sinister. She still found comfort in its primitive rhythm. The strong and quick survived; the weak perished to further sustain them. It was the same with life, with men. To survive what lay ahead, she needed to stay emotionally strong and mentally quick. She needed to keep fighting. Not just for her own sake, but for Amanda Kicklighter's and Sarah's, as well.

She glanced up at the cottage and was surprised that Nick no longer sat on the balcony. After what had happened in the kitchen, there was no way she could continue to lie to herself. For the first time in seven years, she had started to see things from both sides. Nick may have lied to her and to her father, but he hadn't put the rope around her father's neck. He wasn't the one who had stepped off the crate. Her father had done that. She couldn't go on blaming Nick for her father's actions, but, at the same time, she couldn't forgive Nick for not believing her. For not believing in her. For walking away when she had needed him most.

And yet, she couldn't seem to quite get beyond what she'd felt for him at one time. She hadn't been a nun since the night in Key West.

Ten months, three days and two hours after Nick walked out of that hotel room, she'd dispensed with the inconvenience of her virginity. It depressed her even now to remember how it had happened in the cockpit of a small Cessna. All hands and body parts. Steamed windows. A physical release, but nothing more. As she'd crawled alone into her bed later that night, sore and depressed, she realized she'd been trying to convince herself Nick hadn't been any big deal, that he was like all other men. That the only thing she felt for him was hatred.

But even then she'd known she was wrong on all accounts. Collecting lobster wasn't the only reason she'd gone snorkeling. She had to make some tough decisions. Nick was right. She was going to have to trust someone. And that someone was him.

The prospect unnerved her.

Trust the one man she had no reason to trust, who had proven himself untrustworthy in the past.

Worried, she settled into a smooth kicking rhythm, the catch bag held in one hand, the lobster snare in the other. After dinner, she'd find some way to tell him about Amanda's drug. And she'd try one more time to convince him she knew nothing about a man named Binelli. That Ben had been working alone when he'd involved the airline in smuggling.

And then she'd see if he had it in him to trust her.

Below her, her dim shadow skimmed the sandy bottom, then grazed a six-foot nurse shark briefly at rest. In the murkiness twenty feet to her left, the sinister silhouette of a five-foot barracuda moved. She shifted course to avoid the unpredictable predator.

She could feel the tightness in her lungs, the burning in her leg muscles as she swam over the leeward edge of the reef. Once clear of the coral, there was only sandy bottom.

Settling into a lazy kick, she allowed the incoming tide to do most of the work.

A jarring bump caught her by surprise. The barracuda.

Her hands tightening around the lobster snare, she came around to ward off the attack by becoming the aggressor.

Chapter Ten

In spite of Kelly's swift movements, the lobster snare caught only water as Nick kicked backward out of its path.

Coming up next to her, he blinked away the slight sting. The water they both tread was clear, the sixteen feet to the sand below appearing to be more like three or four.

"I didn't mean to frighten you."

She slipped her mask off and tipped her head back, letting the water smooth the hair away from her face, then looked directly at him. "Well, I guess we're even then. Because I didn't mean to miss."

"I'm sure you didn't." He took the catch bag from her. "Is it lobster season?"

"Depends."

"On what?"

"I prefer lobster to bait, so according to my calendar, it's lobster season. If you have a problem with that, you can always eat more bait."

"I think I'll risk it." Nick adjusted his hold on the nylon bag and nodded toward the beach. "We should head in. The sun will be down before too long. You must be chilled. Not to mention tired."

"I'm used to it," she said. "I saw you watching. Earlier. Up there."

"I was keeping an eye on you. I would have joined you, but you needed time to cool down. Apparently, I didn't wait long enough."

"Time isn't always a cure," she offered.

All remnants of her carefully applied makeup had long ago been erased by salt water, revealing the faint grouping of freckles at the tip of her nose, the small cut at the corner of her mouth, the fading bruise at her left temple, and even a deepening of color along her jawline.

Something made him reach out to touch her. An action that surprised him and, he suspected, Kelly, as well. She didn't jerk away, as he would have expected. Water dribbled from the ends of his fingers as he ran his index finger down one cheek, hesitating at the still slightly swollen corner of her mouth. "I want to apologize. I'm sorry about the way I handled everything earlier."

"Which? The radio? Or what came after?"

"Both."

The next wave carried her closer, her legs brushing his inner thigh as she pedaled backward.

He took the lobster snare from her and released it to be carried in by the tide. Her eyes narrowed as she watched it drift beyond her reach. "Why did you do that?"

"Safety," he answered.

Her breath came out a little unsteady, as if she were winded.

When Nick tried to close the distance, she retreated. "How do you like your lobster?" she asked.

"Cooked."

"We don't have any butter."

"Not a problem for me."

Kelly wet her lips nervously with the tip of her tongue and considered her limited options. If she had any sense left at all, she should give up the slow retreat and swim like hell. With the flippers, she'd have the advantage.

But Nick would view the action as running, and she didn't much like that idea. Then, when she had all but decided self-preservation was more important than pride, she realized she'd waited too long. The water had become shallow enough to stand in. Kelly put her feet down, the flippers suddenly more of an encumbrance than an advantage.

Water sluiced from Nick's shoulders as he did the same, closing distance faster now. His hair was slicked back from his face, accentuating the lean hardness of his features. He hadn't shaven in two days, but instead of unkempt and disheveled, he only looked more dangerous. More intensely male.

As another wave rolled against his body, the bruises on his upper chest and shoulder were briefly covered, then revealed once more.

"Running, Kelly?"

"No."

The undertow tugged at her. To keep from wobbling against him, she steadied herself by holding on to his shoulder. This time, it was his muscles that tensed beneath her brief touch.

His heavy-lidded eyes darkened as the smile faded from the corner of his mouth.

"You always were good at taking stands, weren't you? No matter the risks or odds, no matter what anyone else said. Even at nineteen, you seemed so inflexible and sure. But you weren't, were you? And now, you're playing at being tough, but you aren't. At least, not as much as you want to be."

"Given the past two days, anyone with any sense would be scared." She tugged off her flippers and released them to the tide's care.

He wrapped his fingers loosely around her wrist to keep her from turning away from him. "Trust me."

"I want to, but—"

"Trust me," he repeated, his fingers briefly tightening. "Give me the truth before it's too late."

She'd been ready with a confession only minutes earlier, but now felt uncertain about her decision. "Whose truth, Nick? Yours or mine or Binelli's?"

"There is only *one* truth."

She gave a dry chuckle, her uncertainty about her decision to tell Nick everything, to trust him, escalating.

"Still so pragmatic. So sure the world is made up of black and white. I would have thought by now even you would have stumbled into a gray area or two. That you would have discovered at least one thing you were willing to set aside your damned principles for."

Instead of answering, Nick caught a strand of her hair and twirled it around his index finger. He tugged gently.

"What do you think you're doing?" she asked, refusing to give in to the pressure. Her abdominal muscles flexed as if they could somehow keep the sensation, the knot of fear— of excitement—from settling inside her.

"Testing the water."

Kelly sucked in a slow breath. "You needn't bother." In a last-ditch effort to maintain her balance in the surf, she widened her stance. "I can tell you it's damned dangerous."

"Really? Well, there are some things a man has to find out for himself." He watched her intently, his eyes never leaving her face. "Some things are worth the risk."

Kelly felt a slow burn deep inside her as his fingers threaded through her damp hair to lock behind her head. With steady and even pressure, he drew her forward until her body was trapped against his. She lost her breath when the current rocked them together intimately, thigh to thigh, her breasts briefly pressed to his muscled chest, the salt water between them instantly heating.

She struggled to move backward again, but neither the current nor Nick cooperated. "Let me go."

"No."

"This….this won't change anything."

Nick lowered his lips to hers. "Only a fool would want to change this," he murmured just before his lips brushed hers softly, inviting. Unlike the rough kiss earlier in the kitchen and the one two nights ago at her aunt's, this one coaxed, much as his kisses had seven years ago, and because it did, she didn't resist.

They took their time, reacquainting themselves with forgotten tastes and textures. It amazed her they could come together so easily, as if they had kissed often and regularly. And yet there were differences, too. Very appealing ones. Perhaps because she was older and more experienced, she could focus on the physical pleasure of being expertly kissed without expecting more—from the man or from herself.

After long minutes, Nick pulled back just enough to meet her gaze. "Tell me you would change that," he murmured as he parted her lips again, his tongue delving deeper this time, bringing with it the overpowering flavor of salt and male need. The coercion of seconds earlier gave way to something less controlled. Nick lifted her chin. "We left a few things unfinished between us back in Jersey. The timing wasn't right."

"There was more to it than just the timing. If there hadn't been, you wouldn't have just walked away two days later. You would have stayed. For better or for worse. But whatever it was between us, it didn't include trust. It still doesn't." She lifted sad eyes to him. "Even so, I don't think it was easy on you. I think you cared. About my father. About me. I couldn't let myself believe that until now."

Nick's mouth tightened as he listened.

"I think you still care," she added, as she tried to pull away some. "Maybe not like you did back then, but some."

She curled her fists against his chest. "Maybe that was why when everything was over, when the inquest and the funeral were behind me, I stayed awake nights thinking about all the *what-ifs*. I tried to make some sense out of them until I realized there are certain things in life that are strictly without reason. I think, as much as we both might wish it weren't so, *we* are one of those things."

"Question is," he asked, "what are we going to do about it?"

When she thought she was ready to, she met his gaze. No good would come of giving in to him. Perhaps, come morning, she would regret her decision, but she didn't think so. There were some things that just had to be done even if they weren't wise.

She reached up and touched his cheek, liked the rough feel of it beneath her fingers. "We could finish what we started. We could pretend we're back in Key West. We could make believe tomorrow never comes for us."

Nick's lips came down hard on hers. There was nothing soft about him. Not his mouth and not his fingers as he twisted them into her hair, roughly dragging her head back so he could take more from her.

She could feel and taste him everywhere, not just in her mouth, but in her fingers and even in her head. It was as if he'd been there all along, somewhere in her subconscious, in her memory, just waiting for her to find him, to remember.

LIGHT FROM an early rising moon angled through the open sliding glass door as Nick laid her on the unmade sheets of his bed. He followed her down, his hard body briefly covering hers, damp, chilled flesh meeting the same.

Rising to his knees, he peeled away her suit. When he had tugged it to her waist, he stopped, his hands briefly spanning its narrowness. "Most women destroy the mystery with bikinis and thongs. If they only knew just how sexy pale, cool flesh is to a man."

His callused palms skimmed upward over her breasts, stopped to close over them briefly, to knead them gently until she arched beneath the caress, her nipples suddenly hard and aching.

The sound that came from her throat was halfway between a groan and a chuckle. "I think…if my memory… I think we were beyond this point that night. I think…"

"Maybe you should stop thinking so much," he pointed out, his mouth following the path of his hands.

"Good…idea," she said, her voice ragged as his tongue found her nipple.

When his lips reached the barrier of her suit, he peeled it farther, exposing more of her. He stopped to kick off the pair of borrowed shorts, left them on top of her wet suit as he turned to fumble in the dark for something on the dresser.

Then, he was there, stretched out beside her, braced on one elbow, his hand skimming from waist to hip to thigh, and then higher again to settle warmly over her breast.

But as he lowered his mouth to hers, he must have seen the hesitation, the withdrawal in her eyes, or felt it in the tensing of her body, because he pulled back.

"Second thoughts?" he asked, his voice roughened with something that sounded almost like tenderness.

"Maybe some," she admitted.

His fingers played in the soft hair above her left temple. "I want you, Kelly."

"And I want you." She caressed the line of one brow. "Let's keep it simple and uncluttered. Don't make promises that will only be broken."

She pulled Nick's mouth down to hers and felt the restrained tension in his body as he covered hers with his. Then his hard erection against her thigh as he pulled back enough so that his mouth could reach the sensitive skin just beneath her jawline. She pushed her hand between their bodies, finding him already encased in latex. Nick gave a soft groan accompanied by a ragged chuckle as her hand closed around him.

"You're direct—I'll give you that."

"I've always believed a woman should go after what she wants."

"I agree." Nick pulled her hand away, then pushed slowly into her. She watched his face, his eyes briefly narrowed as he filled her. And then, with his first full thrust, all thoughts save one emptied from her mind. Raising her hips, she pulled him in deeper, craving the feel of him inside her. Over and over and over. Hard and deep.

She climaxed first, almost immediately, but Nick followed closely, his deep-chested groan drowning out her softer one. In those final moments, Nick's gaze met hers and they seemed to connect on more than a physical level.

Then the moment was gone.

He rolled onto his back, taking her with him until she sprawled on top. Her skin was as slick as his. When she shivered, he pulled the sheet over them, left an arm draped around her.

"I hope I wasn't too rough," he murmured as he pushed damp hair away from her cheeks. He kissed her gently.

If Kelly had expected anything from Nick, it wasn't tenderness. Not even after what they'd just shared.

Her heartbeat and breathing gradually returned to normal, but in some ways she felt as if nothing would ever be the same again. That she had come home, briefly, but with the rising sun, she would once more be banished. Would once more be on her own.

The thought of being alone had never been quite so lonely as it was now in Nick's embrace.

"You're awfully quiet." His arm tightened across her shoulder, snuggling her to his chest as his fingers idly traveled her back.

"Just thinking." She realized she'd allowed some of her misgivings to filter into her tone. What was wrong with her? Wasn't she the one who'd wanted *simple and uncluttered?*

Nick tipped her chin until she was forced to meet his gaze. "I thought we agreed to avoid using any higher thought processes."

She let her hand glide down his torso until she found him. He was already half-hard when her fingers closed around him, but hardened further almost instantly. "Higher than this?"

"No," he said, the single word accompanied by a low groan of approval. "I'd say that was just about the right level."

"Really?"

Just when she would have pushed her advantage, Kelly suddenly found herself on the bottom again. Nick's knee pressed upward against where she was still damp. His free hand found her breast even as his mouth took hers again. It was as if he stormed her body from all directions. Thinking was impossible. And overrated.

She climaxed against his knee, her sharp groan muffled by Nick's mouth. Instead of pulling back, he pushed her more, his hands and mouth making love to her body over and over again.

Nick's breath was roughened with his own need now. "We need protection."

Her eyes remained unfocused. "Don't you...?"

"No. Just the one. I thought maybe you might..."

Kelly shook her head weakly.

"Are you sure you don't have anything? Not even one tucked away in that bag of yours? Maybe in a side pocket?"

Kelly groaned. "No. Maybe the nightstand or the medicine cabinet. There's bound to be one around here somewhere. Four men, most of them single. They must have brought a girlfriend down here at least once."

She saw his irritation. Which she didn't understand. "Give me a break. I wasn't exactly expecting the best sex of my life."

"The best?"

"Yeah, but whatever you do, don't get a big head."

"I think you're a few minutes too late for that." Nick rolled on his side and flicked on the lamp, but didn't immediately make a move to check the bedside table.

"Besides," she said coming up behind him, resting her chin on his right shoulder, her breasts pressed to his back, "women who carry condoms look easy."

He glanced at her, one brow raised. "Don't worry. No one will ever accuse you of that one." He grinned as he said it and Kelly wondered if she had imagined his hesitation.

"Damn straight."

Nick opened the drawer and sifted roughly through the usual contents of a bedside table.

With a whoop, she scooped up a square cellophane packet that had fallen out from between two pads of paper.

She ripped it open. Elation fell flat as the antacid dropped into Nick's lap.

He picked up the tablet from where it had landed. "I don't think that's going to work very well. Though I have heard if the woman holds an aspirin between her knees, it's generally thought to work as birth control."

Undaunted, Kelly slipped off the end of the bed to check the top drawer of the Formica dresser.

Frowning, Nick leaned back against the headboard as she

continued to root through a third drawer. Half a second later, she gave another whoop and fell onto the bed beside him.

"Saved." She reached across Nick and turned off the lamp. "Let's get you suited up."

WHEN SHE WOKE in the darkness, it took her several moments to realize she was still in Nick's bed, but she was now alone. The room had turned stifling hot in spite of the ceiling fan rotating overhead. The surf was a distant throb that broke the intense stillness of the night and seemed to mimic her own weighted pulse.

"Nick," she called and rolled up onto an elbow to study the room, expecting to see him standing in the opening to the bathroom or silhouetted at the sliding glass door.

She grabbed a clean T-shirt from the top dresser drawer and pulled it over her head. Legs suddenly shaky, she sank onto the end of the bed, recalling just how ridiculous and desperate she must have appeared as she dug through those same drawers. She scraped the hair away from her forehead with both hands. What now? Had she really said those stupid words? Uncluttered and simple? No promises that would only be broken?

But what about hearts?

Sitting alone in the dark, she finally found the courage to admit to herself something she would never be able to admit to Nick. That she loved him. Still. In spite of everything. And there wasn't a chance in hell he would ever believe her.

It would take more than sex to do that. He'd assume she was trying to manipulate him.

She glanced in the mirror as she stood and wished she hadn't. Even without lighting, she looked a mess. Hair matted and sticky with salt water. The dark shadows around her eyes making her look almost as worried as she felt inside.

She should have told Nick about Amanda's drug before

any of this happened. It would have been one less secret between them.

The confession wasn't going to be quite as easy now. Before, she'd only wanted Nick to believe her. She now wanted him to understand, as well.

She found him upstairs, balanced on the balcony rail as he had been earlier when he'd watched her snorkel. His back braced against the side of the house, he stared out into the night, his jean-clad legs stretched out before him as if oblivious to the dangerous drop to the coral rock below.

There was a harshness to his expression that hadn't been there hours earlier when, with their bodies still joined, he'd looked down at her. There had been a question in his eyes even then, she realized. But it wasn't until that moment that she realized just what the *question* had been.

He'd found the Ocularcet.

"Come out and join me, Kelly."

There was nothing inviting about the sound of his voice.

She tried, but failed to take a steadying breath as she crossed the metal door track. "Can't sleep?"

"No."

"Want to talk about it?"

"Why the hell not?" He avoided looking at her.

Arms tightened in front of her, she waited, the ball of fear in her gut expanding into her chest.

"You must take me for a real fool," he said between clenched teeth and held up the fistful of foil packages, then let the strip unfurl square by damning square, until they hung there between them.

"I can explain."

"I just bet you can."

Chapter Eleven

Kelly had wanted Nick to learn the truth from her almost as much as she'd wanted those few hours until dawn to be free from the ugliness of the real world.

The ache in her expanded as his fingers tightened into a fist around the strips. In a brooding silence, he continued to stare at what he held, his brows drawn down.

He wore the same jeans he'd shown up in two nights ago, the material over the left thigh marred by a bullet hole, a bullet he had collected while saving their lives. His chest remained bare, moonlight bisecting the hard-ridged line of his abdomen, the bruising there almost appearing to be shadow.

"You know, when I found these I assumed they were just what they appeared to be." His lips formed a wry twist. "Imagine that."

"When…" Kelly swallowed and tried again, her voice stronger this time. "When did you find them?"

"This afternoon. After the business with the radio." He studied the packets. "It seems I should have taken time to examine them a bit more closely."

He looked at her then, his expression harsh. "Intriguing, isn't it? What appear to be condoms are in fact packages filled with a cheap, new high. I bet Binelli thought he had a real winner here, didn't he? He must have been damned mad when you didn't deliver."

"Whatever Binelli's after, I can guarantee you it's not that."

"Stop lying!" His facial muscles flattened. "I guess I don't need to ask how far you were willing to go to convince me of your innocence."

Kelly took a sharp, uneven breath. "You can't think—"

He dropped his head back against the rough-sawn cedar siding. His eyes narrowed to dark, thoughtful slits as he let the packets flow from one hand to the other, like a card shark shuffling a deck. "Why wouldn't I?"

She watched his hands, the fluid motion of the packets as they piled again in his palm, his fingers closing over them as if in preparation to deal. He gave a little twist of the wrist. See. *Nothing up the sleeve.*

And yet, at the moment, she felt as if he held all the aces and the hand he'd dealt her was a sure loser.

"I suppose you're right. As far as you're concerned, the only reason I'd let you touch me was if I wanted something from you." She straightened. "Well, you're right. I wanted something from you. But not what you think."

"Yeah. I'm always wrong about you." Nick stacked the packets in his palm again. "After I found these, I spent hours watching you, telling myself who you slept with was none of my business. That I had no intention of getting too close. That no matter what had happened back in Jersey, there was nothing between us." He looked up at her. "You'd think I'd have learned after the last time. But you come around and bam. I can't seem to think straight." He looked at her again. "I even bought that crap about a girl who carried condoms looking too easy."

His words hurt more than she'd expected. "You're a real gentleman, Nick."

He dropped down to the deck and, shoving the packets into a pocket, closed the distance between them in measured, easy strides.

The rough wood snagged her T-shirt as she started to shift away.

She didn't get far before he crowded her to the rail, his arms braced on either side of her, keeping her trapped there.

The heat from his body seeped through her T-shirt, reminding her of how naked she was beneath, reminding her of what they'd been doing only hours ago. The way his hands had moved over her, the way his mouth had taken her lips and her body with such heat and need, the way he'd held her afterward.

Nick's gaze dropped from her face to her breasts and she knew his thoughts kept pace with her own.

"I never claimed to be a gentleman, Kelly. As far as I'm concerned the word's old-fashioned and overused. My father claimed to be a gentleman. Even on the night he walked out on his family after learning his wife of twenty-three years had breast cancer."

Kelly tightened her arms across her middle and raised her chin to meet his condemning stare. "You never told me that."

"Why would I? You don't know me," he taunted. "We don't know each other. Isn't that what you keep claiming?"

"Yes. But we both know you haven't listened to me, that you aren't even remotely interested in the truth."

"What truth? That you lied to me? That you used me?"

"Used *you*?" She nearly spit the words at him as she tried to shove him away. "You used me, too. Seven years ago to get near my father, and again now because you think I can get you close to Binelli. And don't tell yourself you did it for any other reason. You want Binelli for what he did to your friend, and you don't give a damn who gets hurt in the process."

"Oh, I tried to use you. But you have me beat there, sweet-heart. I was going to take you to bed for one night. No prom-ises. No expectations. Simple, straightforward sex. As much as I hate to admit it, that's not what happened tonight."

He looked at her, his gaze lingering on her face. "What scares the living hell out of me is that I don't care any more what you've done. That, when it was put to a real test, every-thing I believed to be true about myself was simply fiction. I'm no better than my father."

Nick turned away, but she remained where he'd left her. The anger inside her having drained with his words, with the admission that whatever had happened tonight, it hadn't been casual sex. For either of them.

"You're right about it being a drug. It's not a narcotic, though." She took an uneven breath before continuing. "If you have it tested, you'll find it's Ocularcet." She faced him, wanting Nick to see the truth in her eyes. "Physicians in Eu-rope have been using it for several years to treat a rare type of blindness."

"Let me guess," he said with cynicism, "you know some-one with the disease?"

"My five-year-old goddaughter." She pushed the hair away from her face where the breeze kept tossing it. "It's medicine, Nick. For a child."

He just stared at her for the longest time. "You don't know how much I want to believe that. But even if that's true," he said, "it doesn't make what you're doing right."

Kelly momentarily closed her eyes, willing away her irri-tation. Blood pounded at her temples as she tried to control the anger and frustration.

"Since you seem to have all the answers, Nick, why don't you tell me what's right. Is it right that a child goes blind be-fore she has to because the FDA refuses to approve a drug? If there's anything right about that, I want to know what it is. Better still, try explaining it to that scared little girl and her parents. You look them in the eye and then try to sleep nights."

She paused, took a deep breath. "The Kicklighters are good, decent people with three children and one income. They don't have the kind of money it takes to fight bureaucrats."

Nick grabbed hold of her arm and pulled her in close. "Kicklighter? So that business with the radio was a lie, too. There was no code. You weren't expecting Rod to be listening in, were you? He's well beyond anyone's reach by now, isn't he?"

"What is it you think you know, Nick? Do you think Rod is somehow part of what is going on? Do you think he's messed up with Binelli? You're wrong."

His fingers tightened, and he pulled her in closer, until their gazes were level with one another, until she could see the anger in his steel eyes.

"How many lies, Kelly? Let's get them all out in the open. No more holding back."

"How many?" she repeated the question. "Just the ones you wanted to hear, Nick. Wanted to believe."

"What in the hell is that supposed to mean?"

"It means I don't know anything about a man named Binelli. It means I can't help bring to justice the killer of your friend. It means you've been wasting your damn time keeping me alive. Or keeping my aunt safe."

He stared at her for several long seconds, stunned. Then his hands loosened and he released her. "You really don't know anything about Binelli, do you? Or the smuggling?"

Her voice dropped to nearly a whisper. "That's what I'm telling you. And it's exactly what I've been telling you from the beginning. Just as seven years ago I told you I didn't know about a shipment of guns. Or about my father's involvement with a terrorist organization. An organization he didn't believe in. I had nothing to hide then. And the only thing I had to hide this time was medicine for a child."

Nick rubbed his face, then scrubbed it again, using the heels of his hands to massage his closed eyes before roughly combing his fingers through his hair.

He shook his head slowly, almost as if he couldn't get his mind around all of it, or even part of it. "But the evidence was all there," he said and paced away. "Your bank account. The surveillance tapes of Binelli's attorney boarding your planes. And then there's the fact Binelli is after you."

"For something he thinks Ben gave me." She turned away. "Why now, Nick? Why are you so willing to believe me now? Just like that."

"What's important is that I do. I'm sorry I didn't before."

There was a time only hours ago when she wouldn't have been able to accept his apology. A time when she would have thrown it back in his face. That time was past. They'd both made mistakes, she perhaps more than Nick.

"So where do we go from here?" she asked.

"I get you someplace safe. Then I sort out this mess." Nick shoved his hands into his pockets. "In the morning, we'll go back to square one, go over the details, decide how to proceed."

It wasn't the best time to ask more of Nick, but she couldn't afford to wait, either. "What do you intend to do with the Ocularcet?"

"I can't let you take it into the country."

And she couldn't let it go that easy.

Kelly walked back into the living room to where Nick had dumped her satchel on the sofa. It didn't take long to find Amanda's photo. The then four-year-old sat astride the secondhand tricycle her father had found in a trash pile and had spent several days carefully sanding and painting.

Amanda loved two things. Her daddy and the color pink, so the bike had been painted flamingo sunrise. Streamers in a paler shade fluttered from the end of the shiny handlebars. And from its seat, Amanda grinned proudly. She wasn't a beautiful little girl. She had short red curls, dusty, bare feet and skinned knees.

Over the past six weeks, the edges of the photo had become ragged from repeated handling.

Nick was waiting when she returned. Wordlessly, she pressed the picture into his hand, then walked away.

Instead of Nick's bed, Kelly returned to the cramped, hot room where she'd spent the first night. She had wanted him to come after her, to hold her in his arms, but he didn't.

Maybe it was just as well, she decided.

Resting her head against the headboard, she closed her gritty eyes and tried not to think. About Amanda, about Ben, about Binelli or even about her mixed-up feelings for Nick.

When she'd asked him where they went from here, she hadn't just meant the mess with Binelli.

Much later, she heard Nick come down the stairs. He hesitated outside her door for several moments. Long after she had convinced herself he had retreated, that she had missed the sounds of his leaving, the door opened quietly. He crossed to the bed to stand over her in the shadows.

Lifting a hand, she held it out to him. When he hesitated, she entwined her fingers around his, felt the heat and strength there.

They were good hands, she decided, to place a life in.

"Stay with me," she murmured and made room for him.

Nick placed his weapon on the bedside table and then stretched out facing her. "In the morning, we'll get to a phone."

"Even if you believe me, Nick, no one else will. The evidence is the same. And even if you can sell my innocence to the government, can you sell it to Binelli?"

MYRON RICHARDSON calmly stood by while the door to Nick Cavanaugh's condo was forced open. It had taken some time for the necessary paperwork to be completed, for the investigative team to be assembled and briefed.

In another few hours dawn would arrive, but for the moment, what was left of the night was humid and still. The moon floated full overhead, bright enough to cast shadows in the small, enclosed entry-patio.

Myron settled back, letting the brick wall support him as he watched what went on inside. Room by room, the lights came on, revealing the modern furnishings, the uncluttered decor of a man who was rarely home. A man whose life had always been the job.

A techie handed him a cup of coffee and he took it, sipped as he watched. He found himself wishing he were somewhere else.

He knew when they found the first cache of evidence. Like a hound alerting its human master with excited yelps, the volume and tenor changed inside the condo.

It was only a matter of time now, Myron realized, and wondered if he'd be able to live with what he'd done.

USING HIS FOREARM, Nick swiped the sweat off his forehead, then resettled his cap. He glanced down at the boat's speedometer. Twenty-one knots. Not great, but not too bad, either, given the mechanical problems.

Kelly sat nearby, a red baseball cap swiveled backward to keep it out of the wind's reach. She wore another borrowed T-shirt, this one depicting a sailfish in midleap. The wind tugged at the cotton material, pressed and molded it to her slim figure.

Last night had been a mistake. His life and the situation were already overloaded with complications. He didn't need any additional ones added to the mix, and the last thing Kelly needed was him. She'd been through enough already.

By tonight, they could be back in Florida. Unfortunately, Kelly would be in custody. It was unavoidable. And unsafe. Nick didn't doubt Binelli's ability to get to someone behind bars. Which meant Nick was just going to have to come up with some way to keep her out of jail and with him. Without breaking any laws.

Less than an hour after leaving the cottage, they rounded a point and followed the nautical markers and a large green turtle into Conch Haven. The area looked deserted, the thigh-high brown grasses growing beneath wind-formed trees appearing lifeless. In the distance, an old lighthouse, long out of service, stood against the sky.

As they idled closer, he saw several rough, low-slung buildings clustered along the beach, forming a pseudo-compound, the newest of which had been constructed of unpainted concrete block. Large, crude black letters over the door identified it as Conch Haven Foundry and Museum.

A few small cottages of weathered clapboards climbed the slope just behind, though the elevation wasn't much except when compared to the flat topography of the other islands. At one time, the settlement might have prospered. At the moment, it resembled the film set for *Gilligan's Island.*

Kelly rotated the bill of her baseball cap forward, pulled it low to shade her face as Nick maneuvered the boat to a vacant slip.

Nick cut the motor. Up close, the jumble of buildings looked like abandoned properties. "The foundry contracts with you?"

Kelly nodded.

He didn't like it. Binelli would know about the connection. Nick glanced at the boats already tied up at the dock. Only one, a thirty-eight-foot Donzi, was built for speed; the rest were geared for fishing and diving.

Pretending to check the aft line, Nick did a slow, thorough scan of the area. A family, a father and three barefoot young boys, strolled out of the foundry and toward them.

"Where's the phone?"

"Hell's Pub." Kelly motioned toward a structure some distance along the beach, a glorified, oversized thatch-roofed hut without walls. Flags, tattered and faded, hung out front. "The phone's at the back. It's usually working."

Nick adjusted the set of his sunglasses. "It might be better if you waited here. Just in case Binelli has sent someone up here to look around. Even in that hat and those glasses, you won't go unrecognized for long."

Kelly's fingers caught the edge of his unbuttoned shirt. "Oh, yeah. And what about the disguise you're wearing, Investigator? I may be a marked woman, but they're looking for you, too. And the only thing you have they want is me."

He grinned slowly, the power in his smile only barely visible. "What's your point?"

"Be careful, Nick."

The smile faded from his lips. "Don't worry about me. I know how to handle trouble. Just keep alert."

"You got it." She sat down on the edge of the dock to wait. "Don't forget to ask about Sarah, though."

"First thing."

"And something cold to drink," she called after him.

He headed across the hard-packed sand. When they were back on open water, he'd feel a whole lot easier.

Nick stepped out of the glaring sun and into the shade of the open-air pub. He allowed his eyes to adjust to the dimness. Several foundry men stood at the bar, their feet and chests bare. As they turned and stared, he acknowledged them with a nod.

"Phone?" he asked.

The better dressed of the group indicated the back corner.

All three had tall, colorless drinks sitting in front of them. It was only nine thirty in the morning, and, yet, Nick would bet his life it wasn't ice water they sipped.

A couple, rich tourists by the look of them, slumped at a table in the back of the structure. They probably belonged to the fast boat.

Typical of the local phone service, it took the call some time to go through, but once it did, Douglas picked up on the second ring.

"Talk to me."

"Nick." Willcox sounded surprised. "You had me worried. I expected you to get back to me yesterday."

"You have the aunt, don't you?"

"No. She hasn't been on any of the incoming flights."

The news startled Nick. "What do you mean?"

"I've checked every one coming out of the islands. She seems to have just dropped out of sight."

"That's not possible. Eighty-year-old women don't just drop out of sight."

"Unless they have help," Doug pointed out. "Binelli may already have her."

"I hope not."

"We all do. But it is a possibility, isn't it?"

"Sure it is," Nick admitted.

"What about Kelly Logan, then?"

"That can wait. Just give me what you have."

There was a brief hesitation on the other end. Maybe Douglas was checking his notes.

"I checked Ben Tittle out. It wasn't easy. He was part of the Witness Protection Program. He was kicked out just after everything went down with the Logans back in Jersey. Seems he wasn't playing by the rules."

"Any chance he was involved in gunrunning?"

"You means with the Logans? Possibly. The marshals

would have been monitoring him. Maybe they weren't too happy about getting caught with their pants down and decided to cover it up to save the embarrassment."

Scanning the group of men near the bar, Nick realized he was being watched. Perhaps just idle curiosity, but getting *noticed* could lead to more uncomfortable complications.

"You haven't heard the best part, though, Nick. Ben was an accountant for Benito Binelli's brother. Back in the late nineties, Ben turned state's witness on Ramon Binelli, supplied dates, names, enough evidence to put Ramon away for life."

"Damn," Nick whispered. Every time he turned around, the situation became more confusing.

"I'm still working on the dive shop owner. So far I haven't come up with much. He raced offshore boats for a few years in South Florida. Stopped suddenly and disappeared. Resurfaced over there soon after with enough cash to set him up."

"Where did the cash come from?"

"I'm still working on it."

"Any chance he was doing more than racing boats?"

"Wouldn't surprise me."

Nick glanced behind him at the sound of a boat motor starting. One of the fishing boats pulled away. And one of the men who'd been standing at the bar was no longer there. Shit. Maybe the guy was just making a trip to the outhouse. Or using a shortwave radio.

"I'm out of time here, Doug. What kind of transportation did you arrange?"

"You need to talk to Myron on that one. He's handling everything from his end."

"You went to him?"

"Yeah. I wished I hadn't now."

"What do you mean?"

"There's been some new developments in Ake's case. The ballistics check came back."

"And?"

"It matches the thirty-two you killed the kid with four years ago."

Nick shifted the phone to his opposite ear. "That's bull-shit!"

"Sure it is. But you have to admit it's damn good bullshit. To anyone who didn't know the two of you, it would appear to make sense. Ake was too good to let anyone follow him and too cautious to let anyone he didn't know get close enough to leave powder burns. You said as much. He knew whoever killed him. The way the guys over at the FBI are playing it, Ake discovered evidence of your involvement with Binelli and called you. He would have figured no matter how dirty you were, you were still a friend."

"What's Myron saying?"

"Not much at the moment. He wants you to call him."

"And?"

"When you get stateside, there's a cell waiting."

"This is crap. Someone is tampering with evidence."

"Undoubtedly. But who?"

Nick's exhaled. "I don't know?" He tried to recall the last time he'd seen the weapon. He kept it wrapped in a cloth on the bottom shelf in his gun safe, but probably hadn't looked at in months.

"My advice at this point is to turn yourself in. Bring the girl with you."

"Not a chance."

"Don't be stupid. The airports and the marinas are covered. You'll never make it out of the islands."

Without saying another word, Nick hung up the phone.

For several moments, he just stood there, his thoughts a jumbled mess. How could this be happening? To him? He looked over his shoulder toward the boat. It wasn't only happening to him, though, was it?

Kelly stood when Nick made the end of the dock. She could tell by the way he moved something was wrong. Her aunt? God, don't let it be Sarah. Anything but.

"Nick?"

He brushed past her and ripped free the bow and aft lines and flung them into the boat.

She grabbed his shoulder. "What's happened?"

"Get on, Kelly. Now!"

He hopped aboard.

Frightened, Kelly jumped in after him, but glanced back toward the pub. Had they been made? Had Nick spotted one of Binelli's people?

As Nick choked and started the motor, Kelly asked, "Where are we going?"

In answer, he threw the throttle in reverse. "Somewhere I can think."

She didn't say anything for several minutes, not until they cleared the harbor.

"What did your friend say?" Kelly hung on as Nick jerked the steering wheel to the left and opened the throttle wide, the boat slipping across water like a skateboard on ice. "Did he arrange—"

"The only thing that's been arranged for either one of us is a jail cell."

Chapter Twelve

After several more attempts to get information out of Nick, Kelly fell silent. Whatever had taken place back there, it wasn't what he had expected.

An hour later, having left the boat tied up at the cottage's dock, she followed Nick into the kitchen.

"What happened, Nick? I have a right to know!"

He grabbed a glass from the cabinet, crossed to the sink without answering her.

She followed him. "Damn it, Nick, you're scaring me. What did you mean about the only thing waiting stateside was a jail cell?"

He faced her finally, his expression hard. "Did you know Ben Tittle was part of the Witness Protection Program?"

"What? Of course not."

"Back in the early nineties, he testified against Binelli's brother-in-law. It was his testimony that put Ramon behind bars."

"I don't understand?"

"Ben was Ramon's accountant." His expression hardened. "Which makes it damned unlikely Binelli would be doing business with him. None of it makes sense," Nick continued as he turned away. "I thought I had a grasp on at least some of the players. But now…" He stared out the window over the sink. "What would make Ben get involved with Binelli? And under what conditions would Binelli let Ben continue to breathe long enough to be a player?"

"What about my aunt, Nick? Is she okay?"

"She hasn't been on any of the incoming flights."

Kelly punched the heel of her hand against his back, would have thrown another but he turned in time to catch her wrist.

"You said she'd be safe! That you'd make sure Binelli couldn't get to her!"

"We don't know that he has. Let me ask you again. How well do you know Rod? Is there any chance he's working for Binelli or that he'd do anything to hurt your aunt?"

"No. I can't believe he would harm her. Even if he's working for Binelli."

Nick released her wrist. "Then hold on to your belief. Maybe he saw trouble and took evasive action. Maybe he thought he had a better idea for keeping her safe." Nick's lips flattened. "Maybe he's playing the hero to get your attention."

But what if he wasn't? What if she was wrong about Rod? As wrong as she had been about Ben? How could you spend 24/7 with a man and not know him? And then spend only days and hours with another and be willing to put your life in his hands?

"What about the transportation your friend's arranging? Is there a problem?"

"Yeah. You could say that." He gave her a stiff smile. "They found a match on file for the bullet that killed Ake."

The expression in his eyes should have been all the warning she needed.

"Who does the weapon belong to?"

"Me." He said the single word with no emotion.

Kelly was the one who flinched. "I don't understand."

She moved back half a step when he slammed the cabinet door. He stood there several seconds with his hand splayed on the dark wood, his arm taut, his body rigid. "It's called manufacturing evidence. Someone has done a damn good job of framing me. Not that I'll be able to convince anyone. I'm not sure I would believe it, either, given the evidence."

"That's not possible. Anyone who knows you…you couldn't…you wouldn't…"

"Thanks for the vote of confidence. But you're in the minority. The whole agency, not to mention the FBI, thinks I killed Ake. Even my supervisor has bought into it, and Myron knows me better than the rest, so the evidence must be damned convincing. Every marina and every airport between here and hell is being watched."

"But why frame you?"

He saluted her with the glass. "Someone has been trying to neutralize me since I stepped off the plane two days ago. They just hit on the perfect way to accomplish their goal."

"But how is any of this possible?"

"Binelli has someone inside."

He must have noticed the way her hand shook as she pushed the hair away from her face because he crossed the room to where she leaned against the door frame.

He looked as if he wanted to touch her and she willed him to do just that, to touch and hold her, to kiss her and make love to her until she couldn't think, until his touch made the world go away. But he didn't do any of those things. Maybe because he understood that nothing was going to make the nightmare disappear. For either of them.

"I'm sorry I wasn't there for you seven years ago," he said. "That I didn't believe in you. In your innocence."

As she believed in him now.

He didn't say the words, but she *heard* them just the same. In his eyes and in his voice.

"All that matters is that you believe in me now." She glanced away. "What are we going to do?"

"*I'm* going to find out who set us up."

"What if you can't?"

His fingers combed aside a stray strand of hair from her forehead. For the first time, the guarded look left his gray eyes. They warmed from the cold, dead steel of a stormy Atlantic to a softer shade. "I will, Kelly." He stepped past her. "Or die trying."

THE NIGHT WAS unbelievably still, suffocating, the cottage a small oven where daytime heat lingered like unwanted company.

Kelly sat on the floor in front of the large, square coffee table where she'd dumped out a puzzle depicting autumn leaves.

So far, she'd completed only a small portion. But then, the goal wasn't to finish the puzzle, but to keep her mind occupied.

Kelly took another sip of wine. She'd found a small stash in the mechanical room downstairs. Not the cheap stuff from the kitchen cabinet, either, but a good vintage. She didn't figure Steve Cameron would mind if she sampled a bottle or two. After all, the night was still young.

In fact she already had a nice little buzz going, not enough to really dull her thoughts, but enough to keep her from going stark, raving mad. And, who knew, maybe Nick would even help her empty one of the bottles. There was something oddly pathetic about drinking alone. Maybe it was her Irish background.

She looked over to where Nick sat a short distance away, obviously having no problem concentrating on the pad of paper in front of him. He'd been making notes for hours now, rarely doing more than looking up to ask a question about the airline or Ben or Rod, before returning to his own thoughts. Any attempts on her part to pull him into conversation about their predicament went unanswered.

As she used a fingernail to pick up another puzzle piece, the shortwave radio's static gave way to a transmission. Kelly's breath slid out slowly as she turned and listened.

Nick's voice startled her. "It's just a couple of fishermen."

"For a moment…I thought…I thought one the voices was Rod's."

All afternoon, she'd been battling her fear by not thinking too far ahead. But now, in the room's silence, with the shadows pressing in, her thoughts were becoming more difficult to fend off. Even with the help of some mighty fine wine.

Her fingers slid upward over the slender stem of the wineglass to cup the fuller dimensions of the globe. She traced the rim, then allowed her finger to drift downward.

Sensing she was being watched, she looked up. Nick stared at her, his eyes dark and unreadable. It wasn't fear kicking just beneath her skin now, but awareness. He hadn't touched her all day, and she was starting to feel edgy. Bitchy, even. It was as if he'd turned his emotions off and closed her out and wasn't even aware of it.

She straightened her spine as if to loosen the kinks. "Care to join me?"

"No. Thanks, though." He went back to the tablet.

Needing to move, Kelly picked up her glass and wandered. She stopped in front of the doors to the deck. How many times had she stood here? How many times had she put a puzzle together on the table behind her, never knowing this moment would come, never realizing that even when you thought you'd caught every curve life was capable of pitching you…there was always another one?

Her gaze skipped to the radio as it once more scratched

to life, and she stepped closer to catch the coordinates of the storm system. At the current rate, it would blast through the islands within the next few hours.

Kelly stiffened when she felt Nick behind her, but didn't turn around. "My father used to move like that. So quietly I wouldn't hear him until he was right next to me."

Nick put his hands on her shoulders and pulled her back against him. She let her body relax, his nearness calming her, easing the knot in her middle.

His lips pressed the top of her head in a kiss, then moved against her hair just as his breath did. "Sounds as if we're in for a bit of a storm. How about some sleep?" He tightened his arms around her.

She locked her free hand around his forearm and looked up at him. "Did you come up with anything?"

"Only more questions." He released her, stepped back. "Ones I can't answer from here. I need access to the evidence. To files."

"So you think there's more than the gun?"

"I'm sure of it."

"Your friend didn't tell you what, though?"

"No. But the only reason we're not locked up at this very moment is because of him. He's put more than just his career on the line."

"So you think he's done all he's going to, then?"

"Doug's not only a good friend, he's a good investigator. No matter where the evidence currently points, he'll keep digging."

"And you're hoping he turns up something?"

"Sure. But I'm not counting on it. Somehow, I need to get stateside where I can do my own investigating. From the sound of it, though, for the next few days the seas are going to be too high to cross in such a small boat."

"What about a plane? And an experienced pilot?"

His eyes narrowed. "Where would you get a plane?"

"Rod bought one last year to fix up. Up until several weeks ago, I kept it in my hangar while Ben worked on it."

"Where's the plane now? Assuming Rod doesn't currently have it?"

"He won't have taken it. It's at the airport. Tied down outside. Which means it would be tricky getting it fueled and checked over before taking it out of there, but I imagine it will be the Bird of Paradise hangar and the commercial airlines they're watching. And the weather will be bad. Visibility poor. That could play to our advantage. At least until we're airborne."

"So you're suggesting we just walk in and fire the bird up?"

"Unless you have a better plan."

"I only wish I did. What happens on the other end? How do you plan to avoid the Air Defense Identification Zone?"

"As you well know, it can't be avoided, not completely, but we can fool it and buy some time. They'll come looking for the plane, but we could be several miles away before they find it."

Nick paced outside and leaned at the rail. Kelly followed and stood next to him, her elbow barely brushing his.

She turned to him. "Do we have any other choice?"

"No," he said and straightened. "After the conversation with Doug this morning, we can't stay here. Binelli will pull out all the stops to get to us first, and at the moment he has a head start on both Customs and the FBI. And unfortunately, my guess is no matter who gets to us first, we'll end up dead."

She somehow managed to swallow the gulp of wine she'd just taken. "What do you mean?"

"Whoever Binelli has working inside will make damned certain he's on the front lines. Neither of us can be allowed to talk."

He remained silent for long moments, just staring out at the reef, then turned to her. "You're right. The sooner we get out of the islands, the better. So how do you propose we go about it?"

"We get an early start. Arrive around four or so. Just before most of the crews come in to do prep work. We blend."

"Blend," he said, his expression skeptical.

"Which is something you did very well seven years ago."

"My cover wasn't blown then."

"So it'll be tougher this time."

"More dangerous," he said and looked worried, almost as worried as she was.

"You should try to get some sleep," he suggested.

"I don't want to be alone. Not tonight."

Nick pulled her into his arms, an embrace filled with comfort. "Sounds like an invitation no gentleman could refuse."

"I thought you didn't claim to be one?"

"I have my moments." He released her and stepped back, but his gaze stayed on her face.

"You have lots of them." She reached up to cup his beard-roughened cheek. "You're harder on yourself than you should be. We'll get through this. Somehow." Standing on tiptoe, she pressed a kiss to one corner of his mouth, then the other. "Let's go see if either one of us can sleep."

She twined her fingers through his and turned toward the stairs. "Don't worry, I'm too tired to seduce you," she murmured as he gave into the pressure of her fingers.

NICK LAY IN THE DARK, listening to the rhythmic sound of Kelly's breathing beside him. He had no problem staying awake, listening to the rustle of palmettos just outside and the nearby pounding of the surf.

In his mind, he'd made lists of the pitfalls they'd be facing. Once they got stateside, they'd need transportation, a safe place to stay. And that was only the beginning of what it was going to take.

He closed his eyes to rest them, but saw the notes he'd been working on earlier.

Maybe Ben hadn't been directly involved with Binelli. Maybe there was an intermediary, someone who made all the arrangements. Rod, perhaps. He didn't like to think about what that might mean for Kelly's aunt.

And then there was the inside man, the one bought by Binelli, the one who manipulated the evidence. It would have to be someone close to the investigation. Most likely someone in the FBI, but he couldn't rule out someone in Customs.

Nick shifted, tugging Kelly spoon-fashion against him. The heat of her body and the scent of her skin and hair were powerful reminders it wasn't only his neck he needed to save.

He'd let her down once.

He wouldn't this time.

KELLY CAME AWAKE with a start, her heart feeling as if it might break through the wall of her chest, her breath coming in soft, harsh gasps. Every time she closed her eyes, she was confronted with Ben's wide staring ones.

Even now, she was afraid to check her hands, afraid they'd be covered in blood. Which she knew was ridiculous.

She looked around the room, first wondering where Nick was, then wondering how many more hours or minutes until 2 a.m., the time they'd need to leave to reach the airport.

She opened the bedroom door and looked out into the narrow hallway.

She checked the upper level, found it empty. On her way back downstairs, she glanced at the time on the kitchen clock. Eleven. They wouldn't be leaving for more than three hours and yet her nerves were on edge. Kelly slipped outside.

Chances were Nick had walked down to check on the boat or was too restless to stay indoors.

Cloud cover obscured what had only last night been a nearly full moon. The overhead canopy of trees shivered as a breeze whipped through it. In the distance thunder grumbled.

The air had already turned heavy and hot and laden with moisture. With expectation.

She descended the steps to the dock where water slapped the sides of the empty boat.

"You shouldn't be out wandering." Nick's voice startled her and she spun to where he leaned against the trunk of a nearby tree. She'd nearly passed him without having seen him. He was a silent, dark apparition that moved freely through the night.

Watching.

Protecting.

His shadow pushed away from the more massive form of the tree.

"What are you doing out here?" she asked.

"Just making sure the lines were secure on the boat." He walked toward her. "Storm will be here soon."

"I suspect the worst of it will have cleared out by two."

"That would be good," he commented. She could barely discern his face, couldn't read his eyes, but for some reason felt… Felt what? His edginess? Or hers?

As the breeze caught at her T-shirt, the slide and tug of the soft material across her breasts sensitized her whole body, as if the touch was that of Nick's hands gliding over her. Softly. With erotic intent.

"That shirt makes an easy target."

She shifted, the bottom of her feet scuffing the step. "My wardrobe is a bit limited. It was either this," she said and tugged on the hem, "or nothing at all."

He smiled. "I vote for the latter."

He moved half a step closer. She could feel the heat of him now. He lowered his head. "How do you feel about storms?"

She raised hers a fraction. "What do you mean?"

She watched his well-formed mouth approach hers, felt the tightening low in her body, the hitch in her breath.

"I mean, how do they affect you?" he whispered just before kissing a corner of her mouth.

The stubble of his beard chafed her cheek. He angled her mouth to his, tasted her slowly, sensually.

She pulled back enough to murmur, "I don't know. I never thought about it. How do you feel about them?"

He made no move to pull her closer or to even touch her with anything more than his mouth. It was oddly erotic, to have all sensation so focused. He continued to nibble.

"I like them," he murmured against her mouth, the vibration of sound fluttering against her lips, sending a shock of sensual heat deep into her belly.

Kelly moistened her lips before she tried to speak. "You like what?"

"Storms. Especially the thunder." The soft enticement of seconds earlier disappeared just as thunder rumbled overhead. The sound pulsated to the very core of her as his tongue swept across hers.

The sudden shift in wind caressed her bare legs, molded her T-shirt to her thighs, whipped her hair with stinging force around them.

When he shifted his lips to the line of her jaw, she willingly lifted her chin, her breath as ragged and uneven as his. He lightly bit her chin, then her lower lip. Her ability to think, to reason, faded, pushed aside by intense wanting.

"What are you doing?" she asked weakly, already knowing.

"Seducing you," he murmured, his thumb caressing her

jawline, her throat, the side of her breast. "How am I doing so far?"

"Just fine," she answered and swayed into the hard, lean length of his body as the first heavy drop of rain penetrated the tamarind trees.

Tentacles of lightning snaked across the black sky and she saw Nick's face briefly, saw the desire. Thunder rolled again, closer this time, the sound resonating through her.

Nick brushed the back of his fingers over her breasts. Her nipples instantly tightened.

Her hands slid up his hard biceps, slick with moisture, to tangle in the wet hair at his nape. She dragged his lips down to hers. She wondered if he knew exactly what he was doing.

He did. He knew all right. Somewhere, distantly, in the back of his mind, Nick remembered he'd sworn he wouldn't touch her. That he wouldn't hurt her again.

That when this was all over, if they both survived, he'd walk away, leave her to rebuild her life without any reminders of her past.

She moaned, and he gave up analyzing what was likely to happen….

He stroked her mouth hard with his tongue as he reached down with his hand to find the warm center of her. Tugging up her wet T-shirt, he pushed aside her panties. He found her hot, damp. She shifted her stance wider for him, taking his fingers in her with the same raw sexuality she'd displayed the first time he'd made love to her.

He kept his rhythmic touch moving within her as rain pounded against them, as wind swirled around them. She moved against his hand and fingers, taking what he was offering with such abandon that he didn't know how much more of it he could stand.

Thunder growled as she climaxed. Her fingers dug into his shoulders for support as she gasped his name.

He swung her up and carried her inside. With unsteady hands he tugged off her T-shirt, then peeled down wet panties, dragging them off over her ankles. His fingertips fanned back up the slick skin of her inner thighs, his thumbs brushing across her.

Kelly groaned and her reaching fingers tangled in his hair. "Please…"

"Please what?" he asked

"I need to feel you inside me."

"I can't, Kelly. I don't have any condoms."

"Don't say no. Not tonight."

Kicking his way out of his soaked jeans, he blanketed her wet body with his own, drove into her. And, for the moment, the world seemed all but wiped out except for his need for her. And her need for him.

Chapter Thirteen

Civil twilight, that period of time just before the sun breaks the horizon, was more than two hours away when Kelly finished a hurried preflight check on the vintage Cessna 182.

The worst of the storm system had moved through the islands, and yet the wind still gusted twenty to thirty knots out of the west.

For the moment, no one seemed to notice the action around the small plane. On the other hand, Kelly knew she couldn't be certain she hadn't missed something in the dark. Taking a plane up without doing a thorough inspection was equivalent to playing Russian roulette.

She wiped her hands on a rag as she stepped out from behind the Cessna. A stiff, salty breeze hit her in the face and tried to pull off her cap.

In the distance, she could see the Bird of Paradise hangar. She'd worked hard to build the airline and, up until two days ago, she'd considered it the core of her life. The very reason of her existence. She'd been worried about what she would do if she lost it. Losing the people in her life, her *family,* had never entered her mind. Considering what had happened to her father, it should have, she realized.

A man walked in front of the building, stopped and looked toward where she stood. She knew he couldn't see her amongst the planes, but for a blur of a moment, the way he stood there, the way he moved when he turned away, she was reminded of Ben. The wave of nostalgia hit her full throttle.

She'd been edgy since they'd left the cottage over two hours ago, as had Nick. But there was no going back now. Whatever course it was that they were on, it would ultimately lead somewhere.

Feeling apprehensive, realizing each small action led her closer to the unknown end, she opened the plane's door and climbed inside the cockpit to where Nick waited.

The interior of the plane had yet to be refurbished and showed signs of severe neglect. Split cloth on the seats, grime-covered windows and an over-riding stink of mildew.

"Is she safe?" Nick asked.

Kelly worked the ignition. "She hasn't been up in months."

"How about the fuel situation?"

"As long as the head wind isn't too great, we have a good chance."

"Good chance? Right about now, a lie might be nice."

"I'll keep that in mind," she said dryly.

Kelly revved the engine, checking the oil pressure. She flicked on the radio and donned headsets before taxiing between two planes, a tight fit, and then cutting across the tarmac toward the end of the empty runway.

As the rpms climbed, the Cessna shimmied.

"Is that normal?"

"Normal? No." She glanced at Nick. "Either she's just cold-natured or she's being coy about some mechanical problem. I'm sure she'll let us know which very soon."

"When? When we have sixteen thousand feet of air below us?"

Glancing at the radio, she waited tensely in spite of everything that told her to keep moving. With her reflexes already compromised by lack of sleep and the high levels of stress over the past few days, she forced her thoughts to stay keenly tuned to what lay ahead.

"Now," Nick said, "would be a damned good time to get out of here."

Her mouth flattened. Still she didn't move. "I'm doing the best I can here," she responded through gritted teeth. "So give me a break."

Radio static cleared. "The Cessna 182 on the tarmac. Hold your position. Please identify yourself."

"This is nine, two, two asking for immediate clearance. I have a medical emergency on board."

There was a brief pause where Kelly felt the ball of tension in her gut tighten. She counted slowly to herself. If they didn't give clearance in the next few minutes, she'd have to go for it, have to risk the possibility that, halfway down the runway, they'd find themselves playing chicken with another plane.

"Nine, two, two, you are cleared for takeoff."

As they hurled down the runway, a vicious crosswind rocked them and had Kelly silently swearing even as the ground fell away.

The cockpit turned cooler with altitude, and Kelly rubbed one hand against her bare leg in an effort to stay warm. She tried the heater, but wasn't surprised when it spewed only cool air. Ben, who, over the past ten months, had spent his spare time working on the plane, would have left that type of repair until the more important ones had been completed.

Kelly flashed on the last time he and Rod had worked on the plane together, the good-natured banter among the three of them when she'd shown up between gigs. They'd been close. At least, she'd thought they had been. The events of the past few days had shown her the error in her thinking. Now one of them was dead, and she didn't know what to think about the other.

Was it possible Rod worked for Binelli? That he could hurt Sarah? Everything inside her refuted both possibilities, but she no longer trusted her instincts. Even when it came to Nick.

She and Nick had made love over and over in the night. The last time had been slow and easy and with tenderness in his touch and in his eyes. Almost as if he were saying good-bye to her.

And maybe he had been. When he looked at her now, the warmth was gone. And he avoided physical contact.

She felt bereft. She was experiencing the loss of something she had only recently discovered. Had she really said those words? No expectations. No promises. Simple and uncluttered. She'd been a damned fool then, hadn't she, to think she could walk away so easily?

"She seems okay," Nick commented, breaking into her thoughts.

"Yeah," Kelly agreed. Staring at the gauges, she gave herself a mental kick. So he didn't feel about her the way she felt about him? She'd forget in time, wouldn't she?

Time isn't always a cure. She'd told Nick that and believed it now more than ever.

Ten minutes later, when they cleared the worst of the weather, the ride smoothed out. Kelly glanced over and noticed the signs of fatigue in Nick's eyes.

"There's nothing you can do. You might want to get some sleep."

"You're right. It doesn't look as if you need me."

Nick pulled his ball cap down to shield his eyes and slumped in his seat.

"You're wrong about that," she said softly, the drone of the engine making it inaudible.

Nick's voice startled her. "Oh, by the way, Kel. Your father was a damned good pilot, but you're a better one."

She flexed her grip on the stick. "You're just saying that because at the moment I hold your life in my hands."

He never lifted his head or glanced in her direction. "Just hold steady, sweetheart, and damned tight."

She planned to. Unfortunately, it was going to take more than a firm grip to make the upcoming landing.

Before taking off, she'd contacted Calvin Kicklighter, the only person beyond Nick she currently trusted. He'd be waiting on the other end with transportation for them and some cash and other supplies.

He'd asked about the Ocularcet. She'd tried to soften the blow, but had heard both disappointment and fear in his voice when he'd learned it was no longer in her possession but tucked in the borrowed knapsack a Customs investigator carried.

Kelly could only imagine what Sue Kicklighter must be feeling. Pretty much the same worry Kelly faced when she thought of her aunt.

She focused her eyes on the instruments, checked heading and airspeed, checked the fuel. *Live in the box,* she cautioned herself. *Control what you can. Leave the rest for later.* It was the same method she'd used to get through each day following her father's suicide, and it would get her through the next twenty-four hours.

"Coffee?" Nick asked more than forty-five minutes later. She'd been so wrapped up in her own thoughts again she hadn't realized he'd straightened in his seat.

"Sure," she responded, checking airspeed and the directional gyro once more before reaching for the mug.

She took a scalding sip and glanced over at him. He'd taken the ball cap off and slung it over his kneecap. He held his own mug between his spread knees, took a careful sip occasionally.

"Did you sleep?"

"Maybe some. Where do you plan to set her down?"

"A small field."

"How small?"

"Small enough no one will think of it when they start coming up with possible landing options for us. I wish I could tell you there was nothing to worry about, but…"

"Just tell me there are lights?"

"Sort of."

"Hell," he said and looked out his window.

Kelly found herself smiling as she flicked the transponder switch off, then on quickly, her fingers shaking subtly.

"What are you doing?"

"Buying time." She worked the switch again, leaving it in the Off position for several seconds as she slipped the radio headset back into position over her ear. She pushed the silver transponder switch up, then down, then back on.

She glanced out her side window as she spoke into the radio microphone. "The signal's going in and out?"

Kelly glanced at Nick now. "No, there doesn't appear to be a problem on this end. Maybe an electrical short," she told the air traffic controller, her voice unsteady. "I'm about thirty miles out on a heading that puts me into Melbourne in about ten minutes."

"Altitude?" She checked the gauge. "Seven thousand feet."

She checked the other gauges, then the fuel level. Kelly tapped on the glass to see if the indicator would creep up.

"There was no time to fuel up and I've hit some strong headwinds, so I'm coming in on fumes."

She listened for several seconds. "You were notified? Appendicitis. Stable for the moment."

Nick leaned across to look at the fuel gauge, then wordlessly sat back again.

Waiting five tense minutes, she then shut the transponder

down for the final time and spared Nick a single glance. "Hold tight."

She forced the plane into a steep dive to four hundred feet. Air turbulence rocked them. A sudden, sharp downdraft pushed them seventy-five feet lower before she got control again. When she was able, she banked the plane sharply to the north.

"For someone who claims not to have done any smuggling, you're damn good at it."

Her lips tightened. "They'll figure we ran into real trouble and were diverted to another field. But when they don't locate us, they'll assume we either crashed or we were carrying drugs or illegals." She took a deep breath. "And I'm damned good at a lot of things the first time out," she added. "Or had you forgotten?"

Nick was smart enough not to say anything more.

Eight minutes later, she peered through the black in front of the windshield, searching for lights on the ground, for the few landmarks she recalled from the last time she'd been forced to make an unexpected landing here. Though the previous situation had been just as dire, a mechanical problem, the weather had been better and there'd been enough light for her to find the ground.

Lights suddenly came on below. Headlights first and then several marine flares. If she'd thought the fuel would last for another pass, she would have circled once, taken the time to line up, and to allow Jim to get a few more flares out.

Nick swore softly, more to himself than at her.

She couldn't really blame him. What she was attempting to do was just short of insane. As she dropped down, she amended the thought. If they walked away from this one, it was going to be a miracle.

The field was a narrow, grassy trail between an alley of scrub oaks that seemed to have grown some in the past few years. As the altimeter reading dropped, her stomach kept pace. She still fought the disorganized gusts.

The left wing clipped branches. Kelly pushed hard on the right rudder and felt the plane's sluggish response. The opposite wing caught vegetation and she made another adjustment.

Problem was, the field wasn't meant for airplanes, but for cows.

"Brace yourself!"

With a sharp jolt, the wheels found grass meadow. Then a gopher hole. Her body jerked forward, then was thrown back and to one side as the nose plowed into soil. And kept moving.

There was no controlling the plane at this point. They were just along for the ride. A very bumpy one that seemed to go on and on and on as they skidded toward the headlights.

And then the motion, the momentum, finally stopped. For several moments she sat there, her eyes closed, the silence deafening. She felt the touch on her shoulder, the brief, comforting squeeze. But when she opened her eyes, there was no hand resting on her shoulder.

And Nick was busy undoing his safety belt.

She closed her eyes again and smiled. *Thanks, Dad, for being there.*

"What are you smiling like some fool about?"

She calmly reached up and flipped off the engines. "You know what Dad used to say, don't you?"

"No."

She turned toward him. "No guts, no glory."

"No one, Flygirl, has ever accused you of being short on courage."

In an unexpected gesture, he tucked a strand of hair behind her ear again. "And I'd fly with you anytime. And anywhere."

It wasn't what she'd expected him to say, and she was about to thank him when he added, "Just don't ask me to do it anytime soon." His smile took any bite out of his words. For several seconds, he seemed to study her face, and there was warmth there.

He looked as if he were about to say more when the shadow of a man cut across the glare of the headlights. "We should put some distance between us and this plane."

A man of medium height and medium build walked toward them. He held the hand of the young girl from the photo.

Kelly grabbed her satchel. When she would have shouldered it, Nick took it from her.

He followed her out. "This is no place for a child," he commented.

"And a world of blackness is?" she tossed back as she strode ahead.

He couldn't read her expression when he caught up. The grass hissed against his jean legs and her bare legs, the uneven ground beneath still spongy and slick with the recent rain.

As they drew closer, Jim released his daughter's hand, and she came racing toward them. Kelly went down on one knee. Capturing the girl, she swung her up into the air, then held her close as she kept introductions between the two men short.

"I couldn't get a sitter on such short notice," Jim offered as he led them back to the Blazer, stopping only to grab the metal pails containing the still-ignited flares.

"How's the baby?" Kelly asked and took one of the buckets while Nick sprinted to collect several others. "Last week when I talked to Sue, Emily had a cold."

Jim grabbed a gallon jug of water from the back of the mini-van and started dousing the flares. "Yesterday, Sue took her and went to stay with her mother."

He stopped what he was doing and looked Kelly in the eye. "You don't have to go with him. He can't help you, at least not right now, and being anywhere near him could get you killed. We can figure something out. Maybe Rod could—"

"Thank you for worrying, but you're wrong. I do need Nick."

Jim's eyes narrowed. "You say that as if there's more to it than this mess. Are you two involved?"

"One of us is."

Jim silently shook his head and went back to dousing flares.

The men loaded the pails in the back while Kelly strapped Amanda into the back seat.

Nick slid in front, Kelly in beside Amanda.

"I rented a car for you," Jim said as they left the narrow dirt lane behind. "And a place to stay."

"I'm really sorry for getting you involved," Kelly said.

Jim gave the vehicle a bit more gas as the road improved. "You'd do the same. We both know it."

"Thanks anyway."

"The car's just a basic sedan," Jim said. "The motel isn't as nice, but it's in a section of town where I doubt anyone will look for you."

Nick took the keys Jim held out and dropped them into his shirt pocket. "Thanks. For everything."

Jim didn't acknowledge Nick's words, just continued, "There are two duffel bags and a sack with toothbrushes and other basics stashed in the trunk, enough for you to get by on for a few days."

Nick caught Jim looking in the rearview mirror and did the same. Instead of Kelly, though, it was the little girl who confronted him. For the past few minutes, she had been entertaining herself by singing "Starlight, Star Bright" over and over again as she stared out the window.

He still carried her picture in his pocket. And now he would carry the sound of her voice in his head. Just one more regret, one more demon to add to the others.

He looked down at the bag at his feet. Maybe there were some grays in the world, some principles worth compromising. Some laws that needed breaking.

He took the three T-shirts he'd borrowed from the cottage out of the satchel and stuffed them into Kelly's.

When they drove away thirty minutes later in the car Jim had rented for them, Nick's satchel still sat on the van's front seat.

"Thank you," she said. "I know how hard that was for you to do back there. It was the right thing, Nick."

He looked over at her. "It really wasn't as tough a decision to make as you might think."

Kelly reached out and took his hand in hers. "Just the same, thanks."

His fingers tightened. "I hope it makes a difference."

"It will."

They stopped at the first outdoor phone booth they came to. While Nick got out to make the call to Willcox, Kelly sat in the car.

Twenty-five yards away, a convenience store on one side of the road was the only obvious sign of life in the area.

A restroom, a cup of coffee and a bottle of aspirin for this headache of hers would do the trick. Kelly glanced at Nick once before climbing out of the car.

It was early still, not yet six, and the store's fluorescent lighting seemed a harsh environment.

The male clerk behind the counter looked up, but went back to watching the morning news as Kelly found the restroom. Inside she stopped to use one of those vending machines that sold a buffet of protection. The machine used all her single bills. She'd always wondered what kind of loose woman buys protection in a dirty convenience store restroom. Now she knew.

She was paying for the coffees when Nick's face flashed across the television screen, just visible over the clerk's right shoulder. Her New Jersey mug shots was next on the screen.

"Thanks," she said and hurriedly picked up the coffees with hands that now shook.

She was three steps away, when the clerk asked about her change. Returning because it would draw too much attention not to, she took it and stuffed it in her pocket with the Red Zinger, the Black Voodoo and the Mellow Yellow Tickler.

Nick had pulled the car up by the front door. Maybe she was overreacting. She just hadn't been expecting it. To see her face there on television like one of the Ten Most Wanted.

Nick leaned across to shove open the passenger door for her and she slid inside, both hands still full.

"Everything go okay in there?"

About to tell him, Kelly glanced toward the plateglass window crowded with advertising billets. The clerk stood there watching them.

"We've made the morning news. I think the kid may have recognized me."

"I should have warned you to stay put."

"And I should have checked with you. I'm sorry."

Nick backed the car away slowly. Then cut behind another vehicle pulling in. The maneuver blocked the rear of their car until they were nearly on the road.

"Chances are," Nick said, "without a license plate number, the kid won't be sure enough of himself to make a report."

"You're not surprised, though, are you? About the bulletin? That they think we're in the area?"

"No. Whoever is framing me knows I'll come back to clear myself."

Kelly opened the aspirin bottle, was tempted to take the whole thing, but stopped herself at three. She burned her lips with the coffee.

"Any luck?" she asked and checked the side mirror, almost expecting to see a cop following. Somehow, the fact that they were being hunted, that they were on the run, seemed more real now that they were in the States. Hiding out in the Camerons' cabin already seemed distant. Secure.

"Did you reach your friend?"

"No answer. Probably out jogging. I'll try again when we get closer to town."

They drove for another twenty minutes before Nick stopped at a phone booth positioned well away from any buildings. It was light out now, though the low cloud cover made it feel like a heavy, gray winter day.

Kelly waited in the car this time. Even before he opened the car door, she knew by his closed expression that he'd been unsuccessful.

"Maybe he had an early meeting," Nick said as they pulled back out on the highway. "We'll make another call this afternoon."

"And in the meantime?"

"I could use a shower and some hot food. And maybe some sleep."

Chapter Fourteen

Nick unlocked the door and held it open. "Home sweet home."

She stepped carefully inside and briefly scanned the motel room.

Well off the beaten path, the Auto-Court's heyday was long gone, yet someone had attempted to keep it clean if not appealing.

The furniture was the blond stuff popular in the fifties, the bedspread and drapes a turquoise, green and yellow geometric print. The small table near the window bore a plastic vase and flower.

She set her suitcase on the bed. "It's a little too *Twilight Zone* for comfort."

"But not bad for what we need." Nick tossed his duffel on the spread and the sack of cold burgers next to it. "We'll eat first. Then sleep."

"I need a bath," Kelly announced and headed for the bathroom, her fingers already tugging off the T-shirt.

She turned on the faucet, watched the tub fill as she finished undressing, then slid into the too-warm water.

Closing her eyes, she willed her mind to tune out questions and uncertainties. Don't look forward or backward. Concentrate on the moment. Feel it. Believe in it and in nothing else. Worry was a waste of energy better used for action.

The pep talk was a rotten failure, yet she recalled sitting in another tub of warm water, telling herself the same thing after her father's death. She'd gotten through then. She'd get through this.

Ten minutes later, she came out of the bath with a towel wrapped around her. She dug a nightshirt out of the suitcase and pulled it on before making eye contact with Nick.

He was propped against the headboard, a fast-food wrapper in his lap. He'd shed his shirt. Looking at him, Kelly couldn't help but think of the condoms still stuffed in the pockets of her shorts, of wanting to feel him deep inside her where she still felt alive.

But amazingly, she was frightened of making that first move. By doing so, she would give over one more piece of herself to Nick.

What did he see when he looked at her? A responsibility? A complication? Or someone he might consider building a future with?

She sat on the corner of the bed and started brushing out her wet hair. "What if you reach this Doug and he's not willing to help?"

"You take the car and start driving. Don't look back."

"And what about you?"

"I stay and see it out."

She'd expected as much. "But they won't let you live. They can't."

"Maybe I'll get lucky," he said and offered a tired smile.

"Dad used to call *luck* the most dangerous of four-letter words. Start believing in it when you're in the cockpit, he used to say, and you'll find yourself dead. Rely on it outside the cockpit and you're likely to find yourself hugging a bottle in some dark alley. His words, not mine."

"What happened to the luck of the Irish?"

"As mythological as leprechauns and unicorns." She tossed the brush on top of the towel. "And what about Sarah, Nick? What if Binelli does have her?"

"If you're out of the picture, there's no reason for Binelli to hold Sarah. He's not a stupid man. He'll hedge his bets. If, at some point in the future, you're apprehended, she has to be alive for him to use her to keep you quiet."

"You mean if the feds catch up to me before he does, he'll need her? To make sure I don't talk?"

She could see the answer in his eyes. He thought likely that, if Binelli did have Sarah, he might continue to hold on to her. Did Nick really think she would leave her aunt in the hands of a brutal killer?

Kelly's fingers tightened on the brush. "We might as well get one thing straight between us. I won't leave here until I know she's safe, that he doesn't have her and can't get to her."

"The hard truth is that the only time she's going to be safe—the only time any of us will be safe—is when this is over." Nick wadded up the hamburger wrapper and tossed it on the bedside table. He swung his legs off the bed. "You think you have a choice now, that staying will help, but it won't. And Sarah wouldn't want you to put yourself in harm's way for her."

"How the hell do you know what my aunt wants or doesn't want?"

"If you love someone, you want what's best for them. Even if it isn't the best thing for you." He shook his head. "You're so damned transparent at times."

"I don't know what you're talking about."

"You think there's a chance that you might able to convince Binelli to trade your aunt for you. He won't."

"How can you be so sure?"

"I know his kind."

Nick stood and began pacing beside the bed. "Maybe we won't have to worry about that angle. Perhaps Rod's a straight arrow, and he's got Sarah with him. Right now, because of what happened with Ben, you don't trust your instincts. But you need to. Often it's your instincts and your wits that keep you breathing."

She looked up at him. "Well, right now they're telling me it's unlikely Rod has her. By now, he would have contacted me or Jim."

"That's rule number two. Don't discount the survival instincts of others. He may have realized any attempt to get in touch with anyone close to you could be dangerous."

She rubbed her forehead. "I hadn't thought of that. You don't think…"

"No. I don't. There's no reason for someone to have made the connection between you and the Kicklighters."

She only managed a nod.

"I'm going to grab a shower. You should eat something."

"Sure." As the door to the bathroom closed, Kelly chewed on a hamburger and washed it down with a lukewarm soda.

She ate half of it, tossing the rest into the trash. Kelly dug through the discount store's bag and came up with two toothbrushes and some paste.

As she turned on the faucet, Kelly confronted her image in the mirror. At what point during the past three days had she become gutless? She'd never walked away from anything she wanted. Not without trying. And she realized she wanted Nick. Not just physically, but in other ways, too. Seven years ago, she'd fallen in love with him. She'd never fallen out of love with him. Even with everything that stood between them.

Spitting out the remains of the toothpaste, she straightened. So what was stopping her now?

She was pulling the condoms from the pocket of her shorts when the shower went off. She hurriedly unbuttoned the nightshirt, let it drop around her feet as the door to the bathroom opened.

Nick's eyes darkened as his gaze swept down the front of her.

She opened her hand, let the packets drop from the left into the right, the motion very similar to the one Nick had used the other night when he'd confronted her with the Ocularcet.

"In case you're wondering, these are the real thing. The only liquid inside is a lubricant."

He smiled. "Jim?"

"No. The vending machine at the convenience store."

When he tried to grab her, she backed away, toward the bed. "One of us looks to be overdressed for the occasion."

Grinning, Nick released the towel from his waist, let it drop.

He was already hard, his erection swaying as he advanced.

"Look's like a Red Zinger to start, then maybe a Black Voodoo, and after that, if you're still up to it, there's Mellow Yellow."

"I'll damned sure still be up," he said and smoothly tackled her, taking her back onto the mattress.

She smiled up at him and he smiled back briefly before his expression turned more serious. He touched her lips. Then he kissed her slowly and thoroughly over and over.

Her fingers found him, stroked up and down. When she started to reach for a condom, he rolled her to her stomach. "Not yet."

Nick started kissing her all over again, pushing her hair aside to devour her nape, his teeth and lips everywhere at once, his hands finding her breasts, then lower. He put his mouth next to her ear and whispered "Relax. Just enjoy the ride."

His breath was uneven.

When she didn't think she could take much more, and yet at the same time was too relaxed to do anything but greedily accept each caress, each sensation, he pulled back. She heard the tearing of the packaging, managed to look over her shoulder to watch him slowly roll the Black Voodoo down the length of him.

When she again tried to roll over he held her steady. "Not yet." Spreading his knees, he straddled her, then lowered himself over her.

He sank into her slowly, filling her by degrees, then withdrew at an equal pace. "Relax," he said again as he filled her once more. "Let me do all the work this time."

On the sensitive skin where her neck met her shoulder, Kelly felt Nick's lips and then, unexpectedly, his teeth.

She came immediately. Hard. Nick changed the pace, forced her into a second and third climax. He leaned down and gently rubbed his beard-roughened chin along her jaw. "I'm still standing—how about you?"

"Not a chance," she said.

Still hard inside her, Nick wrapped a hand around her waist and lifted her around and sat on the edge of the bed, Kelly in his lap now. When she opened her eyes, she met Nick's gaze in the dresser mirror.

She felt another raw rush of desire as one hand dipped to touch her between the legs, the other covering her breast. And then he was moving inside of her, not gently as he had before, but with one solid thrust after another.

She knew the moment he came. The harsh in-drawn breath, the hand tightening over her breast, the pulsing of latex-captured semen.

They sprawled on the bed, both out of breath and too weak to want to move. Nick smoothed the hair away from her cheek. "Not bad for our third try."

She smiled. "Ready for number four and number five?"

"How about we sleep for a few minutes," he said.

"Sure. After I get a drink."

"SDS, have you?"

"What are those?"

"Sexual dehydration syndrome," Nick said and got up to get the water.

By the time he came back, she'd curled on her side and fallen into an exhausted sleep.

Her brows drew tight as if, though her body slept, her mind refused to give over. He knew she wouldn't leave when the time came. Perhaps she wouldn't want to leave him, either. And he didn't know what he was going to do about it.

But then he seemed to be uncertain about a lot at the moment. Like what he was doing here. To Kelly. To himself.

He could no longer fool himself into believing she wasn't important to him. Yet there were so damned many reasons why it couldn't work out for them. The past most of all.

He remembered her words from the other day. *All the family he'd left her.* A father who was dead because he hadn't been observant enough; an aunt who might be dead because he hadn't been careful enough.

He should never have taken Kelly to Key West that weekend. It had been Myron who'd ordered the trip. He'd "wanted the girl out of town". Not that Nick had hesitated.

He turned on the television but muted the sound. They were showing the report again, both his and Kelly's faces briefly filling the screen. He could almost read the reporter's lips. Armed and dangerous. Thought to be in the area.

Someone was damned sure they were back in town. Otherwise there wouldn't have been the need for such an intense media blitz.

But who? Did they work for Customs, the FBI or even another branch of law enforcement? With Doug's help, access to information or a look at the evidence, Nick might be able to at least pinpoint the agency.

Closing his eyes, he allowed his head to rest against the headboard.

Ake's words haunted him now more than they had the night he'd been murdered. Similarities in the cases. MO? Principals? Evidence? What?

In the early stages of both investigations, the evidence had been largely circumstantial. There had been little else to go on. With Princeton Air, the only pieces of evidence that hadn't been circumstantial were John's fingerprints on the weapons and the suicide note admitting guilt.

It had seemed like enough. Now he wasn't so certain. Kelly was being set up. Had John also been?

It was a line of thought he'd been examining since his last conversation with Doug Willcox.

The only prop needed to turn a lynching into a suicide was a note. But what kind of inducement did it take to make a man write something like that? Especially knowing he was already a dead man?

And how was Nick ever going to live with himself if that were true? Knowing that, if he had been there, John Logan might still be alive?

NICK HELD the telephone handset. The heat of the late-day sun radiated from the pavement and the cement block of the strip mall's wall.

"I need you to get Douglas to the phone. I can't risk my voice being recognized."

Nick dialed the number then passed Kelly the phone.

"Douglas Willcox, please."

She waited for the call to be forwarded.

"Supervisor Myron Richardson."

The voice was familiar to her. He'd interrogated her back in New Jersey. Kelly glanced at Nick. Saw the question in his eyes.

"Hello?" Nick's supervisor said again.

She decided it would be unlikely he could recognize her voice after all these years. "I was attempting to reach Douglas Willcox."

"Is this in reference to an investigation?"

"No. Is he available, or do you know where I can reach him? It's rather important."

"Are you a friend?"

"Why does it matter what my relationship is?"

There was a pause. "He was murdered this morning."

Kelly's fingers tightened on the phone. "How did it happen?"

"Car bomb. Just before seven." Myron paused as if waiting for another question, then, when none came, continued. "Kelly?"

She hung up the phone without saying another word.

Nick supported her when her knees gave way and supported her weight as she slid to the ground. She was shaking inside. Hell, she was shaking on the outside, too.

He squatted next to her, his expression worried. "Kelly?"

"He's dead."

Nick got to his feet and walked a short distance away. He stayed like that, his back to her. When he returned, the expression in his eyes was cold and lifeless.

"How did it happen?"

She told him. They'd been sitting outside the convenience store when it happened, she realized. Or maybe she had been putting money into a vending machine when a man had lost his life.

Nick sat next to her, pulled her into his arms. This time she couldn't keep the tears from coming.

"Let it go," Nick murmured. "Don't hold back."

He was holding back, though. Douglas Willcox was nothing more than a name to her. She didn't have a face to go with it. No shared history. Nick had both those things.

"He had a family, didn't he?" she asked because she wanted to feel what Nick was feeling.

"Two kids. He's separated from his wife," Nick said his expression grim. "I wished to God I'd never gotten him involved. He didn't deserve this."

"You don't deserve what's happening to you, and it's happening because of me."

"No, it's not." He forced her to look at him. "Ake maybe, but not you. I know that's what I suggested, but it's not true. Whatever is going on here, we're involved because we were both meant to be."

It was then it hit him how true the words he'd pulled out to comfort Kelly were. He wasn't involved because of Kelly and maybe not even because Ake. It was because from the start someone had wanted him involved.

Nick tightened his hold on her, forced her gaze to meet his. "I want you to leave. Take the car and the money." He pulled out his wallet, passed her his ATM card. "Wait to use it."

"Wait?"

"Once I've turned myself in, or…"

"Or what, Nick? Once you get yourself killed? Is that what you were going to say?"

He ignored her words. "They won't be monitoring the account. Just keep moving. Midwest, or even Canada if you can make it."

"I'm not leaving."

"I'll try to locate your aunt. If I do, I'll find a way to place an ad in the L.A. *Times.* I'll use the name Christopher McMann."

She tugged free of his hold. "You're not listening. The only way I'll leave is if you come with me."

His expression filled with pain, he said, "I can't do that." He stood, pulled her up after him. "There isn't going to be a happy ending, Kelly. Not now."

"I know. I just want an ending."

Nick studied her for several moments more. "Okay. I guess I can't make you go."

"No, you can't." She leaned back against the wall.

"Then we wait for dark. Then we go in."

"Go in where?"

"Myron Richardson's."

"You trust him?"

"No. Not any more. It was Richardson who Doug had been talking to. And it was Richardson who ordered our trip to Key West."

"And it was Richardson who was taking Doug's calls just now."

"Monitoring his calls would be more accurate. He had to know I'd make another attempt to talk to Doug."

"He knew it was me, Nick. He said my name."

Nick's hand checked the weapon at the small of his back. "Maybe you were right about the luck."

"SOMETIMES," Nick said, "you think you know someone. Then you learn just how wrong you are. You discover they're capable of things you never thought possible."

He didn't say it, but Kelly suspected he was thinking of her father, too.

It was just before one in the morning and they were parked half a block from the Myron's home. For the past twenty minutes, they'd watched the house.

"So you thought you were close?" Kelly asked.

"Yeah. I really did. Myron hired me."

"He told me. During the interrogation seven years ago. He also warned me to stay away from you. He was afraid your career might be ruined if I didn't."

"As if you were likely to forgive me for deceiving you? For what happened to your father?"

"One was your job," Kelly pointed out. "The other wasn't your fault. I think I've finally come to terms with that. And a lot of other things, too." She glanced out the window at the quiet neighborhood. "How did Myron get from New Jersey to Florida?"

"Relocated about five years ago. It was supposed to be semiretirement, but it didn't last."

"And you came with him?"

"No. In fact, we didn't have much contact for almost a year. One night, he calls, says it's for no particular reason, but, of course, it wasn't true. He'd heard about the shooting."

It wasn't the words that made her look in his direction, but the tone of his voice. And yet the interior of the car was too dark to really read anything in his face.

"Shooting?" She shifted so she faced him, her back against the door. "What happened?"

He remained silent for so long she thought he wasn't going to answer her. Perhaps because even now, after all they'd been through in the past few days and the intimacies they'd shared, he still didn't trust her. And that bothered her.

She reached for the cup of take-out coffee that sat on the dash, pretended to look out the front windshield. Pretended that his closing her out didn't matter.

"We got a tip," he said after several additional minutes. "Some shipping cartons being off-loaded late one night contained more than pottery. It was a routine take down. We showed up as the last carton hit the dock."

He sipped the coffee. "There were seven of them. We

took them into custody after exchanging gunfire. Nothing serious though. I remember thinking how smoothly it had gone, and that I was in the mood for a good steak.

"We were putting the last two in a car, when this young kid comes rushing out of nowhere, waving a semiautomatic. He was the younger brother of one of the perps. Fourteen. He'd come to help." Nick looked away. "I shot him. In the chest." He stared down at the nearly empty cup. "He lived for almost a day."

"It wasn't your fault."

"Maybe not. But I still regret it." He looked at her. She couldn't see his eyes, but she knew if she could have, they'd been filled with pain.

"So Myron calls," she prompted.

"Yeah. He called. Suggested a change of scenery might help. I refused at first."

"What made you change your mind?"

"The fact that I couldn't do my job. I spent more time analyzing each move I took in an investigation. I told myself I was being thorough. What had really happened, though, was I'd stopped trusting my instincts."

"And that's not understandable?"

"It nearly got another investigator killed." He emptied the contents of the cup out the window. "So I took Myron's advice. Figured I had nothing to lose."

Tentatively, she reached out to touch the side of his face. The skin was firm and resilient beneath her fingers, as resilient as the man.

Their gazes locked for several seconds before he spoke. "So you see, it isn't easy for me to contemplate the possibility Myron is behind any of this. Or that there might be a connection between what's happening now and what happened to your father."

Kelly's fingers curled as she withdrew her hand. "What

are you saying? How could Myron have had anything to do with what happened to my father?"

Nick rubbed his eyes. "I don't know what I'm saying anymore. And the past isn't nearly as important as the future. I just want you to know how damned sorry I am that I didn't trust my instincts where you were concerned. If I had, things might have turned out differently. Very differently."

"Maybe. Or maybe it would have been exactly the same, Nick. It was my father's decision to end his life, not yours."

"What about Aidan Gallagher? Did he ever contact you afterward?"

"About six months later. Not in person, though, but by mail. I was surprised the package ever caught up to me."

"What was in it?"

"A note telling me how sorry he was about my father. He never admitted he was in it with my father, but I always considered the cash he sent a guilt payoff." She smiled sadly.

"Cash?"

"I burned it. Every single hundred dollar bill. Can you believe it?"

"Yeah. I can." There was understanding in Nick's eyes when they met hers.

With both hands now, he framed her face and, for the briefest of moments, seemed to study her before lowering his mouth to hers.

When he released her, they both sat back, their spines pressed to opposite doors.

"That was for luck," he said and turned to reach for the handle. "Wait in the car. If I'm not back in ten minutes, get out of here."

He seemed to contemplate her silence for several seconds. "I don't suppose you'll do it, though, will you?"

"Probably not."

"Didn't think so," he commented as he climbed out and

turned back again. "Myron's house is midway down on the left-hand side. When I turn the porch light on, make your way around to the back. The kitchen door will be unlocked."

"What are you going to do? Pick it?"

"I thought I'd try the spare key first."

Kelly watched Nick stroll up the street, cut across to the opposite side. He disappeared between two of the houses.

Chapter Fifteen

The homes in the neighborhood stood close, shoulder to shoulder. At one time, it would have been a working class community. Now yuppies and financially secure retirees, anxious to downscale, inhabited the quaint residences. In the distance, Orlando traffic hummed; nearby crickets and a small, window air conditioner roughened the night.

Nick pushed open the door to the utility room and quietly let himself inside. He allowed his eyes to adjust to the room's dimness before stepping into the kitchen. A small amount of light from a neighbor's yard fixture reached across the sink to the wood floor and to the chrome leg of the vintage table.

Nick glanced down as Myron's cat brushed against him, then moved cautiously toward the den door.

He opened it no more than six inches at first, his weapon in hand. The light he'd seen beneath the door came from the desk lamp. Myron sat, slumped over the surface, his cheek resting on the blotter.

Red wine leaked from the neck of the overturned bottle to soak like blood into a pile of shredded papers on the floor.

Obviously, Myron had been working just as hard at emptying drawers as he had been at draining the bottle.

Reaching past him, Nick picked up what appeared to be an airline ticket. He fingered it open.

"What is it?" Kelly asked.

He didn't bother to mention she'd failed to wait until he'd signaled her with the porch light.

"He's set up an escape route. South America." Nick glanced over his shoulder. "I want you outside."

"I have a right to be here."

"And I don't need the distraction."

Myron picked that moment to lift his head. Turning, he focused bleary eyes on the man standing over him.

"Nick? What are you doing…You shouldn't…"

Coughing, Myron reached for the glass of wine, and Nick realized the older man wasn't as drunk as he'd initially thought.

Tossing the ticket on the floor, Nick stepped back and brought the gun up level with the man he'd once considered a mentor.

Myron's eyes narrowed. "What are you doing?" He started to reach for the center drawer.

"Don't move." Nick jerked the chair, with Myron still in it, away from the desk. "Keep your hands where I can see them."

Myron's gaze skipped to Kelly and then settled on Nick again. Wiping his face with a broad hand, he sat back in the chair, let out a deep breath. "I was just looking for something for this cough. What's go—"

"That night," Nick interrupted. "It was you who made the call for the hit on Ake. From your office. I stood outside while you did it."

"What are you saying? I called my daughter. Hell. I didn't know who you were meeting. You were damn careful. Didn't want me to know it was Ake on the phone. Didn't you think I might remember as much later?" He paused for half a beat. "And wonder about the reason?"

Nick dragged Myron from the chair, shoved the gun under

his chin as he pinned him to the wall. The two men weighed the same, but there was more than thirty years and half a foot difference in height between them.

Even as he thumbed the trigger back, he tried to rein in his temper. "No more lies!"

"It was your gun!"

"And you knew where to find it. I've gone over and over it in my head. When Ake learned you were in the room that night, he became nervous. Because you were the one Binelli bought."

"No!"

Nick picked up the ticket and all but crammed it in Myron's mouth. "Then what is this?"

"A way out. *For you.*"

Nick turned the ticket so he could read the name. Nathan Carmichael. "This is bullshit. I said I'd get Ake's killer. Doesn't look like I'm going to able to now with all the heat breathing down my neck, does it? But I've got the next best thing. I've got the bastard who set it all in motion. I'd let you call your daughter and tell her goodbye, but you didn't give Ake that chance!"

"If you don't believe me, there's a passport in the top desk drawer. I'll get it."

It was the second time he'd tried to go for the drawer.

Nick tightened his hold on the shirtfront. "Not so fast."

"Kelly?" he said over his shoulder. Blood pounded at his temples. He didn't want any of this to be true, wanted it to be some kind of mistake. "Take a look."

As she slid it open the first thing that came into view was a small revolver encased in a holster.

"Nice try," Nick said and tightened his hold. "Now start talking."

His hand trembled as he contemplated pulling the trigger, thought about killing a man whom he'd considered one of his closest friends. He'd held Myron while he cried after he'd buried his wife. And had cried with him for the wonderful woman lost to both of them.

"What gets me is you're the last person I would have expected to be involved in any of this. I thought you were incorruptible. Hell, I always thought more of you than of my own father."

"Nick?" Kelly said softly.

He noticed her puzzled expression. She held out what appeared to be a new passport. "I think you better have a look."

Stepping back, Nick took what she passed him, but kept his attention focused on Myron. Nick sensed the other man's relief even before he opened the passport.

His own picture stared back at him. The name below was Nathan Carmichael.

Myron sagged against the wall. "At first, I couldn't believe you were involved with Binelli. But then, when Willcox told me you were with the girl…" His voice faded as he retook the seat Nick had dragged him from. "Hell. People do things they wouldn't think themselves capable of when it comes to someone they love." He studied his hands briefly. "Look at me," he said and glanced up at Nick. "You're the closest thing I've got to a son."

Nick stepped back, but didn't put away his weapon. He wanted to believe Myron, but after what he'd been through, he didn't trust anyone but Kelly.

"So you thought I was involved?" Nick asked.

"Not until the ballistics report. Then there seemed no denying it. I had hoped you would get in touch with me."

"That's why you told Willcox you needed to talk to me?"

"Yeah. The arrangements weren't quite made, but I thought, if you could hang tight in the islands for a few more days, I could complete them."

"What about Willcox?"

Myron closed his eyes, rested his head against the chair.

"I don't know. The blast took out half the windows of the building, left nothing but a twisted pile of metal where the car had been. With dental records, they may be able to make a positive ID."

"Any witnesses?"

"No. And so far no real leads. It appears he slid the key in the ignition, and…" Myron shook his head. "He never knew what hit him."

"It's not Binelli's usual hit."

"No," Myron agreed. "Binelli normally wants them to see it coming."

"So it was someone else?"

"Binelli's inside man would be my first guess."

"Which agency?"

"Everyone's too busy pointing fingers right now. FBI thinks it's someone inside Customs, but then they would."

"Nick," Kelly interrupted and held out a second passport to him. When he flipped it open it carried Kelly's picture. A nice photo taken from a surveillance shot.

Nick met Myron's gaze.

"I figured if you loved her enough to kill Ake, you wouldn't be willing to leave her behind." For the first time, he addressed her directly. "Hello, Kelly. It's been a few years."

"Like I told Nick when he showed up in my place, it hasn't been long enough."

"Maybe if you didn't keep such bad company."

"That's just it, I don't. Excluding the two of you."

Nick broke in. "It's not just me who's been set up. Kelly isn't any more involved with Binelli than I am. But someone has gone to a lot of trouble to make it appear she is. I initially suspected the mechanic."

"Who is now dead," Myron finished. "It still could have been him. Binelli might have been warned the government was getting close, that he should start tying up loose ends."

"Maybe. But he wasn't dealing with Binelli directly."

"How can you be so sure?"

"Ben's testimony put Ramon Binelli behind bars ten years ago."

"Hell," Myron said softly. "Where'd you come by that piece of information?"

"Willcox." Nick studied the passport. "Good workmanship. Can't say I'm not grateful, but why South America?"

"No extradition. Nice weather. And no one would be suspicious if I decided to take an extended vacation to do some fly fishing." He smiled. "You didn't think you were going to get rid of me that easily. Not after all these years."

Nick put away the gun. "I owe you an apology for what just happened here. I want you to know it just about killed me to think you might be involved."

"Why me, Nick?"

"Ake talked about similarities in the current investigation and the one seven years ago. But he was concerned he might be seeing something that wasn't there."

"Seeing what? What kind of similarities?"

"He didn't want to say on the phone. Especially after you walked into the room. He wanted to see if I saw the same thing he did."

"And you withheld all of this during the investigation."

"Yes. It wouldn't have done anyone any good. I got my hands on the reports from Princeton Air and on some of Ake's notes."

"And?"

"Nothing. I didn't see anything. As far as I could tell at the time, the only repetitive element was Kelly."

"Who claimed she and her father were innocent and now claims she's being set up." Myron clasped his hands. "You didn't believe her before. Why now?"

Kelly interrupted. "You could at least wait until I leave the room before talking as if I wasn't here." She stood. "Where's your bathroom?"

Myron nodded toward the kitchen. "In the hallway. Second door on the right."

Nick waited until he heard the door close behind her before continuing the conversation. "Why I believe her doesn't really matter. What does is the fact that someone is doing a great job of setting us up." His lips hardened.

"Why bother, though. What are they getting out of it?"

"You mean other than the chance to see me burn?"

Myron rubbed his face again. "You do have a few enemies, Nick. In both the FBI and Customs." Myron gathered up the passports and the tickets and handed them to him. From the bottom drawer, he pulled out a thick envelope. "It's all I could get on short notice and without raising suspicions. After I sell the house, I'll get you more. And Nick, I'm sorry for thinking it even possible that you could have hurt Ake."

"I suppose, with the evidence, you didn't have much choice."

Nick took the envelope and looked inside at the cash. "You don't think there's any other way."

"Honestly? No. I think if you want to live, you should plan to do it outside the country. With any luck, they'll get tired of looking someday."

"That's not living. That's running."

Myron nodded. Nick realized just how tired his friend looked. "Your health, it's good, right? You took a few days off recently." Was there more to Myron's fatigue than he let on?

"I'm fine. Just had some tests done."

"Tests?"

"Yeah. Bev made me promise to get checked out. It was one of the last things she asked of me before the cancer took her, so I figured, hey, if she's looking down right now, she'll know I'm still keeping my promises to her." He glanced toward the darkened kitchen. "What about you and Kelly?"

Nick didn't pretend not to know what his friend asked. "Too much bad history. Even with the chemistry."

"There's more there than just that. Haven't you ever wondered why it didn't work with anyone else?"

"You think it's because I've been in love with Kelly all this time?"

"I don't know. But ask yourself why it was you went to the Abacos. It wasn't strictly to find Ake's killer. You didn't really think Kelly would have the answer to that question, did you? I think it was because, no matter what she'd done, you couldn't stand the idea she might get hurt."

Nick knew there was some truth in Myron's words. "I suppose we'll have lots of time to figure it out."

"Then you'll take her with you?"

"I have no choice."

"There's always a choice."

A noise near the door had both men looking in that direction. "You should listen to him, Nick," Douglas Willcox said as he stepped through the doorway, his weapon wrapped in the hand hanging at his side. He faced both men with a confident expression. "Just can't keep a good man down," he offered as he took another step.

Instead of his usual dress shirt and slacks, he wore jeans and a T-shirt. He'd dyed his blond hair a dark brown and added an earring to one ear.

The shock of seeing a *dead man* passed quickly enough, but Nick still didn't attempt to go for his weapon. It would take a second and a half to get the automatic out and the safety off, while all Douglas needed to do was lift his arm and pull the trigger.

Better to pick his moment, Nick decided. When Douglas

was distracted enough, the odds would be evened. And when he knew Kelly's location, could factor her safety into the equation.

"Who was in the car?" Nick asked.

Douglas massaged the recently pierced ear. "Just a body."

Myron spoke for the first time since Willcox walked in. "They'll figure it out when the dental records don't match."

"But they will match. That's the beauty of planning ahead. A few weeks ago, I went shopping for my stand-in. At the dental office of Lee Caboda." He grinned. "For a hundred and seventeen bucks, I bought a body and the corresponding set of X-rays."

"Another patient's?" Nick felt his gut tighten with disgust and anger.

"Yeah. He'll turn up missing. They'll suspect foul play, but without a body and without witnesses, it will become another unsolved case. If the widow can convince the insurance company her husband didn't just slip out of town with another woman, she'll undoubtedly collect a nice little sum. Enough to put the kids through college."

"You bastard," Myron said and started to rise.

Douglas had the muzzle of his gun level with his supervisor's nose before the larger man's backside cleared the chair. "I wouldn't do that."

Douglas backed a step. "I know the odds seem in your favor, hotshot, but they're really not." He glanced toward the door to the kitchen. "Bring the girl in."

A second man kept a muscled arm wrapped across Kelly's neck as he pushed her into the room. She struggled, her heel connecting with his shin more than once, the blows bringing only an amused expression to his heavy-featured face. He carried a sawed-off shotgun in the other hand, a cute little toy that left very big holes.

Tightening his hold, he lifted Kelly's feet clear of the

floor, the pressure choking off her windpipe. With her hands, she fought ineffectively to loosen the grip.

As soon as Nick started for Kelly, Willcox's gun was planted at eye level.

She stopped struggling, and as soon as her feet hit the floor, Willcox pulled her in front of him and pressed a gun to her temple. "Make any fast moves, she dies first."

"What is it that you want?" Nick asked.

He recognized the other man, figured Myron did as well. Danny Nagel. In the past he'd done mostly contract work. Until Binelli had come along. Now it was rumored Binelli kept him on his private payroll.

Nick knew he was looking at Ake's killer. Ben's, too, though he'd never known him to use a knife. But MOs weren't necessarily static. "Why come here tonight?"

"The girl, for starters." Douglas rubbed the muzzle of the gun over her cheek. "She really is a looker, Nick. I can see why you went back for more. But, of course, it would have been much healthier if you hadn't. You forced me to do some improvising."

"Is that what you call murder these days?"

Nick glanced at Danny. "I thought you were Binelli's boy. Must have had it wrong. But why knife the mechanic, Danny? It's not your usual style."

"It wasn't Danny's hit," Douglas commented.

"Yours then?"

"Yeah. First blood I've had on my hands since I worked the stockyards during college." He rubbed the knuckle of his index finger down Kelly's cheek. "I hadn't realized how much I'd missed seeing it. The slow leaking of life from a warm body. The eyes, at first shocked, going dim." He looked up. "It's a real rush, Nick."

"Which makes you a sick bastard. Even Danny here probably doesn't really enjoy what he does. He's just too stupid to do anything else."

"In his case, you may be right. You're probably telling yourself right now that you and I are different, that you had no choice with that kid. It was you or him."

Nick remained silent.

"We all are capable of killing, Nick. If the payoff is the right one."

Nick still said nothing.

"In your case, you wanted to live. For me, it's that I want to *live* well."

"And to live well, you had to kill Ben?"

"Yeah. Who would have guessed he'd grow balls so late in life? Stupid man thought he could blackmail me into backing off, leaving Kelly here alone. Unfortunately, that wasn't possible."

"How can she be of any value to Binelli?" Myron asked.

It was Nick who answered. "I don't think Binelli knows what's going down. I think he's getting scammed just like the rest of us."

"Good guess, Nick," Douglas said.

"No guess. I figured it out. Binelli will, too."

Douglas tightened his hold on Kelly. "Enough talk. Nick, I want you to pull out your weapon using the thumb and index finger of your left hand." He waited while Nick complied. "Kick it over here."

"Arrogant to the last," Nick commented. With no other choice, he shoved the gun across the carpet. The only remaining weapon was in the desk. Once Kelly left this room with Willcox, there was a good chance Nick would never see her alive. He thought of the gun, of his chances of getting to use it. He looked over at Myron, knew he was thinking the same thing. Weighing the same options and chances.

It was Myron who shook his head, but Nick silently concurred with the assessment. To make any moves now was to put Kelly at further risk.

"Pull the car around back," Willcox ordered Danny. He changed his gun to his left hand. "Kelly, I want you to bend down and pick up the weapon."

Douglas tightened his hold on her upper arm. "And, just in case you're thinking on any fast moves, it will be Nick I kill first."

Kelly straightened, gun in hand. Douglas pulled her back against him and smiled. "Isn't this a fun little game? Now, Kelly, Simon says put your finger on the trigger."

"No."

"Put you finger on the trigger!"

She shook her head. "I can't."

"Sure you can. Because if you don't, I'll kill you."

She shook her head again.

Douglas laid his own gun next to her temple. "You better talk some sense into her, Nick."

"Go ahead, Kelly. Do it. Do what he says."

"But—"

"You have no choice," Nick said softly. "He's not bluffing."

She rested her finger on the trigger. "Now point the gun at Nick."

"Noooo!"

Willcox wrapped his hand over hers and lifted the automatic until it was aimed at Nick's head. "I think the girl really loves you, Nick." With that he swung the weapon to the right and squeezed off two quick rounds, the first hitting Myron in the head, the second in the upper chest.

Chapter Sixteen

Kelly stood there, shocked, her brain refusing to believe her eyes.

Myron sprawled on the floor, blood leaking from his head, the front of his shirt soaked with the same.

She couldn't look away, couldn't quite register that she still held the gun, the hand of the man who'd forced her to pull the trigger still wrapped over hers.

She'd killed a man.

Forcing her eyes from Myron's face, she looked into Nick's eyes, briefly saw the pain there before hate and determination buried it. The pressure in her chest expanded. She couldn't breathe. It was all happening too fast. She needed to think.

Leaning in, Douglas whispered in her ear, "You should never pick up a loaded gun unless you're prepared to use it."

Déjà vu. The night in the hangar. Nick using almost the same words.

She tried to pull away, but the pressure of Douglas's grip thwarted any escape. "It gives you a real rush, doesn't it?" Douglas added. He straightened. "At this rate, Nick, you're not going to have any friends left. But then dead men don't need friends, do they? Except for pallbearers."

Nick looked down at Myron, then up at Douglas. "Before

I die, you're damn well going to regret that." He said it so coldly, so calmly.

Instead of pointing the gun at Nick when he took a step toward them, Douglas put it to Kelly's temple. She didn't fight him. There was no more left in her at that moment.

Douglas shifted his hold on her as her knees weakened and motioned Nick to move back. "I think it's time I lay out a few of tonight's ground rules.

"Rule number one, Nick. You do anything stupid, Kelly gets a bullet. So be damned careful with every move you make." At the sound of a car door slamming, Douglas glanced toward the kitchen. "Rule number two," he continued. "This one is for Kelly. Do anything but follow instructions, I'll put a bullet in Nick's head."

"Let her go."

"Now that I can't do. Unfortunately. If there's anyone here who is expendable, it's you, Nick. The only reason you get to live a bit longer is because it'll make for such a poetic end." Douglas smiled. "And you know how damned serious we Irish take poetry and wakes."

Nick's eyes narrowed.

"Oh, I suppose I forgot to mention that, didn't I? The Irish blood. Small matter, though." He shifted his hold, his forearm coming up to nudge Kelly's breasts. "Maybe we should have a little test now. See if both of you were listening." Kelly stood there unmoving while his touch became even more bold, his long fingers brushing across her breasts, stopping to squeeze one and then the other.

Kelly wanted desperately to close her eyes, but instead kept her gaze level with Nick's. "Don't," she said when she saw the muscles in his arms bunch.

"You better listen, Nick." With the gun, Douglas caressed the side of her neck. His lips replaced the barrel.

Kelly shuddered.

"Does she tremble when you touch her?" Teeth replaced lips, and Kelly jerked, but didn't pull completely away. "What makes her moan?"

He turned at the sound of the second man just behind. "Take him on out." He used the gun muzzle to motion Nick toward the door. "Kelly and I have a few things to take care of before we join you."

"What if someone heard the shots?" Danny asked.

"In this neighborhood? They'll think they're left over fireworks. Wait outside."

Kelly saw Nick's hesitation, the look of hard fury in his eyes. "Go on," she said. "I'll be fine."

"I'm sure you'll be more than fine," Douglas said.

DANNY SHOVED NICK out the door, the sawed-off shotgun planted against his spine, then pulled the door after them.

Careful to keep his hands up, Nick walked ahead. He had no doubt he could take him. He just needed to pick the right moment. It all came down to who was the most patient.

Danny popped the trunk. "Climb in."

"Damn." Nick sat on the trunk's edge. "And here I thought my ticket was for a window seat."

"Just get in."

"What? No beer nuts and soda? No pretty flight attendants to flirt with?"

Danny lifted the butt of the shotgun as if to strike Nick in the side of the head. "You have a real smart mouth."

"And you might want to consider shifting some of that muscle in your neck a bit north. Use it to figure the odds."

"What odds are those, sport?"

"Which one of us is going to survive the longest." Nick ducked under. "You better think about it. Willcox has never been much of a team player. Think of him as the quarterback calling the plays. In order to score, he'll do damned near anything."

"So will I."

"You won't see it coming."

"Don't be too sure."

The trunk was pushed closed over his head.

KELLY TREMBLED.

Because she knew she had to, she forced a deep breath. She had to get it together. She needed to act instead of react. Needed to start thinking about survival. Nick's and hers. And to do any of those things, she damn sure needed to appear tough.

"Alone at last," Douglas said.

"Only if you ignore the body on the floor. But then you're used to stepping over the dead, aren't you? As if they aren't even there." What was happening with Nick?

Ignoring her, Willcox took the clip out of the gun, shucked the remaining live round on the floor, then carefully wiped the automatic. "It wouldn't pay to get any ideas," he said. "I don't need a gun to kill you."

"I'm sure you don't. My aunt? Do you have her?"

"You ask too many questions."

"Does Rod work for you?"

He held the unloaded gun out. "Take it. I want the prints to be nice and clear so there isn't any doubt."

She did as told, while he pulled out a pair of latex gloves and slipped them on. He took the gun from her, shoved in the clip, loaded a round in the chamber.

"Now sit on the couch and be quiet."

She did as ordered, glad to put even that small distance between her and this monster.

She watched Douglas go through the desk. He came up with the revolver from the drawer, tucked it into his waist and continued his search.

"What is it you're looking for?"

Again Douglas didn't answer.

"You weren't ignoring me a few minutes ago," she said and scooted to the edge of the couch. If she could distract him, get the gun away from him, she might have a chance to at the very least dial 911.

She tried a smile. "I had hoped, without an audience, you might pick up where we left off."

"Don't flatter yourself. I was just enjoying the novelty of forcing Nick to watch. Not that you don't have the right lines, but at the moment, the only thing that's going to give me a real hard-on is the seventeen million I'll be collecting tonight."

"You plan to steal a shipment of cash."

"That pretty much sums up the high points of tonight's festivities. Though killing Nick ranks up there, too."

"Why? What has he ever done to you?"

"Done? Nothing. Except get in my way a time or two. Not that he realized it, of course. Real Boy Scout. But then you know all about that, don't you"

Kelly faced him in stony silence, still trying to figure the angles, the possibility this corrupt agent of the federal government didn't have her aunt. Did that mean Binelli did? Or had she and Rod escaped unharmed?

Douglas tossed the automatic with her fingerprints next to Myron's body.

"Aren't you forgetting something?" she asked when he took her by the upper arm.

"No." He shook his head. "I don't think so."

She could almost see how a woman might be drawn to and even taken in by his boyish smile, the well-kept body. If you didn't look into his eyes, didn't see what they now revealed. A cold-blooded sociopath.

"Aren't you worried about the item Ben gave me for safekeeping?" she bluffed.

The look of confidence remained on his lips, but not so much in his eyes. He was trying to fight his way through it. Did she have whatever it was? What risk did it pose to him if she did? Especially if she were dead.

"You don't have it," he said finally. "If you did, you would have given it up that first night at the marina."

"And lose my only bargaining tool? I'm not totally stupid. It's going to be hard to spend seventeen million," she added, "with Binelli breathing down your neck."

"Move it," he ordered and shoved her toward the door. Her hand was on the knob when he jerked her around. She barely had time to gasp as his fingers twisted into the collar of her T-shirt. The material gave under his assault. He pushed her back against the door, kissed her hard. Her lower lip was bleeding when he pulled back. "I always give a female what she's asking for."

Shocked and sickened, Kelly slapped him.

His hand immediately connected with the side of her jaw. Her head snapped back with the impact, but she managed to lift her chin. She wouldn't cower. Not in front of this man.

"Now move it!"

THE NIGHT WAS peaceful as they stepped out the back door. Douglas's muscled accomplice sat on the trunk, his knees splayed, his knuckles resting against the car, the shotgun cradled in his lap.

"Where is he?"

Danny banged on the trunk lid. "I tucked him in for the night," he said as he hopped down.

"Good idea. It'll keep the prick quiet."

Danny slid in the front seat. Douglas shoved her in the more roomy back and followed. Kelly glanced at the seat back, wondered if Nick was conscious, or hurt.

"Don't worry. He'll be fine."

She gave Willcox a cold stare.

"I think you may actually have it in you to kill," he said.

"Why don't you give me a gun and we'll test the theory."

"You really are a little hellion." He seemed amused by the idea. "What do you say? Want to help me spend the cash?"

She smiled. "You have a better chance with Danny the Goon."

"And you would have a better time of it with me. Contrary to what I suggested the other night, I like my sex straight up, where as Danny Boy is into heavy kink."

"Whatever it is you're saving me for, it isn't Danny."

He nodded, but made no comment this time.

They were on the road for more than an hour, first major highways, then secondary roads that took them north, past neglected orange groves and small, darkened towns.

She could occasionally hear Nick curse as a tire fell into a deep rut.

Kelly tried not to think about what would happen when they stopped. Instead, she stared out the window.

She was resigned to her own imminent death, as resigned as anyone who desperately wants to live could be, but it was more difficult to accept Nick's death. He was going to die because she'd gone to his room that night. Because she'd involved him. He'd tried to tell her otherwise, but she didn't believe his words.

The car took a sudden, sharp turn off the secondary road, the headlights briefly skimming the gnarled, black skeletons of citrus trees, then the thigh-deep grass bordering the narrow dirt track. She could hear Nick being thrown around in the trunk.

In the front seat, Danny chuckled. "Shake 'n Bake." He looked at Douglas. "Get it? Shake 'n Bake?"

"Just drive," Douglas ordered.

She could see Danny's eyes in the mirror, and he looked

less confident than he had earlier. Douglas, on the other hand, seemed almost relaxed.

The car came to a sudden stop. Douglas dragged her out behind him. "We walk from here."

She stumbled half a step before planting her feet. "What about Nick?"

"Move it!"

"I'm not taking one step—"

He shoved her ahead of him and, taking the shotgun from Danny, wordlessly leveled it at her.

With no other choice, she did as she was told.

When they cleared a line of scrub oaks, she saw where they headed. A plane sat waiting on the short runway. The lights were on inside. A short distance away, a vehicle waited with its engine running.

Douglas motioned toward the steps. She climbed them because it seemed pointless not to, but managed to look back once, saw Danny carrying Nick over his shoulder. Another wave of panic slammed over her. She grabbed the rail to steady herself. Too fast. It was happening too fast.

"You have me. Let Nick go. You said it was me you needed, that Nick was unimportant."

"And that's true. But I still can't let him live."

"Why?"

"Because I don't plan to spend the rest of my life looking over my shoulder."

"You're going to do that anyway. Once Binelli receives the package."

"Which will be mailed to him by a third party when something happens to you?"

"That's right."

He nudged her with the shotgun barrel. "Good try, sweetheart."

There was something not quite real about the night. The

damp, rain-slickened air. The light leaching down from inside the plane.

When she looked up, reality became a lead weight crushing her chest and heart.

"Hello, Kelly," Aidan Gallagher said from where he waited above her.

"Aidan," she answered coldly. She hadn't seen him since the day following her father's funeral. Her fear turned into a hard knot of hate as she realized just what his presence here tonight meant. The money he'd sent her had been out of guilt. Over her father's death. And she was to be his next victim. Used and discarded when the usefulness no longer existed, when the gain from her death was more cost-effective than whatever part she had unwittingly played in his plans. But how had Doug's and Aidan's paths crossed?

"I see you met my nephew."

She hid her shock. "Are you sure I didn't just squish him under my shoe?" She lifted her foot, pretended to check the sole.

"And you were such a charming girl once. There was a time when I thought of orchestrating a meeting between you and Dougie."

With his accent, the name came out sounding almost like doggie.

Kelly knew Aidan had spent little time in his homeland over the past twenty years, and yet the heavy accent remained intact. Probably because it was better to promote the cause.

Kelly forced a frigid smile as she climbed the remaining steps to stop in front of him. Up close, he looked as if a dozen years had passed instead of just the seven. His pale blue eyes were watery and lifeless, his skin wrinkled and sallow. "So what's the plan here?" she asked. "Same as the last time?"

"That's up to you. Just as it was up to your father." He took her by the elbow and escorted her to one of the rear seats.

Aidan waited while Danny carried Nick past them and dropped him in the center of the aisle. He nudged him with a tennis shoe. "Wake up, pretty boy." He nudged a little harder.

"He'll come around soon enough," Aidan said. "Tie up the girl."

Danny placed plastic zip ties—the type cops used—around her wrists, pulling them until the stiff plastic bit into her skin. He shoved her down and did the same with her ankles.

Moments later, Douglas walked in carrying a suitcase in each hand and had to maneuver around Nick. "A hundred thousand."

"Should be enough to convince Benito the rest burned or sank."

Douglas sat opposite Kelly. "I think my uncle had hopes you might want to join us where we're headed."

"And where would that be?"

"Like I said before, the good life."

Kelly looked up at Aidan. "What happened to you? When did it become about the money?"

"It was always about the money."

She stared into his hard eyes, eyes that were not unlike his nephew's. "I can believe that."

"But you don't understand it any more than your father did."

"And yet he agreed to help smuggle guns."

"No. He agreed to smuggle currency to buy supplies for those in need of food or clothing or medicine."

Kelly sat forward. "But there were guns found. Two cases. His fingerprints were on them."

"Yes they were. And willingly placed there. Just as the note was written by him. In a steady hand."

"I don't understand."

"Your father found the guns." He rubbed his chin, looked toward Nick. "I want you to know I gave him a choice."

"What kind of choice?"

"He could either become a partner, or he could just keep his mouth shut and look the other way. But, unfortunately, that wasn't John. He made me resort to a third course of action."

"What are you saying? That it wasn't suicide?"

"He gave me no choice. I couldn't trust him." He looked at her. "Any more than I can trust you. Or Ben, it seems."

She looked away quickly. She should never have believed her father had taken his life. Should have listened to her instincts. That he would never willingly leave her.

But she hadn't. Maybe at first, but not later. Not in the end. She and Nick were no different in that respect. They'd judged with their heads and not their hearts.

"You know what really amazes me—" Aidan broke into her recriminations "—is what motivates each of us to accept our own deaths."

Refusing to let him see just how shaken she was, she met his gaze.

"John willingly gave his life to protect you. Ben, too, in the end."

Kelly remained silent still, her mind reeling as she absorbed the meaning of his words.

"He didn't even have to get involved. He could have kept his mouth shut, but he, too, chose to cash in his life."

It hit her then. Up until that moment, she had believed all the men in her life—her father, Ben—had deserted her. But they had died protecting her the best way they knew how.

And now she would die and take with her the only other man she had ever loved.

Aidan pulled Nick to his feet, shoved him toward the cockpit. "I hope he's worth dying for."

Nick took only two steps before turning to face Aidan.

"Time to get this bird in the air, Nick. Time to meet destiny."

Nick reached for the seat back before glancing toward the front of the plane, then at Kelly, then at Aidan.

Kelly watched mutely as Nick, who had obviously decided he had little choice, slid into the pilot's seat.

Douglas tossed Nick's pistol to Danny. Then a second piece of equipment. "The GPS coordinates for a spot thirty-five miles offshore are already entered. A boat will be waiting. There's a parachute in the back."

Kelly saw the brief hesitation in Danny's eyes.

He looked a little less confident than he had earlier. "You didn't say anything about going along for the ride."

"The agreement was that you'd deliver these two when it came time. You haven't really done that yet, have you, boyo?"

"I don't know anything about jumping out of planes."

"It's easy. At the right time, you just take one large step out the door."

Possibly sensing he had no choice, Danny slid the GPS into his pocket and watched as Aidan and Douglas walked down the steps. He didn't look too happy when he turned back.

"Now take us up," he ordered.

"Or what?" Nick asked, not making any move to do as ordered. "You'll kill us? You're going to kill us anyway. Maybe we should just get it over with now."

Danny leveled the gun at Kelly's head. "There's always an outside chance you'll both live. Or at least one will make it."

"I suppose the same could be said for you. There might be a boat waiting. And there might not be. That parachute back there might open. And it might not."

"Just get this thing in the air."

Nick began the routine of warming engines and checking gauges.

As the plane moved forward, she could see beyond Nick's shoulder to where the landscape bounced past like a dysfunctional film reel.

Just after takeoff, Danny pulled out the GPS and flicked it on. "Turn north seven degrees."

Nick banked the plane slowly, then as she leveled back out, reached for the radio.

"Don't bother. It's not working."

Settling back, Danny studied her. "You might as well just relax. It'll all be over soon enough."

They hit more turbulence soon after they left the Florida coastline behind, and Nick was kept busy handling the plane.

Kelly briefly watched Danny fiddle with the GPS, then closed her eyes and let her body go with the sway of the plane. Time was running out. She knew that much. But not how to stop it.

She still didn't know the fate of her aunt. As she sat there, Kelly realized that, in the last minutes of her own life, she needed to think of Sarah as alive. She allowed images to float through her mind. The first time she'd laid eyes on her aunt. She'd been sweeping the front steps, her apron fluttering in the island breeze. She'd stopped as Kelly approached and had stood there, broom forgotten as she had smiled grandly. Then she'd held open her arms in welcome.

Then there was the kind look in her eyes when she talked to one of her cats. Or to herself. Kelly could smell her now. The lavender. The sweet scent that had clung to her clothes after a day of baking. Then it was Rod and Sarah together. She'd think of them like that. Arm in arm. Both smiling. The sun on their faces.

"I've never seen a woman quite so happy when she was on her way to her death." He smiled. "At least, not recently."

"I've never seen a man quite so stupid on the way to his. Nick's right. I know Aidan Gallagher. The chute won't open. When you hit the water at two hundred miles an hour or more, I expect it's like hitting a concrete wall at the same speed."

"Take the plane down to seven hundred feet," Danny ordered as he stood and retrieved the parachute.

Kelly felt the descent in her stomach. They slipped into the clouds. The panic that she'd managed to keep at bay crept closer now, like a savage predator.

When he finished adjusting the chute, he turned to work on the door.

Wet wind leapt in to pummel the interior as it dropped away. The plane rocked with the increased turbulence, and Danny hesitated at the doorway, his dark, lank hair caught in the breeze.

"You better say your prayers fast." Turning back, he checked the GPS again, then his watch. "Shit. Doesn't look like the two of you will have time even for a long prayer at this point."

"What's that mean?" Nick yelled.

"You're sitting on a bomb." Danny leaped out of the plane.

"Hell!" Nick swore. "Hold on, Kelly!" He forced the plane into a steep dive.

Kelly was thrown forward, her hips and shins and shoulders connecting with every obstacle as she tumbled toward the front of the plane, her hands and feet still bound. She screamed as a crate slammed into her, and then her universe went black.

Nick barely had time to glance down to where she ended in a small pile crammed between the pilot's and copilot's seats. He swore harshly as he fought gravity for control of the plane. The dark water below came toward him at blinding speed.

Too fast.

He'd never get the nose up in time.

Chapter Seventeen

The rush of air shrieked inside the cabin. Nick hauled back on the stick, but the Atlantic came at him like a brick wall.

When they hit, the nose cleaved deep, a wall of water exploding over the windshield. A wing was torn off by the impact, and then suddenly the hull was skipping across the water like a flat stone.

As soon as forward momentum stopped, cold water surged in.

He tried standing. Pain shot through his knee and his leg crumpled. He went down. With a grunt of pain, he staggered to his feet. They had to get out. Fast.

He lurched again as he bent to tug Kelly free. He dragged her through salt water already a foot deep. Snatching up two seat cushions, he anchored them by their straps over one shoulder and jumped into the water, Kelly in his arms.

They went under, the Atlantic devouring them.

Nick floundered back to the surface, then struggled for several seconds just to keep Kelly's head above water.

He shoved her hair out of her face. She was pale. A deep gash seeped blood at the hairline. He couldn't even be certain she was alive. There was no time to check.

She wasn't dead. He wouldn't allow her to be. Not now. Not yet. Not ever.

He kicked awkwardly with his one good leg. In his head, he felt the ominous sweep of the second hand and heard the insistent ticking of a bomb. How much longer?

Seconds?

Minutes?

Waves washed over him. Over her. Desperate for more speed, he tried his injured leg and faltered, going under. Salt water stung his nose and eyes as he adjusted his hold on Kelly and resumed the awkward one-legged pace.

After what seemed an eternity, but what was probably only minutes, a wave lifted them. As they briefly rode the crest, he glanced back.

The explosion heaved a fireball heavenward. Flames licked sky and water. Searing heat blasted across the surface, carrying chunks of torn metal and smoke.

Nick used his body to shelter Kelly from the rain of debris. He held her face buried against his neck, his fingers trapped in her tangled hair. "We made it," he mumbled. "We made it."

After several minutes, only silence and the water remained. Stoically, without room inside him for even relief, he started kicking again, then realized there was nowhere for them to go.

Now there was no hurry. Now they played a waiting game. To be found. Like two live needles in a very large haystack. He didn't kid himself about the odds. Yet the plane would have to be found if Binelli was going to be convinced the cash had simply gone down and not been stolen.

Which meant they had been tracked.

But even if the plane were located, there was no guarantee there'd be an intense search for survivors. Not after the explosion.

The best course of action was to stay close to the original crash site. Which, given that he didn't have a GPS on him, was nearly as doable as swimming the fifty-plus miles to shore.

He tugged on his own flotation device, then, holding Kelly cradled to his body, he worked at the bindings around her wrists. "We'll make it, sweetheart. You just have to believe that."

He pushed her hair away from her eyes again and willed her to open them. Her skin had grown more pale, her breathing shallow and irregular. Maybe a concussion, or something far worse, like internal injuries. He didn't know.

When he managed to free her hands, he struggled to put the flotation device on her, afraid that if she slipped from his grasp and beneath the water, he'd lose her.

He prayed for the first time in years. Making promises he couldn't hope to keep.

Nick caressed her forehead, her closed eyelids, the stiff line of her lips. Her skin was so cool to the touch. Fear like no other he'd ever experienced went through him.

He remembered what Myron said about choices, realized he'd been right. He hadn't gone to the islands just to find Ake's killer, but also to protect Kelly. He tightened his hold on her. Myron was dead.

When it had happened, Nick hadn't allowed himself to feel anything but the anger, the need to see retribution done. Now, the deep sense of loss filtered in. If only he hadn't doubted Myron. He knew just how much that must have hurt the other man. Just as it had Kelly all those years ago. He recalled the look on her face just before he'd turned his back on her and walked away. The pain. The incomprehension.

He'd doubted Kelly. Questioned her morals where she'd never questioned his. Never doubted him. Even when she'd had no reason not to.

Kelly was all about loyalty. Which was the reason she hadn't been able to believe Ben was involved. Had risked her life to go to the hangar that night. Had been unwilling to accept the possibility her father smuggled guns. Had put her life in Nick's hands. The bottom line—Kelly believed in people, in their inherent goodness. It had been a long time since he'd seen anything to make him believe in either.

What of Sarah and Rod? Aidan hadn't gotten to them. If he had, he wouldn't have held back when he'd had the chance, he would have used it to cause Kelly further hurt.

Binelli, though?

Maybe, Nick admitted, but he didn't think so. With Douglas's plans hinging on Binelli believing Douglas was dead and that the millions were now part of the Atlantic's bottom, chances were better Binelli had no reason to suspect he was going to need a hostage.

Because of Nick's assumptions, they'd been looking in the wrong direction the whole time. Just as Binelli would be when he heard about his cash.

After several hours, Nick's arms turned stiff, but he refused to loosen his hold. The straps on the life jacket chafed. He wondered how much longer before the cushions became waterlogged and useless.

KELLY FOUGHT AGAINST consciousness, preferring the comfortable, black oblivion of seconds earlier. In spite of her wishes, though, pain edged in. An explosion went off in her head when she tried to move, and she groaned.

Cold. So damned cold.

The pain…intense now…sucking the air from her lungs as it intensified…then, after several seconds, fading away like a bad dream. For as long as possible, she held on to that idea. That it was only a dream. A nightmare. Nothing real.

But when she roused herself, the pain returned.

She felt weightless and heavy at the same time. She vaguely managed to register that she was floating, but was unable to grasp where or why.

An unknown period of time later, the mental fog lifted away, and she opened her eyes to the emptiness of night.

Terror impaled her. Alone. She was alone.

"Nick," she cried and grabbed ineffectively at the water in front of her. "Nick!" She had to find him. She didn't want to face this alone. Didn't want to face anything without him ever again.

"Here." His arms tightened around her. "Take it easy. I've got you."

She registered that he held her from behind. "How long?" she asked, her headache making any type at thinking impossible. She carefully licked the saltiness of her own lips. "How—"

"It should be dawn in a few hours." He caressed the hair off her face with trembling fingers, needing to touch, needing to convince himself he wasn't hallucinating. "You're okay," he repeated.

Seeming to accept his words, she succumbed to unconsciousness once more.

Time crept by.

His arms became numb. Finally, scared that if he dozed off he might lose her, he used the cord from her wrists to anchor them together. But he didn't sleep. He held her, murmuring soft words of comfort.

Sometime later, she roused again, slipping toward consciousness as she had before, but this time there was no comforting hope that it was only a bad dream.

"My legs, I can't move them." She struggled again.

"Easy," he soothed. "They're still tied. I couldn't reach them."

"I want… If we don't make it…" Her voice faded.

"Hush," he said, the word barely escaping his tight throat. "We're going to make it," he said, his voice hoarse and raw at the thought they might not. That *she* might not make it.

"Just in case," she whispered. "Nick?"

"What?" he murmured, his fingers touching her, feeling the cold immobility of her skin. Hypothermia was setting in.

"Kelly?"

She closed her eyes and gave herself over to the long, dark and silent shadow of blackness, welcoming its warm absence of pain. *I love you.*

Nick held her tightly to him.

The hours that followed were endless. He knew he would shortly reach a point when he, too, would pass out. He fought it by forcing his brain to work on the intricacies of survival.

Bleary-eyed, cold and exhausted, Nick watched dawn creep silently toward them, bringing with it hope.

The sky overhead showed signs of a cloudless day and of milder seas. He watched shades of peach and plum and red stain the morning sky. And then it wasn't the sunrise he studied but the dark speck marring its beauty.

He watched the helicopter sweep closer, then over them, the harsh metronome of its rotor beating the air and water. Nick squinted against the down blast and waved.

He glanced down at Kelly. "We're going home."

Chapter Eighteen

Sixteen days later, Kelly rose slowly from the desk chair and walked toward what had been the airplane hanger's storage room where she'd found Ben.

With her hand on the knob, she hesitated. It was a nightly ritual, this testing of herself. Someday she might be able to forget, but not yet. She still woke up from nightmares where she was floating in a great abyss.

Alone.

Unconnected.

Filled with a nameless terror. Searching desperately for a safe harbor.

Kelly turned the knob and reached inside to flick on the overhead light before she stepped across the threshold. Having been turned into a brightly lit waiting area for her passengers, the room bore little resemblance to what it had once been.

She retrieved a soda and a cold-cut sandwich from the small refrigerator, then returned to the chair and the company checkbook.

The radio played softly in the background. She'd flicked it on in an attempt to fend off the late-night shadows and to fend off the raw sense of loneliness that seemed to find her whenever she was alone.

She wouldn't go home, wouldn't try to sleep until she could be certain her exhausted body would win out over her mind.

Kelly took a bite of her ham and cheese, chewed with little appetite.

Since she'd been released from the hospital, she'd been staying with Sarah. As Kelly had suspected, Rod had been unwilling to let her aunt out of his sight and had taken her with him to the Caymans.

Kelly had never spoken to Rod about those moments and hours when she had doubted him. It would only hurt him. As it humbled her.

At every turn he'd proven himself a good man, a great friend, and yet she'd questioned him.

As Nick had suspected Myron Richardson. Perhaps that was one of the few bright moments in the past several weeks. Myron had miraculously survived his wounds, though he had just been moved from critical care only two days ago.

Danny hadn't been so lucky. The parachute hadn't opened. Search and Rescue had fished his body out of the Atlantic only hours before their own rescue.

Aidan Gallagher and Douglas Willcox had been arrested when they tried to leave the country, while Benito Binelli had been apprehended as he sat down to dinner with his wife and daughters. With the help of Ben's journal, which had turned up in her mailbox a week after his death, there was every possibility all three men would do time behind bars.

Kelly pushed the half-eaten sandwich away. Business was booming for her. She'd hired a new mechanic, a young kid. She should be happy, but she wasn't.

Nick was the problem.

She was hopelessly in love with him. "When will you finally learn, Logan," she muttered.

Up until yesterday, he'd called her daily, giving her reason to hope. They had talked about Myron's improving condition, about the upcoming indictments, about the need for her to testify.

Though she had relished the sound of Nick's voice, she had wanted to hear other words from him. The same words he'd whispered against her cheek as they'd floated in a cold ocean.

It was those very words and the memory of his arms that had sustained her for the days she'd spent in the hospital, and they had been the very words that had made it possible for her to face the terror that continued to fill her nights.

But, she knew, they'd been words spoken during the worst of circumstances, when there had been little hope for survival left in either one of them. She couldn't trust them.

Perhaps he stayed away because he now regretted the very words she cherished.

What hurt the most, scared her the most, was that she'd never felt as whole as she had in his arms.

But life went on, didn't it? In spite of all the disappointments and the heartaches. She needed to count her blessings. She was alive, as were Sarah and Rod. Amanda was doing well, the Ocularcet doing its job.

Kelly closed the checkbook and slipped it into the bottom drawer.

In the past several hours, she had been tempted a dozen time to pick up the phone, but she hadn't. It was up to Nick now to decide what he wanted. If he wanted her, well then, he knew where to find her, didn't he?

She had grabbed the small revolver she kept close at hand and was reaching to turn off the radio when she heard the soft mewing at her feet. She glanced down just as a black kitten leaped onto the chair cushion and then the desk, almost as if he were scoping out new digs.

She laid the gun aside and reached out to pet him. "Where did you come from?"

"He hitched a ride with me."

She spun around, her heart climbing into her throat at the familiar voice, hope already surging uncontrollably through her.

"Nick," she said her voice barely above a whisper.

He stood there in the collected shadows near the door. When she couldn't move, couldn't respond any further, she realized how starved she'd been just for the sight of him.

Unlike the last time he'd stood in this doorway, there was no duffel bag slung across his shoulder. Which could mean he planned to stay only long enough to break her heart one final time.

"Hello, Flygirl," he said as he closed the distance between them. She watched his lithe movements and felt her heartbeat kick up unsteadily. Her mouth went dry.

Still ten feet away, he stopped, the mellow glow of the desk lamp enfolding him.

He wore jeans and a Polo shirt. His usual cocky grin, though, was absent. Bad news, then, she decided. All the prayers in the world hadn't changed her Irish luck.

His dark hair was neat except where it fell forward onto his forehead. She wanted to reach out and brush it back with her fingers, but she was afraid to even touch him—afraid that if she did, she might just make a fool of herself and throw herself into his arms.

"What brings you to Marsh Harbor?" she asked. She smoothed her hands against her shorts, for the first time feeling grungy and mussed and in need of a long, hot shower.

He took a step toward her. "I had unfinished business."

Something deep inside her twisted into a hard knot. Some small seed of hope found a small corner of her heart to put down roots.

"How's the investigation going?" She tried to keep the disappointment from her voice, but suspected she failed miserably.

"With the help of Ben's journal, well enough. It's the first time the government's had a decent shot at Binelli."

"So you think you'll be successful in putting him behind bars?"

"I'm not involved in the case anymore."

"Oh." She searched for an additional comment. It was so damned hard to find inconsequential conversation when all she wanted to say came from her heart. "How's Myron?"

"Doing fine. Really good. If he continues to heal at the same rate, he should go home in another few days."

Kelly felt her insides continue to shred as she looked at him. Only ten feet separated them, but it might as well have been the Atlantic Ocean. She didn't know how to bridge that gap, felt as if she was once more drowning, this time alone.

"How's Rod and Sarah?"

"Good. Sarah's glad to be home, though. And I think she's decided traveling's not for her."

"And Rod?"

"He'll be here in a few minutes to pick me up."

Kelly realized her ability to stand here pretending everything was fine was quickly ebbing away.

"I went by and saw Amanda this morning," Nick added. "The medication seems to be working. At least for now."

Kelly managed a small smile. She didn't need any reminders he was a good man. "What you did meant a lot to me. To Calvin and Sue, also. I know how hard it was for you."

"Not nearly as difficult as it should have been." He shrugged. "You know you were right."

"About what?"

"There are a few shades of gray left."

He stuffed his hands into his pockets and took several additional steps toward her. His gaze caught hers and held it steady.

"How are you really doing, Kelly?"

I'm lonely. I miss you. I wish I wasn't such a coward. "Fine." She lifted her chin. "How about you?"

"Better," he commented.

She glanced away. "Business is good."

"So I heard. I also understand you hired a new mechanic."

"Yeah. A kid. He's thorough...." Her voice faded and she looked away. Alone. Without Nick, she would always feel this way.

"But he's not Ben?" Nick prompted after several weighted moments.

"No," she answered and shook her head. "No, he's not."

Kelly was the first to retreat by picking up her keys from the desk. "I was just heading out. It's late and I have an early flight in the morning."

His gaze on her halted any further movements. "Is it too late, Kelly? For us?"

"I don't know," she answered softly, suddenly wondering if he'd ever be able to look at her and not see the past. Maybe neither of them would be able to. Maybe that's what surviving meant. What loving meant, also. Accepting the past, but living in the present.

"I wanted to give you some time alone to think. I needed time to think, too."

Nick closed the distance.

He didn't deserve her. He knew that. And there was still the fear one morning she'd wake up hating him for what had happened to her father, what had nearly happened to Sarah. That she would walk out of his life, would leave him as he had left her. He didn't know if he was nearly as strong as she was.

He wasn't certain that if she walked away now, or ever, he could survive. Maybe that was why it was so hard for him to say the words. What if she said no?

She inhaled the clean scent of his aftershave and the warm male scent of his skin. Though several inches still separated them, she could feel the heat of his body seeping into her. She'd nearly reached that safe harbor she'd been searching for. All she needed to do was toss a line out, snag a cleat and she would be home. She kept her gaze locked on Nick's face, on his deep steel eyes. "What are you asking me, Agent Cavanaugh?"

"I'm no longer an agent. I retired."

"Why?"

"Because I heard there was a commuter airline in need of an extra pilot."

"So you came here looking for a job?"

"No," Nick murmured and closed the few inches still separating them. "I came for you."

"Why, Nick?" she whispered, desperately needing to hear it from him.

He gave her a soft smile. "Because I love you. And because I need you in my arms more than I've ever needed anything else. I need you so damned much that the idea of not having you there scares the living hell out of me."

Nick's fingers shook as he pulled a suede jeweler's box from his pocket and opened it.

The aquamarine stone could have been sliced from a clear Caribbean sky.

"Marry me, Kelly. Marry me and I'll spend the rest of my life making you happy."

Her eyes met his. "Yes."

"Yes? You don't need to think about it? There's so much—"

"I've thought of little else since you walked back into my life, Nick Cavanaugh. I love you. I'm so very much in love with you. I want nothing more than to go on loving you forever."

Anxious to feel the ring on her finger, she took it and slid it in place. It fit perfectly.

She didn't stop to study it, though. Instead, she launched herself into Nick's waiting arms.

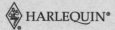

HARLEQUIN®

INTRIGUE®

**Don't miss the third book
in Cassie Miles's exciting miniseries:**

COLORADO
CRIME CONSULTANTS

*For this group of concerned citizens,
no mission is impossible!*

ROCKY MOUNTAIN
MANEUVERS

BY CASSIE MILES

**Available March 2005
Harlequin Intrigue #832**

When Molly Griffith agreed to go undercover to help out
a friend, her boss Adam Briggs wasn't happy with her plan.
Her investigation turned dangerous, and it was up to the
two of them to find the truth and each other. Would they
realize that some partnerships were meant to last forever?

Available at your favorite retail outlet

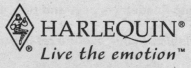

HARLEQUIN®
Live the emotion™

www.eHarlequin.com

ATHENA FORCE

The Athena Academy adventure continues....

Three secret sisters
Three super talents
One unthinkable legacy...

**The ties that bind may be the ties that kill
as these extraordinary women race against
time to beat the genetic time bomb that is
their birthright....**

**Don't miss the latest three stories
in the Athena Force continuity**

DECEIVED by Carla Cassidy, January 2005

CONTACT by Evelyn Vaughn, February 2005

PAYBACK by Harper Allen, March 2005

**And coming in April–June 2005,
the final showdown for
Athena Academy's best and brightest!**

Available at your favorite retail outlet.